Savior

An *Impossible* Novel

By Julia Sykes

D1715172

For everyone who told me they loved Clayton and wanted him to find his own happiness. He is eternally grateful that you saved him from me going all George R. R. Martin on his (exceptionally yummy) ass.

Chapter 1

Rose

It was a simple fact of my life that I didn't have the time or the emotional energy for a relationship. But I could make some time for the blond hottie sitting alone at the bar. I mentally checked my calendar. Yep, I definitely had one night to give this prime piece of man candy. In fact, he was just the fix I needed. A few shots of tequila and several long hours of this man inside me would provide the escape I craved.

My eyes roved over him for the hundredth time, and I wondered if he was kinky. A slightly predatory smile spread across my face. If he wasn't now, he would be by morning.

Flipping my long, platinum blonde hair over my shoulder, I rested one elbow on the bar, angling my body so that I was facing my future conquest. I easily fell into my signature seductive posture and flagged down the bartender.

"I'll have what he's having." I pitched my voice just loud enough to catch my target's attention. He glanced over at me.

Score!

With a few more points, I would win my prize. This was my favorite game. It provided the most wonderful distraction. The sex was usually pretty good too. It was what came after the sex that wasn't so pleasant.

Keep your head in the game, Rose.

I would deal with the emotional consequences later. If I just played the game often enough, I might never have to deal with them.

Shockingly blue eyes met mine, and my concerns evaporated. Sex with this man would be worth whatever consequences I had to face in the morning.

His well-fitted black suit – and the obviously strong body it concealed – radiated a sense of authority. His strong, clean-shaven jaw and carefully styled dark blond hair told me he was a meticulous person, carefully controlled. He had all of the hallmarks of a man who liked power. And I definitely liked a man who wanted to be in control.

Now that I had his attention, I immediately pressed my advantage. I reached out to touch his glass, making sure to brush my fingers along the back of his as I did so.

"What's your drink?" I didn't have to try to make my voice sound low and throaty. The rush of lust that shot through me in response to the interest that flared in his remarkable eyes did the job for me.

"Glenfiddich, neat," he responded easily, as though that word made perfect sense.

What the hell? Was that even English?

"What's that?"

"Scotch whisky," he explained.

The man didn't seem to be much of a talker; he appeared to favor two-word sentences. Not that I was here for conversation, but I needed to keep him engaged for a few more minutes, at the very least.

"Never mind then, Mr. Fancypants," I said teasingly before turning to the bartender. "We'll have two shots of tequila, please." I shot my target an assessing look, my eyes lingering pointedly on his suit before flicking back up to his eyes. "Is Cuervo good enough for you, Fancypants?"

He just nodded, and I smiled at him encouragingly. His answering grin was like looking into the sun. It illuminated his alluring features into something bright and breathtaking.

But it was the intrigued spark in his electric blue eyes that captivated me most. A fire stirred in their cerulean depths that spoke of desire, a sexual hunger. It reflected my own voracious needs. They had driven me here tonight, and they had most definitely been further stoked by this man.

He wasn't the type of guy I usually found in Big Jim's Tavern, my go-to neighborhood dive bar. I had come here looking for a tattooed, brawling bad boy. Someone who took what he wanted and then got the hell out of dodge after he got it. The last thing I wanted was a guy who would hang around in the morning.

I couldn't get a read on this stranger in that regard. The Fancypants types tended to at least pretend to be gentlemen. They would ask for your number and claim that they would call you. Sometimes, they even asked you on a date. Of course, the number of times they followed up on the offer were few. But occasionally... Occasionally I had made the mistake of taking home a Stage 5 Clinger. Getting rid of one of them was messy. And it often involved some cruel words before it was over.

I *definitely* didn't want that. I already knew I was a cheap slut. My mom had told me often enough that I didn't need any reminding.

Better to fuck my way into sweet oblivion than find happiness in the sting of a needle, I reassured myself. Sure, sometimes I did a little coke or E to loosen up at a party, but I was horrified at the idea of doing anything harder. I had seen what had happened to Greg. No way did I want to end up like my kid brother.

The bartender clunked the shots down on the hardwood, and I shook off the dark thoughts. I was here to forget about my problems, not dwell on them. I flashed a smile at the hottie who would be my drug for the evening.

"So, Mr. Fancypants," I said with a mocking smile, intentionally trying to get a rise out of him. "Do you have a first name?"

I was hoping to see a flash of anger, some indication that I had provoked him. But he just smiled broadly and laughed. The sound was melting chocolate, dripping warmth onto my bare skin before being licked away by a hot, demanding tongue.

"Clayton," he responded easily. "And you seem to be misinformed. My surname isn't Fancy-"

I quickly pressed two fingers to his lips, silencing him. I didn't want to know who he was. I didn't want him to know who I was. Hell, I didn't even plan on giving him my real first name. It was better that way, really. For both of us.

"'Clayton' will do for now. I'm Mary." The false name rolled easily off the tip of my tongue.

Clayton smiled. "It's nice to meet you, Mary." As he spoke, his soft lips moved against my fingertips. I wondered what those lips would feel like caressing other areas of my flesh, a thought that elicited a sudden flash of dissatisfaction at the sound of my fake name on his tongue.

Rose, I wanted to say. *Call me Rose.*

But it was too late to correct him. I would seem like a crazy person if I admitted that I had lied about my name. So I just returned his smile and reluctantly drew my fingers away from his mouth. Clayton started to lift the shot of tequila to those full lips, and I found myself licking my own unconsciously. His looked delicious, and I couldn't wait to feel them against mine.

I lightly put my hand on his wrist, stopping him short. I had to suppress the urge to shiver that the contact awoke within me. The intensity of it was almost unsettling. And "almost unsettling" was just what I needed; I wanted to be pushed to the edge, to that elusive place where passion was so intense that I would only barely be able to piece my shattered self back together in the aftermath. In my personal experience, that perfection had yet to be fully realized, but it was a hell of a lot of fun trying.

Keeping myself focused on the game, I gave him a playful but slightly censorious smile.

"You don't drink tequila often, do you?" I asked. "Here, let me show you how to do it properly."

I released him, raising my hand to my own mouth before I slowly licked the sensitive flesh between my thumb and forefinger. My eyes locked with his I did so, and I was pleased to see him shift slightly on the barstool, clearly affected by me. It seemed I would be initiating the seduction here. I could only hope he would turn the tables on me soon. It would be a shame if he turned out to be completely vanilla. He was hot enough that I might be able to make an exception for him, but I wasn't really in to that.

I sprinkled some white granules of salt over the dampness on my hand. Then I licked it off, enjoying seeing Clayton's Adam's apple bob as he swallowed hard. I bit into the slice of lime, pursing my lips at the sour juice that filled my mouth. I took my shot quickly to wash it down, the flavors mingling and becoming something rich and delicious as it slid down my open throat. It burned a little, and I grimaced for a moment before turning my smile back on Clayton. He raised an eyebrow at me.

"Impressive," he said simply.

"I know," I said with a confident shrug. "Your turn."

To my surprise, he reached out and grasped my hand firmly, drawing it towards him and raising it to his lips.

My breathing hitched. "What are you doing?" I asked, confused.

"Doing it properly." He shot me a wicked grin that made my stomach do a little flip just before his tongue snaked out to stroke against my skin. Heat instantly flared between my legs, and to my surprise, I blushed. I never blushed.

His smile was roguish and knowing. Oh, he was definitely turning the tables. I thrilled at the thought.

His thumb traced lightly over the back of my hand as he sprinkled the salt over it. This time I did shudder when he licked it off. I blushed more deeply, embarrassed by my conspicuous reaction. I had wanted him to take control, but this was moving far too quickly. I didn't like losing the upper hand outside the bedroom.

He didn't release my hand as he bit into the lime and took the shot back like a pro. Oh, he was a quick learner. The realization was both thrilling and discomfiting.

"Another?" He asked, that wicked smile still in place as he maintained his grip on me.

"Sure," I agreed breathlessly. I definitely wanted more of this.

We repeated the process again, and I could feel wetness pooling between my legs as I became more aroused by his touch. I needed to get a little of my own back, regain some modicum of control over our interactions. No one had ever elicited such sudden, visceral reactions from me, not even during my kinkiest encounters. Images of Clayton dominating my body, holding me down as he fucked me roughly, ran across my mind.

We would get to that in a little while. But not yet.

"So," I said lightly, trying to cut into the intense sexual tension between us. "What were you sulking about before I came over here?"

He looked affronted, but the playful gleam in his eye let me know that he wasn't really offended.

"I wasn't *sulking*," he insisted.

"Okay, you were brooding then," I shrugged. "Women trouble?" I sincerely hoped that wasn't the case. He hadn't been acting like he was attached, but it wouldn't be the first time some cheating asshole had made his way into my bed without me realizing it.

He surprised me by chuckling. Apparently it was impossible to get under his skin.

"I appreciate the more manly term, but not your perceptiveness," he said. "I came here to brood in peace. Work is a bitch right now." He grinned, eyeing me in a way that made me flush pleasurably. "But things are suddenly looking up." He cocked his head at me. "And what are you doing here, taking shots with a stranger? Man trouble?"

His tone was casual, but the spark of true curiosity in his eyes let me know that he hoped I was unattached too.

"In a way," I admitted. "Brother problems." My tone was casual as well, but I could feel that my smile was a bit tight. Why had I admitted that? I didn't want anyone to know about my brother. He was my dark secret, the thing I was trying to escape from. When I had come home from work earlier, he had been high again, completely strung out. Over the past several months, I had tried to get him clean, but seeing him go through the agony of withdrawal pained me almost as much as seeing him fucked up out of his mind. It was a vicious cycle I couldn't stop, so I did the only thing I could for him: I took care of him. As much as I was able to. But seeing him like that... Nothing made me feel shittier. It was hard to leave him alone, but tonight I hadn't been able to take it anymore. I had hidden his stash so he wouldn't overdose in my absence, and then I had gotten the hell out.

So now I was here, seeking my own fix. I struggled to make my smile more genuine as I steered us away from the subject.

"Things *do* seem to be looking up now, though," I agreed. But man, could I use another drink. Alcohol would dull my wayward thoughts, keep me focused on the here and now. I waved down the bartender and ordered four more shots.

Clayton's eyebrows rose. "That's a bit much, don't you think?"

I forced a sly smile. "Nope," I said definitively. "It's just enough."

He frowned slightly. "One more each. We're not negotiating on this."

My lips parted slightly. The utter gall of him! "You're rather bossy." I had intended for my voice to be hard, but instead it came out low and breathy. I could definitely deal with bossy. I craved it.

His smile was a touch twisted. "Doesn't seem like you mind," he said teasingly.

I shot him my best smoldering look. "Not one bit."

His remarkable eyes glinted, clearly intrigued. I still wasn't sure if he was experienced in this area, but it didn't seem that would be a problem. My clit pulsed in anticipation. We had exchanged enough conversation. It was nice enough talking to him. Perhaps too nice. It was time for him to shut up and fuck me already before I became even more dangerously intrigued by him.

His eyes widened slightly as my hand closed around the back of his neck, boldly holding him in place as I pulled myself up into him quickly. His lips were frozen under mine for the space of a moment, but he soon responded. I felt a strange, delicious lightness fill me like a rush of blood to the head as his lips caressed mine. He was gentle at first, but I didn't want that. I sucked his full lower lip into my mouth and traced the line of it with my tongue before biting down sharply. To my satisfaction, he didn't pull away in shock but instead reacted aggressively, driving his tongue into my mouth roughly and exploring me thoroughly. I had to suppress the moan of pleasure that wanted to escape me. His arm closed around my waist, pulling me off of my barstool until my body was pressed up against his, my pelvis wedged between his legs. I pressed my hands against his chest to steady myself after the sudden movement, but his other arm was around my upper back, holding me to him so I couldn't put any distance between us. The feeling of him taking my mouth was heady, even more intoxicating than the tequila.

Then I felt something hard against my hip, and I gasped into his mouth as I realized that he wanted me. It seemed I wasn't the only one who was strongly affected here. My panties were already soaked with my arousal; I was as wet and ready for him as

I usually was after a long period of foreplay. And from nothing more than his kiss. This was definitely going to be a great night.

Clayton only pulled away from me when the bartender cleared his throat loudly, interrupting us. The stocky man was looking at us disapprovingly, his brows drawn as he hitched his thumb in the direction of the door.

"How about you two lovebirds go find someplace else to do it? This is a bar, not a brothel."

It's dirty enough to be one, I thought acidly, but I bit my tongue. I didn't want to look like a bitch. Delivering cutting retorts was a rather unfortunate specialty of mine. Choosing not to directly acknowledge the man, I kept my attention on Clayton.

"The man does have a point," I said throatily. "How about we go back to your place?"

To my dismay, Clayton pulled away from me slightly. There were small frown lines around his mouth, and he looked distinctly uncomfortable. "Ah, I don't really do that," he told me. But I could see the lust in his eyes, and I was sure I could persuade him otherwise. Besides, I didn't think I could handle his outright rejection. Did he think I was a slut for wanting to go home with him when we barely knew each other?

Probably.

But you are a slut, I reminded myself. I might as well accept what I was. It was easier than fighting it.

"Listen," I said softly, "it's clear that you and I have both had a shitty day. Hell, I've had a shitty year."

Give or take twenty-four years, I thought bitterly. But that was none of his business. He didn't need to know anything more about my life, and I didn't need to know about his. The only thing I needed to learn about him was his body.

I splayed my fingertips across his chest to renew our contact, and the heat within me ratcheted up another notch when I felt the hard planes of his muscles. My tongue snaked out to wet my lips as hunger filled me, and his eyes followed the movement, obviously transfixed.

"So why don't we go somewhere and do something to forget about it?" I purred.

"Mary…" He trailed off indecisively. I could see he was cracking; the twin blue flames of his eyes told me how fiercely he wanted me. Not to mention the persistent hardness against my hip.

"Haven't you ever done anything wild? Reckless?" I asked, allowing a note of temptation to imbue my tone.

His smile was half-regretful. "Not in a long time," he admitted.

"Don't you want to now? I know I do. And if you don't remember how, I'll remind you. 'Wild' is kind of my thing." The smile I gave him was full of wicked promises.

He seemed to deliberate for a moment, reason warring with desire in his handsome features. Finally, desire won out, and he stood, offering me his arm as he did so.

"Shall we?" He asked, every inch the formal Fancypants.

I grinned and looped my arm through his. "Why yes, good sir, I do believe we shall," I said, my voice slightly mocking. But he just took it in stride, chuckling at me. I thrilled at the sound. Nothing ever ruffled this guy's feathers, did it? I found the thought… comforting. Sure, I had gone home with plenty of strangers before, but there was always an element of danger in doing so. Who knew what they might do to me? In truth, that sliver of trepidation, of fear, was part of the allure. But with Clayton I felt safe. And I enjoyed the warmth that flooded me at the thought more than I had ever appreciated the little twist in my gut at the thought of doing something dangerous.

It was a fairly lengthy cab ride from my crummy little corner of Brooklyn to Manhattan's Lower East Side, but Clayton and I kept ourselves busy. Our lips only parted for as long as it took to pay the driver and walk across the foyer of his building to the elevator. As soon as the silver doors slid closed, he grasped me with such intensity that I fell back against the wall. His body was as unyielding as the cool metal as he pressed against me, his fingers tangling in my hair as mine curled around his shoulders. I wasn't exactly sure when or how we made the transition from the elevator to his apartment; he commanded the full attention of all of my senses. Clayton was the only solid thing in the world as we tore our way through it, banging against walls and doorframes as we made frantic progress to his bedroom. There were long minutes where he was kissing me so thoroughly that my head was spinning from lack of oxygen. Instinct told my body to fight him, but I just clung to him more fiercely as I reveled in the resultant rush of endorphins. When he did finally give me the space to draw breath, I breathed in his heady masculine scent and became even more intoxicated by him.

His hands were at the hem of my dress, fisting in the material as he shoved it up my body. I moaned as he began to explore my heated flesh where I desired it most, and I was desperate to touch him as well. My efforts to tug off his suit jacket proved fruitless. He was far too strong for me to manipulate his movements, and he seemed content touching me for the moment. Undeterred, I went for his belt buckle, working quickly to release the bulge that had been straining against his zipper ever since we had left the bar. I barely had a moment to fully realize his impressive size before he let out a low, guttural sound and shoved me hard. Panic shot through me at the sensation of falling, but I was barely jostled when I hit the soft mattress beneath me. The flash of fear only served to keep my adrenaline thrumming, keeping me riding high.

Clayton had pulled a condom from a bedside drawer and was rolling it on. I was soaking wet and beyond ready for him to take me. My dress was bunched up around my waist, and he was still wearing his suit. But I didn't care. What was passing between us now was raw and animalistic, a primal need that demanded to be met.

He grabbed my legs and pulled me toward him roughly, positioning my body where he wanted it. When my ass was at the edge of the mattress, he settled my ankles on his shoulders and leaned forward to grip my hips with both of his hands. His eyes met mine, and I marveled at the electric blue sparks that seemed to crackle in their multifaceted depths. The light I saw there was wild and hungry, but there was still a trace of concern, of compassion, there. He was at my slick entrance, but he hesitated.

I gripped the hands that held my waist and squeezed so his fingers dug into me almost painfully. "I want you to fuck me hard, Clayton."

At my throaty, brash words, that compassion in his eyes was consumed by lust, and his expression twisted into something exquisitely fierce. He shoved my panties aside and thrust into me mercilessly; the intensity of our bodies joining was almost jarring. I was no virgin, but he stretched me wide enough and fast enough that my cry of delight was tinged with pain.

The sound made him pause. The concern was back. But I didn't want him to be concerned, and I didn't want him to stop. Pain and pleasure were a double-edged sword that I would happily die on a thousand times over. I pushed up my hips and ground against him in a circular motion. Bliss flared as the movement caused his cock to rub against my g-spot.

"More," I gasped. "Please…"

He groaned and shifted his grip on me, splaying his fingers across my ass and hooking his thumbs over my hips. Then he pulled almost all the way out of me before driving in swiftly once again. The intensity of his thrust would have moved my entire body, but his firm hold on me ensured I stayed where he wanted me.

"Yes!" I moaned. "Hard. Just like that. Please…"

Whatever vestiges of concern he had left were obliterated. He took me roughly and urgently, using my body as he wished in order to find his release. It was exactly what I had craved:

something so passionate and all-consuming that it claimed the entirety of my spirit.

The head of his cock hit my g-spot over and over again, sending me skyrocketing as the ecstasy of my coming orgasm built within me. I felt his cock twitch, and I knew he was close too. Everything exploded when his thumb pressed down on my clit hard, rubbing in practiced, demanding circles as he wrung my orgasm from my body. His rough shout and my scream were a violent crescendo, a testimony to the fierceness of our shared, desperate passion.

I moaned softly as he pulled out, leaving me feeling utterly empty. But for the first time in a long time, that feeling of emptiness wasn't accompanied by the feeling of being suddenly, starkly alone. Clayton tumbled down on the bed beside me and wrapped his arm around my waist. Little lines of sizzling pleasure continued to slither beneath my skin as he held me against him. We were both gasping for breath in tandem, our bodies still perfectly in sync.

When our heaving chests slowed to a more normal rhythm, Clayton rolled off of me. A cold knot twisted in the pit of my stomach. Being held by Clayton had felt nice, but it wasn't wise to read too much into his actions.

Wham-bam-thank you ma'am. Time to go Rose.

I propped myself up on my elbows and started tugging down on my dress. His hands were on my shoulders, pushing me back down onto the bed. I looked up at him, confused.

"What do you think you're doing?" He asked.

"Um, getting dressed?" It came out as a question. Clayton was throwing me for a loop.

"Don't." It was a simple word, but it was spoken like an order. The clear, commanding tone of his voice made me shiver. My hands fell away from my dress instantly, and my legs parted slightly as I relaxed, my body instinctively offering itself to him. He cocked his head to the side, studying me for a long moment.

My breaths came more quickly as he regarded me in silence, and that all-consuming need he had only just purged from me came growling back to life.

"Stay."

With only that one word, I froze. Clayton left my line of sight. My eyes wanted to follow him, but I didn't move; I hardly breathed. I could hear water running, so I guessed he was in the bathroom. Did he know what he was doing to me? Did he understand the game I thought we were playing?

My body didn't care if he knew what he was doing or not; it just wanted more of whatever this was. It wanted more of *him.*

The sound of his approaching footsteps told me he was coming back. I thought about standing, pulling down my dress, and getting out of there ASAP. That's what any normal person would have done. Hell, that's what *I* would have done.

But when I saw Clayton, all temptation to leave evaporated. He had gotten undressed while I wasn't watching him. And *holy fuck,* was he perfect. I had been with a lot of big, brawny guys who literally put in hours every day at the gym. Clayton wasn't bulky like them, but every part of his body was flawlessly sculpted and balanced. He didn't have beefy arms in order to make up for the tiny calves he hid under his baggy jeans, and he didn't have huge pecs to draw attention away from his doughy stomach. He was breathtaking.

I was overwhelmed by the desire to touch him, to run my fingertips along the contours of him. Pushing myself up, I reached for him.

"I thought I told you to stay," he said sternly.

I gasped in shock, and my body reacted before my mind could catch up. I dropped back onto the mattress, my arms falling to either side of me with my wrists facing upward, willingly exposing my physical vulnerabilities. "Sorry," I whispered automatically.

His grin was both pleased and predatory. "You really do like it when I'm bossy, don't you?"

I smiled back at him wickedly. "You don't know the half of it."

"I'm sure I don't," he agreed easily. "But I'm a quick study." His rough fingertips brushed against my inner thigh, and I jumped as even that slightest contact sent pleasure arcing through me. He instantly withdrew his touch, fixing me with a reprimanding stare. He didn't have to say it aloud again for me to know what that look meant: *Stay.*

This time, it took concerted effort to force my body to relax.

He waited before touching me again, watching my reactions as he drew out the tension. The longer he waited, the hotter I got for him. God, the man was teasing me with nothing but the sight of his body and the mere promise of his touch, and already I was close to begging him to give me what I craved. When his palms finally slid up either side of my waist, slowly peeling my dress off my body, I couldn't hold back a strangled sigh of relief. But my torment was only just beginning.

I shifted my arms compliantly so he could tug the dress over my head, but he suddenly stopped his steady progress. The thick, stretchy material still covered my eyes, and my arms were trapped on either side of my head.

"Stay." The command was a low growl at my ear, and I shuddered in delight at the sound of it. I could easily get out of this makeshift bondage if I wanted to, but I *so* didn't want to. If I had thought my body was alive with need before, all of my nerve endings were positively crackling now that I could no longer see what Clayton was doing to me. He was everywhere and nowhere; his warm breath, hot tongue, and clever fingers roved over my body, but he never quite touched me where I needed it most. All of my muscles tensed until I was taut as a bowstring from the effort of staying still.

"Are you... sure... you haven't done this before?" I panted, my voice trembling almost as violently as my body.

Clayton's warmth withdrew abruptly, and a soft whine escaped me at the loss.

"No. Why?" He asked. "Am I doing it wrong?"

"No!" I cried desperately, yearning for his maddening caresses to resume. "God, no. Please..."

His low, rumbling chuckle moved over and through me like a palpable thing, making me shiver. "That's what I thought." His tongue traced along the bottom of my earlobe before drawing it between his teeth. He bit down, and the sharp little pain contrasted beautifully with the soft flicks of his tongue. The raw, lustful sound that was pulled from my throat shocked me.

"I told you," he said smoothly. "I'm a quick study."

It probably wasn't healthy that I found his smug tone so incredibly arousing. His cocky attitude only further inflamed my desire, and my nipples and clit were already throbbing painfully. "Please, Clayton..."

"I like that part," he commented as he trailed whisper-soft kisses down my neck.

He wanted me to beg? If that was all it would take to get him to release me from this sweet torture, then I would do it gladly.

"Please. Please touch me."

I gasped as he kissed the swell of my breast. He was so close, so close...

"Say my name."

"Please, Clayton!"

Some dim part of me knew that I should be alarmed at the intimacy of what was passing between us. But the entirety of the rest of my being was focused on the gathering storm inside of me.

He grasped my breast and squeezed roughly, pinching my nipple between his thumb and forefinger. At the same time, his other hand stroked my aching clit. He swallowed my ecstatic scream as his lips came down hard on mine. His tongue plundered my mouth as I came, as though he could consume the pleasure that he had harvested from my body.

I had only just begun to come down from my high when he ripped the dress off of me completely. The light that suddenly flooded my world seared my eyes, and I blinked hard to clear the spots that clouded my vision. Clayton's gaze captivated me instantly. He looked... ravenous.

"Touch me," he ordered, his voice harsh. I clearly wasn't the only one who had been suffering while he teased me.

He didn't have to tell me twice. My hands eagerly explored him, roving over the hard planes of his chest and his rippling abs, dipping lower to tug at the trail of light curls that led to his throbbing erection. He let out a low curse and tore open another condom wrapper. As soon as it was on, we tumbled back onto the bed. My legs were wrapped around his waist, inviting him in. I writhed beneath him as he entered me slowly, stretching me. The lingering soreness from our first frantic coupling only make the sensations that much more erotic. A sheen of sweat glistened on Clayton's brow as he visibly held himself back this time.

"Harder," I begged. "Like before."

"I won't last long that way, beautiful," he admitted, his voice tight with strain.

"I won't either. Please, Clayton."

"Fuck!" Those words were like a trigger, and the wild beast within him was back in control. His ferocity, his raw power, when he was like this completely overwhelmed me. I gave over to mindless lust, allowing my body to clash with his instinctively. My orgasm claimed me with a violence I had never known before, and my fingernails raked down his back as I strained to hold him impossibly closer. He roared out his orgasm, throwing his head back as his cock pumped within me.

I don't know how long he lay atop me, still inside me, but I knew I never wanted it to end. But even when he did finally free himself from me, he still held me close. I rested my head on his chest, breathing in his enthralling scent as I fell into blissfully peaceful sleep.

Chapter 2

Damn, he's hot.

Possibly the hottest guy I'd ever hooked up with. Okay, so he was *definitely* the hottest guy I had ever hooked up with. Hands down.

The sun was just coming up, and I knew it was time for me to get the hell out before he woke up. But I couldn't resist lingering for a few minutes longer in order to drink him in, ensuring that the image of him was burned into my brain so I could revisit it again later. My greatest conquest to date.

I frowned at myself. Something about that thought seemed wrong. Although I preferred being controlled in the bedroom, I had always enjoyed the heady sense of power that came with luring a man in. Clayton had fallen into my trap beautifully. But the swiftness with which he had turned the tables on me once I goaded out the Dominant side of him...

No man had ever made me feel so deliciously vulnerable, so utterly possessed. And to be honest, that scared me as much as it thrilled me. For the first time in years, I was tempted to stay in the morning. I allowed myself a brief fantasy where he awoke to my touch and took me again. Maybe we could even have breakfast afterward. He had been a damn good fuck, but I found myself smiling at the memory of our banter in the bar, as brief as it had been.

I mentally slapped myself and shook my head to clear away the fantasy.

Stop being an idiot. You're just some random woman he took home from the dive bar. He won't want you hanging around in the morning.

And *I* didn't want to hang around. I didn't. Besides, I needed to get back to Greg before I had to go to work. I prayed he hadn't found his stash. Although I dreaded seeing him go into withdrawal, he should be okay for a little while at least. I longed to have my baby brother back, if only for a few hours while he was lucid.

I suppressed a sigh so I wouldn't rouse Clayton. It really was time to go. Still, I couldn't help studying his perfection for a few moments longer. I foolishly longed for him to open his eyes so I could look into those electric blue depths that literally took my breath away.

Time to go, Rose.

Drawing on years of experience, I carefully got out of bed in a way that wouldn't jostle him and moved in almost complete silence as I pulled my dress on over my head. I held my high heels in my hand so they wouldn't click on the floor as I left.

"Leaving so soon?"

I jumped at the sound of his deep voice. The way it rumbled with a hungry edge made me want to shiver. I ruthlessly pushed down the urge. My eyes darted to him, and I stopped myself just in time to avoid meeting his stare. I knew if I did I would be helpless to resist him. Unfortunately, this meant that my gaze fell on the sheets where they were tented at his hips, making his impressive erection obvious. I cursed myself for licking my lips at the sight. Images of tasting his cock as he fisted my hair in his hand made my mouth water.

With a great effort, I turned away from him.

"I have to get to work." It was a struggle to force my tone to come out calm and detached.

I barely made it two steps before he was behind me, his hand snaking around my stomach and pulling me back against his broad chest. I could feel his insistent hardness against my ass, and I couldn't help pressing back into him as heat flared between my legs.

"It's early. Stay."

It wasn't a request, and I thrilled at the word.

"No," I said, hating how breathy and weak my protest sounded. "I have to go."

His hands were on my shoulders, spinning me around so I was facing him. I was careful not to meet his eyes. That would be a mistake.

"Okay," he said gently. "I'll take you to dinner then. How about tomorrow night?"

I hated the longing that expanded in my chest, pressing against my heart almost painfully. But I knew he didn't mean it; he was one of those "honorable" types who would make the halfhearted effort just so he didn't look like a dick. He was doing the obligatory song and dance.

"Let's not pretend this was something it wasn't," I said coldly. I couldn't bear to look at him. If I did, I would see that judgmental expression, the one that had *slut* written all over it.

But he clearly wanted to torment me further. He hooked a finger under my chin, forcing my head up so I had no choice but to meet his gaze. My breath caught in my throat as I saw no disdain there, only consternation. He even looked slightly affronted.

"I told you. I don't do one-night-stands, Mary. I want to see you again."

I hated the sound of my false name on his tongue far more than was prudent.

But it didn't matter. Even if he was sincere, I couldn't allow myself to become involved. I had to think of Greg; I didn't have the time to commit to anyone else. Besides, judging by his apartment and his suit, Clayton was clearly successful. And he *was* honorable. He deserved someone better than me.

I couldn't summon up the words to refuse, but I forced myself to shake my head. Clayton's frown deepened, and he reached for my purse.

"What are you doing?" I asked, puzzled.

He didn't answer as he pulled out my phone. I was embarrassed by its age and beaten-up appearance. It screamed *poor.* No doubt Clayton had a fancy iPhone. And I wished I had one too as he started fiddling with the buttons. What I wouldn't give for a locking passcode in that moment. Did the man have no sense of boundaries?

Satisfied, he slipped my phone back into my purse.

"You have my number now. Call me." His voice was stern; he clearly wasn't going to take "no" for an answer.

"Okay," I lied. I would have said anything at that point in order to escape him and those damn entrancing eyes.

It took a great deal of willpower to step away from him. Although I told myself it was a mercy he had released me, I felt a twinge of regret that he didn't pick me up, throw me down on his bed, and ravage me.

"Aren't you going to put on your shoes?" He asked. "There's no need to be quiet now that you're not sneaking out."

I flushed at his words. As much as I wanted to leave, it would look stupid if I walked out barefoot now. I bent down to lace up my strappy black fuck-me heels, carrying out my task as quickly as possible. My cheeks flamed hotter as I could practically feel his eyes burning into me, staring at my ass. Not looking at him, I straightened and gave him an awkward wave.

"Bye," I mumbled as I half-ran for the door.

In the elevator, I found myself bouncing on the balls of my feet as it seemed to descend the ten floors to the lobby at a snail's pace. I was careful not to look at the porter when I exited the building; my clothes screamed "walk of shame". To my great relief, I was able to hail a taxi in less than two minutes. I couldn't really afford a cab, but there was no way I was going to take the bus in this outfit. Although I usually brushed off commuters' judgmental looks with my head held high, oozing nonchalance, I just couldn't face it today. Clayton had really shaken me up and thrown me off my game.

I shoved him from my mind and focused on thoughts of Greg as I was driven to my shabby apartment in Brooklyn, steeling myself to face the condition I might find him in when I got home.

It was almost painful to hand over my credit card to pay the cab fare. I doubted I would meet the next minimum payment with the added expense.

Don't think about that now.

I would just have to beg to pick up extra shifts at work in order to make up for it. If my boss would let me. Cheryl was the haughty bitch who owned Ivory, the ritzy bridal boutique where I worked. Of course, she had a fancy degree from the Fashion Institute of Technology, paid for by her rich parents. It didn't matter to her that I was the best damn seamstress at her shop; I didn't have the piece of paper to prove I was good enough to be promoted. Cheryl acted like I was lucky she even hired me. Hell, I wasn't even allowed in the front of the shop. As though I would scare off the wealthy customers with my obvious white-trashiness.

So much for the American Dream, I thought bitterly. Anyone who thought there was opportunity for upward mobility in this city was seriously deluded. I would never be considered a person of value, would never make more than minimum wage, and I just had to accept that. Grudgingly.

Okay, so maybe I had a chip on my shoulder. But sometimes I couldn't help resenting the shitty hand life had dealt me. Then I would just get pissed at myself for being sulky. So I sought my escape in partying and fucking, preferring to ignore my problems rather than dwell on them. Sure, bottling things up led to the occasional emotional explosion, but I always tried to aim it at someone who deserved a good verbal smack-down.

But not Greg. Never Greg. Even though he was probably the most deserving person I knew. He shared my painful past, and that was what had driven him to the drugs. If I took out my frustrations on him, it would only make things worse. Besides, I had always been fiercely protective of him, doing my best to shelter him from my mother's nastiness and shield him from her string of lovers, some of whom had been abusive. She had always blamed us for our father walking out on her. I had only been five years old, and Greg was just a baby. But somehow, in her mind, it was our fault he had left. If only we hadn't been such disappointments, he would have stayed.

The rational part of me said that wasn't true. But that shit leaves scars and can become a self-fulfilling prophesy. Now Greg was an unemployed nineteen-year-old junkie, and at twenty-four I was an irresponsible underachiever who was barely scraping by for the both of us.

I couldn't deny we were a pair of fuck-ups. But we were going to survive. I would make sure of that.

Taking a deep breath to brace myself for what I might find waiting for me, I unlocked the door to our crappy little studio apartment. The "kitchen" was nothing but a sink with a couple of cabinets underneath it, and the ancient mini-fridge barely worked. Greg and I each had our own twin bed pushed against opposite walls, and there was a tiny bathroom with the barest necessities. It was the only place where we could go to have any sort of privacy, and the water ran ice cold about half of the time. But it was the best I could afford. Besides, it's not like it was much worse than the hellhole we grew up in, so we didn't know anything different. At least our apartment was tidy. I had spent days scrubbing off the grime when we had first moved in, and I had repainted the walls a cheery pale yellow. It wasn't much, but I did my best to make it livable. I was even secretly a little proud of it.

My eyes did a once-over of the small space, searching for Greg. He was lying on his bed, utterly still. Not for the first time, terror shot through my gut as I feared the worst, and I rushed over to him. The relief that flooded me when I saw he was breathing nearly drove me to my knees. If he had overdosed while I had been off having my brains fucked out…

He was okay. That was all that mattered. The question was: had he used again while I was gone? I walked to the bathroom as quietly as I could, not wanting to wake him as I checked my hiding place. Careful to make as little noise as possible, I lifted the loose tile on the bathroom floor and heaved out a sigh when I found the drugs right where I had left them. Greg must still be sleeping off the effects of his high from the night before. Sliding the tile back in place, I prayed I would make it another day without him discovering where I had hidden it. I hated that I had to leave him to go to work; there was always the very real possibility that I would return home to find the apartment overturned and Greg in a crazed rage as he tore through everything he could get his hands on looking for his stash.

But I didn't have a choice. It was either leave him or let both of us starve. There were no friends or family I could call to help watch over him. We only had our mother, and she would do more damage than good. I had lots of friends, but they only knew me as the carefree party girl. Hanging out with me was supposed to be fun, not depressing as hell. I didn't want anyone to know what my life was really like. Besides, if anyone found out about Greg, they might go to the cops. I couldn't risk that.

I checked on him one more time before I mechanically got ready for work. It was a small blessing that the water was hot. The warmth of it on my skin as I washed away the evidence of my night with Clayton made me want to linger, the soreness between my legs a delicious reminder of our night of passion. But I resisted the urge to touch myself. It was a long commute to work, and I didn't have time for such luxuries. Maybe later.

Nope. That's a bad idea.

What I should do was go out at the first opportunity and find another man to fuck away the memories of Clayton. It was disturbing how unhappy the thought made me. Maybe I should call him…

I rolled my eyes at myself. Finding someone different to screw was definitely at the top of my priority list. Maybe I would go to Decadence, my favorite BDSM club. I had a feeling it would take a true Dominant to knock Clayton out of my mind. Maybe the infamous Master S would be there. I'd wanted to snag him for years. He was definitely one of the hottest, most experienced Doms on the scene, and the fact that he always wore a black mask that hid the upper half of his face only made him even more intriguing. Yes, he would definitely be my next target.

I turned my mind from sex to my workday, practicing my saccharine smile that I always plastered on as I endured Cheryl's condescension. I might hate the bitch, but I needed this job. Having the prestigious boutique on my résumé might even get me a higher-paying job somewhere else one day.

A girl can dream.

As I rode the bus to the shop, I kept my mind occupied by sketching my own designs in my journal. Occasionally, I glanced around to make sure no one was looking at my work; I had never shared my designs with anyone, and I intended to keep it that way. It wasn't like they would ever come to anything, but I couldn't help indulging in the practice. Nothing calmed me like sketching, creating. And I could definitely use something to calm me down today.

I found myself drawing furiously on the commute back home that evening. The dress that flowed out onto the paper was all hard lines and sharp angles. The product of my anger had a harsh beauty to it.

I had heard Cheryl talking shit about me in the break room at lunchtime, and Lisa – my supposed friend at work – hadn't come to my defense. She didn't spew the same vitriol as our boss, but her "Mmmhmms" and soft sounds of agreement had cut me more deeply than Cheryl's words ever had. I guess it was my own fault. I never should have invited Lisa out for drinks after work.

Apparently my habit of over-sharing after one too many lemon drop shots had damned me in her eyes. The prude.

I was definitely going to Decadence as soon as possible. The BDSM crowd was the least judgmental group of people I had ever encountered. I supposed we were all on the fringes of society in that respect, so we all had uncommonness in common. It tended to foster an accepting atmosphere.

But my mood only darkened further when I got back to my apartment.

"What the fuck, Greg?!" I shouted as I slammed the door behind me.

My brother was sprawled out on his bed with his eyes half-closed, a euphoric expression on his face. The apartment was destroyed; he *had* been searching for his stash in my absence. But what alarmed me most was the trail of dried blood that ran from the corner of his mouth down his chin. There was an angry purple bruise on his jaw and a needle in his arm.

"What happened?" I demanded, advancing on him. He just gave me a lazy smile. I grabbed his shoulders and shook him hard. "Who did this to you?"

He didn't answer me; he was too far gone. "God damn it, Greg!" My voice broke as tears threatened. I blinked them back. Breaking down now wouldn't do either of us any good.

I glanced in the direction of the bathroom. The tile was still as I had left it. Fear spiked through me, and I shook him again.

"Where did you get the drugs, Greg?" I demanded. There was no way he could have afforded them. In fact, I wasn't sure how he had been supporting his habit for the last several weeks. I had stopped keeping cash in the apartment. But this was the first time I had ever come home and found him injured. Had someone been in our apartment? Did they know where we lived? The thought made my gut twist. I didn't want to have to move, but that was what I would do if I had to. Maybe it was time to take Greg to rehab. It was one thing to see him destroying himself with his addiction, but knowing that someone out there would physically hurt him was far more terrifying. At least I could keep him alive when it came to the drugs. Maybe I should think about buying a gun.

A knock at the door made me jump. I pursed my lips, hardly daring to breathe. Maybe if I was quiet whoever it was would decide no one was home and leave.

The second knock was sharper and more insistent.

"Greg Baker? Open up."

Shit. Someone was here for my brother. What the hell had he gotten himself into? I walked to the door on shaky legs and pressed my eye to the peephole in order to get a look at my enemy. All of the wind was knocked out of me when I saw who was on the other side.

What the fuck? How did he find me? Had he followed me here? And how in the hell did he know about Greg?

"I don't know what you're trying to pull, Clayton, but I want you to leave," I called out angrily so he could hear me through the door. "Are you stalking me or something? Get out of here now or I'll call the police."

To my great satisfaction, he took a step back, his jaw hanging open in shock. Good. I had scared him.

"Mary?" He asked hesitantly.

"Do you know this woman, Clayton?" The feminine voice drew my gaze away from Clayton, and I noticed the short, dark-skinned woman with a mass of curly black hair standing behind him for the first time.

Clayton didn't answer her, but his shocked expression was replaced with one of determination as his jaw tightened. "Open the door, Mary," he said sternly.

"I'm giving you three seconds to get out of here, or I'm calling the police," I threatened.

The woman made an exasperated sound and shouldered her way in front of Clayton. She pulled a wallet out of her pocket, and she unfolded it so I could see the official-looking credentials inside.

"I'm Agent Silverman with the FBI. And this is Agent Vaughn." Her tone was acerbic as she glared at Clayton.

No way.

"I don't believe you. I don't know what this is, but you both need to leave. Now."

"If you don't open the door, we will use force to enter, ma'am. We have a warrant," the woman said tersely.

I bit my lip, unsure. They said they were here to talk to Greg. What if they were lying? What if they were here to hurt him?

But what if they were telling the truth? How much deeper shit would he be in if they had to force their way in? Greg was clearly high out of his mind, and he would be in trouble for sure if they saw him like that. Maybe it was time to get him into rehab. Maybe I could beg Clayton to get him clean rather than throwing him in jail.

It didn't seem like I had a choice.

My fingers trembled as I slid back the lock and opened the door. Even though Clayton had already figured out who I was, his eyes still widened slightly as though he couldn't quite believe I was standing before him. To be honest, I couldn't believe it either. What were the chances he would end up here? Had he known who I was? Had he been following me before I had approached him at the bar?

But he had just called me Mary, not Rose. He couldn't possibly know who I really was. This was just the most fucked-up coincidence of my life. I should have known that a Fancypants like Clayton wouldn't have been in my neighborhood without a good reason. He might not have targeted me intentionally, but the reason I had met him was because he was in the area looking for my brother.

The woman – Agent Silverman – pushed against the door insistently, forcing me aside so they could enter. When she saw Greg, her eyes filled with pity. And a hint of disgust. My hands curled to fists as rage washed over me.

"What do you want?" I snapped.

Agent Silverman spared me a cursory glance before turning her attention back on my brother.

"Mr. Baker," she addressed him loudly. "Can you understand me?"

Greg didn't respond. She pulled out her cell phone and dialed.

"I need a bus here," she said, her tone cursory. "The perp needs medical attention before we can bring him in."

Perp? Bring him in?

Oh no. That wasn't going to happen. I wouldn't let it. I turned to Clayton, desperate. I wasn't above begging.

"Clayton, please. He just needs help. My brother is a good person." He had to listen. He had to believe me.

Clayton looked distinctly uncomfortable. "He's involved with bad people, Mary. I'm sorry, but we're going to have to arrest him." He stepped forward to brush past me. He was going for Greg. They were going to take him from me.

The fury I so often suppressed came bubbling up. "No!" I shrieked. "I'm not letting you take him!"

Hardly aware of what I was doing, I drew my hand back and cracked it across his cheek. He didn't even flinch. I had a moment to register that his eyes had narrowed angrily, and the next thing I knew my body was pressed up against the wall, my arm twisted behind my back as he trapped me in place.

"Mary Baker," he half-growled in my ear, "you are under arrest for assaulting a federal agent. You have the right to remain silent. Anything you say can and will be used against you in a court of law. You have the right to an attorney. If you cannot afford one, one will be provided for you. Do you understand your rights?"

Cool metal encircled my wrists as the cuffs clicked closed around them. In other circumstances, this would have been pretty hot. But this wasn't kinky role-play. Right now I was pissed off beyond belief, and I jerked against his hold on me. Which of course accomplished nothing.

"Do you understand your rights?" He demanded again.

"Oh, I understand," I hissed. "I understand that you're a heartless jackass. And my name is Rose, asshole."

I felt him stiffen behind me, and his grip tightened incrementally. He said nothing as he stepped away from me, but he didn't release my arm.

"You good here, Sharon?" He asked his partner.

"Yeah," she nodded. "Medics should be here any minute."

Clayton returned her nod jerkily. He didn't look at me as he ushered me out of the apartment and down the three flights of stairs to the street. He helped me into the back of a black sedan. Like a criminal.

Occasionally, he shot me a glare through the rearview mirror. I returned it, seething in silence.

The truth was, I was at a loss for words for the first time in my life.

Chapter 3

I had been sitting in the uncomfortable metal chair in the grey-walled FBI interrogation room for what seemed like an eternity. My hands alternatively twisted in my lap and balled into fists as worry for Greg warred with my anger at Clayton. Why did he have to turn out to be such a bastard? I had almost convinced myself that he was a genuinely good guy. But apparently he was a cold douchebag who could fuck a girl senseless one minute and then tear her life apart the next.

I was going to lose everything: my job, my brother, and probably my freedom. What was the penalty for "assaulting a federal agent"? My actions had been rash and stupid. If I had just kept my cool, I might have been able to sway Clayton. But my temper had gotten the better of me, and I hadn't been able to hold back.

I only wish I had actually inflicted some damage, I thought resentfully. He had hardly blinked when I slapped him. I had enjoyed how helpless I had felt in his strong arms, but now I was considering taking up weightlifting. They had gyms in prison, didn't they? I didn't want to be weak; I wanted to be strong enough to hurt Clayton like he was hurting me. But that would only land me in deeper shit.

Still, it took effort to stop myself from lunging at him when he finally entered the room. All of my muscles coiled and my fingernails bit into my palms.

"I want my lawyer," I snapped. No way was I going to talk to him without someone there to look out for my interests. And maybe they could even help me figure out a way to get Greg off the hook.

Clayton sighed heavily when he sat down across from me. He leaned forward, resting his forearms on the table between us as he studied me carefully.

"You don't need a lawyer," he told me simply.

"You told me I could have a lawyer," I insisted. "That's my right. I'm not talking to you without one here."

When he spoke, his tone was low and calm. The richness of it threatened to wrap around me like a warm embrace, but I shoved the sensation away. "You don't need a lawyer because you're not under arrest," he explained. "I arrested *Mary* Baker. I read *Mary* her Miranda Rights. Rose Baker was never actually arrested." He gave me a small smile. "I got you off on a technicality."

"*You* got me off?" I said angrily. "You're the one who arrested me in the first place! Am I supposed to be grateful towards you after you treated me like a criminal?"

His smile was gone instantly, and his eyes narrowed. A part of me hated that I had wiped that smile away, but the fierceness of his harsh expression made something delicious stir to life at my core. It was a sensation I tried my best to ignore.

"I didn't expect your gratitude. But I was hoping for a hint of remorse. Do you want to tell me what possessed you to slap an FBI agent? To aid a wanted criminal?"

"I slapped you because you deserved it," I said staunchly. "And my brother isn't a criminal."

His expression softened, and the kindness in his eyes almost penetrated my righteous anger. Almost.

"I'm sorry things turned out this way, Rose. It's not what I wanted." His tone was regretful, but he was spearing me with a level look. "But your brother *is* a criminal."

"He's just an addict," I said desperately. "I know buying heroin is illegal, but he just needs help. He needs to go to rehab, not prison."

I thought I saw a hint of sadness in the depths of his blue eyes, but he continued to regard me seriously. "I'm sorry to have to tell you this, Rose, but Greg has been working for the Latin Kings for more than a month now."

Clayton's words hit me like a blow to the gut. I shook my head vigorously. That wasn't true. It couldn't be.

"You're wrong," I insisted.

"How do you think Greg affords his habit?" Clayton asked pointedly.

I had been wondering that myself. And then someone had beaten him up today. Who would have done that? Why would anyone do that to Greg?

"The Kings are recruiting, Rose," Clayton continued ruthlessly. "Your brother owed them money, and he was desperate for more heroin. He's been selling for them in order to pay for his habit."

I shook my head again. "Greg wouldn't do that."

"Your brother might be a good person, Rose. But addiction can drive good people to do bad things."

Greg didn't have any money. And I hadn't given him any. What Clayton was saying made sense. And I hated him for it. I fixed my eyes on a spot just over his shoulder, refusing to look at him any longer.

"I'd like to leave now," I said coldly.

"I'm afraid I need to ask you a few more questions, Rose."

I folded my arms over my chest. "Well I'm not going to talk to you," I snapped. A part of me knew I was acting childish, but I couldn't bear to be near him any longer. And if I couldn't leave, then he was going to have to.

"Okay, Rose. I understand."

And damn it if he didn't sound like he understood. I would have almost preferred it if he had acted like an asshole. That would have made it easier to hold onto my anger. If I let it go, I knew grief would overwhelm me. And I wasn't going to break down. Not when Greg needed me.

I refused to watch him leave, but out of the corner of my eye I saw his female partner enter the room as he left it. The woman's expression was cool and professional when she sat down in Clayton's vacated seat. She looked competent and controlled in her neatly tailored white button-down shirt and black pinstriped slacks. I scowled at her.

"I'm Agent Silverman," she began.

"I know who you are," I snapped.

"But you can call me Sharon," she continued on over me as though I hadn't spoken.

Like hell I would. Were we supposed to be *friends?* Did she really think she was going to have a girl-to-girl chat with me? This bitch had arrested Greg and hardly spared me a second glance when Clayton had arrested me.

"What do you want, *Agent Silverman?*" I emphasized her official title, letting her know I wasn't up for chitchat. Although I knew answering her questions was necessary in order to get out of there, that didn't mean I had to play nice. This was an interrogation, not a cocktail party. And I wasn't going to pretend otherwise.

Despite my caustic tone, she appeared unruffled. "Okay," she said coolly. "I get it. I'll cut to the chase." She looked at me levelly. "I know this isn't what you want to hear, but Clayton was telling the truth: your brother *is* involved with the Latin Kings."

The calmness with which she confirmed this horrific news infuriated me. But this time I didn't deny it; the evidence was stacked against Greg. Still, I needed more proof before I was prepared to believe the worst.

"How do you know?" I demanded. "What do you have on him?"

"I can't tell you everything, but I won't lie to you," she promised solemnly. "We received a tip that Greg had been dealing for the Kings, so we've been watching him. There is photographic evidence. I can show it to you if you need to see it."

I didn't want to see it. But I needed to. I had to know for sure. My nod was jerky, my movements reluctant. Agent Silverman flicked open the manila folder that she had been holding and slid it across the table so I could see its contents. A series of photos were paper-clipped to it, and I pulled them free with shaking hands, spreading them out before me. My heart twisted at the images: Greg being discretely passed something by a hard-looking Latino guy who was covered in tattoos; Greg handing off a small package to a woman who looked like she was wasting away, her eyes wild; and the same Latino guy shoving Greg up against a brick wall, clearly threatening him. Was this the man who had hurt him earlier today? Was my baby brother truly so far gone that he would do terrible things and willingly take a beating just to get his next fix?

I felt sick; I could taste the burning tang of bile in the back of my throat. I swallowed hard and shoved the photos away from me, disgusted and heartbroken. My entire life revolved around protecting my brother as best I could. But I had failed. I had let him down.

"How long? How long has this been going on?" I asked quietly.

When I glanced up at Agent Silverman, I noticed her eyes had softened, her professional manner slipping. Maybe she wasn't such a cold bitch after all.

"About five weeks to our knowledge," she answered gently. "Listen, Rose. We know that Greg has been coerced into this. The Kings are ruthless, and it's obvious that they have threatened him and manipulated him into working for them."

I just shook my head, defeated. "I should have given him money." I hated the way my voice broke. "I just wanted to help him, to make him stop. But I couldn't stand seeing him in pain when he went through withdrawal. So I ignored the problem; I didn't question where he was getting the drugs." I hung my head in shame. "He should be in rehab. But I'm an enabler. I should have been harder on him, should have done the right thing. I just couldn't bear the thought of him hating me if I betrayed him like that."

Agent Silverman – Sharon – reached out and placed her hand over my clenched fist, squeezing gently. "I can understand that."

I glanced up at her, disbelieving. I was shocked to see nothing but sincerity in her rich brown eyes, and there was a hint of pain in her tightened features that convinced me she truly did understand.

My fingers unfurled, some of the tension leaving me. "Thanks," I said shakily, accepting her comfort. The sensation was completely unfamiliar. No one had ever treated me like this. Certainly not my mother. And my friends didn't know me on a deep enough level to know that I needed this. The bond I shared with Greg was the closest thing I had ever known to this feeling, but I was always the one supporting him, protecting him. And our lucid interactions had been few and far between over the last year since his addiction had claimed him. I hadn't allowed myself to fully realize how much I had missed him. It would have hurt too much. But now the pain of my loss crashed down on me, and I couldn't hold back the tears. Even worse, I was going to lose him completely; the FBI were going to lock him up, were going to take him away from me. As destructive as our relationship was, Greg was my whole life, and I didn't know how to function without him.

Sharon let me cry, and the sobs that wracked through me were almost painful. I wasn't sure if it was from the heaving of my lungs or the ache in my heart. Eventually, I pulled myself together. I had to convince Sharon to help Greg.

"What can I do?" I asked, my voice wavering as I blinked hard to clear my vision. "How can I help him? Please don't lock him up. You said yourself he's being coerced. He doesn't deserve to go to jail for that."

Sharon looked a little uncomfortable now. "We're willing to cut him a deal," she admitted slowly. "The Kings are ruthlessly expanding into new territories, and they are becoming more violent. It's more than we can handle. There are too many people like your brother who are being victimized and forced into helping them. But Greg can help us stop this. He can vindicate himself."

"How?" Hope bloomed in my chest.

She watched me carefully as she spoke. "We need him to spy on the Kings, to pass us information about who is involved and where they meet. We need names and concrete evidence in order to bring them down."

I shook my head forcefully. "No. They'll hurt him if they find out. I can't let you put him in danger like that."

Sharon's expression hardened. "He won't be any safer in jail. There are members of the Kings who are currently incarcerated. They'll kill him to keep him from talking. They know he owes them no loyalty, but they're willing to serve more time for murder in order to protect their friends. The Kings have tightly-knit communities, and they would rather die than take on the shame of betraying their friends. Even if they were willing to give evidence against their compatriots, they know they wouldn't survive long enough to go to trial to give evidence. We need people like Greg, good people who are just victims of circumstance. We *will* let him walk free if he's willing to work with us. And we'll keep a surveillance team on him at all times. At the first hint of danger, we'll pull him out. I won't allow him to come to any harm."

What she was saying made sense. I hated the idea of putting him in the line of fire, but it truly did sound like he would be safer with the FBI watching him at all times than he would be in prison.

"But if he keeps working with them, he'll keep using," I pointed out.

Sharon looked sad again, regretful. "We can't stop him if he chooses that. Maybe you can talk to him. If he agrees, we can put him through rehab before he does this. But if he refuses, I promise you we'll get him clean as soon as we get the information we need. Whether he wants to or not. We can get a court order."

I took a deep breath and nodded my agreement. "I'll do what I can," I promised. "And I'll convince him to help you. It's the only chance he has. I have to keep him safe, even if he hates me for it."

Sharon squeezed my hand again. "Thank you for understanding. This really is the best way."

"I know," I admitted. Now that it had been decided, I was anxious to get on with it as soon as possible. "Where is Greg? I need to talk to him."

"We'll send him home to you when he gets out of the hospital. He'll feel safer there and you'll have a better chance of convincing him. But I'm afraid I'll have to send someone with you in order to make sure he does choose to cooperate. And to protect both of you."

"Why would I need protecting? I'm not involved."

"I'm afraid you are," Sharon said evenly. "The Kings might not know about you, but we can't take the chance that they do. They might use you to get to Greg if they find out what he's doing. We can't take that risk."

Fear clenched my gut. I hadn't thought of that. But I would do what I had to in order to help my brother, even if it did mean having some annoying FBI agent breathing down my neck.

Sharon shifted slightly in her chair, looking uncomfortable again. "I'm not sure what's going on with you and Clayton, but I feel I should warn you that he's been assigned to your case."

"What?!" My voice was a few octaves higher than I would have liked.

"You can always refuse, but he was rather, ah, *insistent* about maintaining the assignment." She rolled her eyes. "To be honest, even if you do refuse, I'm pretty sure you'll need a restraining order to get him to back down. And he's not afraid to use underhanded tactics to get his way. The liberties Homeland Security grants us can be a bitch sometimes. Believe me, it will be much easier to save yourself the hassle."

I crossed my arms over my chest and cursed under my breath. "Asshole."

I had thought I liked his controlling side, but it seemed I had made a major mistake in coaxing it out of him.

Sharon shot me a small smile. "I couldn't agree more. But when he gets like this he doesn't really let anything get in his way. He can be very… tenacious when he wants to be. It's part of what makes him such a good agent. It's also what makes him a total ass sometimes."

Just then, the door opened and Clayton entered, a scowl plastered on his face. "Thanks for the glowing assessment of my character. You know I can hear everything out there."

Sharon just looked at him coolly. "I know."

I smiled at her, and she winked at me. Okay, so maybe she was winning me over.

Clayton was glaring at me. "I'm taking you home now."

"Fine," I said snappishly. "But I'll have you know that I don't appreciate the imperious tone."

He said nothing, but the roguish smile that spread across his face told me he knew very well that I *did* enjoy his imperious tone. Damn it, why the hell had I ever slept with the bastard? He knew far too much about me for my liking. And I most certainly *didn't* like the heat that flared in my belly at the sight of his knowing smirk. I didn't.

I was still pissed while Clayton was driving me home. At least I got to ride in the front seat this time, and I wasn't wearing handcuffs. That was *so* not the scenario I might have fantasized about involving Clayton and bondage.

Not that I was going to fantasize about him. I wasn't. Not only was he a heartless bastard, but it would be foolish of me to revisit the memories of our scorching hot night together. Unfortunately, my body wasn't exactly cooperating with my mind. The sexual tension that filled the small space of the car was almost stifling. His cocky air was maddening in an infuriatingly sexy way; he knew he had me backed into a corner, and he was in complete control of the situation. It was clear he was enjoying my predicament far too much for my taste. I was again struck by the realization that he was messing with my usual M.O. Although I was sexually submissive, I never truly lost control. I used my looks and my body to lure in my targets, my conquests. But now Clayton was taking the reins. It seemed he was going to get his way no matter what my wishes were. The thought pissed me off and unsettled me. And it got me hot for him. This new feeling of helplessness, of captivity, was darkly thrilling. I liked to push things to the edge sexually, to find my sweet release in extremes. And Clayton was definitely one of the most extreme things I had ever experienced. He wasn't going to let me get my way, and although a part of me railed against the idea, my lustful side reveled in exploring this new territory. How far would he push me? I longed to find out. I didn't have to like him, but I could certainly use him. If he was determined to stay close to me, then I would keep him close to my body.

With that resolution, I found myself almost eager to get back to my apartment where we could be alone. I had seduced him once before. How hard could it be to do it again? Judging by the hungry glances he was shooting my way, it wouldn't be too difficult. I kept my silence, deciding to play coy. Hopefully that would draw out his aggression.

But my lust was deflated like a popped balloon when we entered my apartment. Greg was home, and he was sober. Even though I was deeply disturbed by the situation he had gotten us into, I couldn't help feeling overjoyed at seeing him as his true self. It was a rare sight. I left Clayton's side in a heartbeat, launching myself at my little brother and grabbing him up in a tight embrace.

"Greg! Thank god you're alright. I was so worried about you."

He was stiff in my arms for the space of a moment, but my heart swelled near to bursting when his arms closed around me as well. He rested his chin on the top of my head as I buried my face in his shoulder. My tears of relief at seeing him safe wet his t-shirt.

"I was worried about you too, Rosie," he admitted tremulously. "They told me they had arrested you for trying to help me. I'm sorry. God, I am such a fuck-up," he groaned.

I pulled away from him slightly so I could look up into his eyes. They were the same as mine: pale green ringed with indigo. That was our only physical similarity. Where I was pale-skinned and platinum blonde, he was tan with an unruly mop of curly brown hair. Apparently he took after my father, but I honestly couldn't remember what he looked like. Right now I was thrilled to look into those eyes that were a mirror for my own. They were clear for the first time in I didn't know how long.

My fingers curled around his arms, unwilling to let him go. "You're going to be okay, Greg," I said firmly. "I'm not going to let you go to jail."

Fear flashed across his face. "I'm not going to jail. Am I? They let me come home. And they let you go too. We're fine." His eyes darted to Clayton where he stood just inside the doorway. "What's he doing here?" Greg asked suspiciously.

I gripped him harder, drawing his attention back to me. "He's here to help us, Greg. Clayton is with the FBI. He told me..." I tripped over the words. "He told me about the Latin Kings. I know what they're making you do, and it has to stop."

Now anger flashed over his features, and he jerked away from me. I hated the distance he put between us.

"You don't know anything," he hissed through gritted teeth. The addicted monster that had possessed my sweet brother was coming to the fore. Usually, this would be the point where I would back down. But not this time.

When I spoke, I made my tone forceful, determined. "I know you're dealing for them. I know they hurt you. And I'm not going to let that continue. You're going to help the FBI take down the Kings. It's the only way to keep you out of jail; it's the only way to keep you safe."

"Are you crazy?!" He half-shouted, his rage taking over. "They'll kill me if they find out I've turned against them!"

I glowered at him, my own anger rising to meet his. This person before me wasn't my brother; it was some twisted demon that wore my brother's face. And I would be damned if I didn't force it out of him. "You're going to help the FBI, or you're going to jail. That's the deal. If you choose jail, you're as good as dead. And I'm not letting you choose that."

"Fuck you! You don't get to tell me what I can and can't do!"

"Don't you dare talk to her like that." Clayton's voice was soft, but the coldness of his tone gave it a much more dangerous edge than if he had shouted. Greg froze, his eyes riveted on Clayton. His muscles were tense, bracing for a fight, but one look at the imposing FBI agent made him back down.

"Your sister is right," Clayton continued sharply. "I will arrest you if you don't cooperate. You should listen to her. And you sure as hell should treat her with more respect after everything she's done for you." The threat of violence that pulsed around him was nearly palpable. The force of it almost made me take a step back. Clayton might seem sweet and easygoing on the surface, but this was a man you most definitely did not want to fuck with.

Greg dropped his eyes. "Sorry," he mumbled. He looked almost petulant, like the child I had known for so many years. In that moment I was struck by just how young he still was. How had I allowed him to be reduced to what he had become? I had been too easy on him, had let him get his way. Yes, I had wanted to protect him, but now I realized I was so terrified of losing him that I had let him walk all over me. I had let him destroy himself rather than risking pushing him away by reprimanding him. But that was all going to change now.

"I know you're sorry," I said gently. "And that's why you have to make things right. You can't keep helping the Kings, Greg. They don't just deal drugs. They're violent, and they hurt people. They kill people. And I'm not going to let them hurt you."

He hung his head, defeated. I hated the way he unconsciously ran his hand up and down over the crook of his arm. He had only been sober for a few hours, but already he was craving his next fix.

"Okay. I'll do it." He sounded weary and more than a little scared.

I lightly touched my hand to his cheek, a reassuring gesture. "Don't worry. The FBI will be watching you. They'll keep you safe. But I need you to get clean before you do this."

That furious, twisted expression was back in an instant. His hands closed around my shoulders, and all of the air was knocked from my lungs as he shoved me harshly against the wall. "No!" His fingers dug into my flesh painfully. "I'm not going to quit. You can't make me," he snarled.

"Greg. Please. You're hurting me." My voice was weak as I gasped for air.

Almost as quickly as he had pinned me, he was torn away from me. Greg was on the floor, his face pressed into the hardwood. Clayton had twisted his arm behind his back, lifting it away from his body. Greg cried out in obvious pain.

"You're going to break my arm!" He wailed.

Panic shot through me. "Clayton! Let him go!"

He ignored me. "Apologize," he ordered, his voice tight with suppressed fury. As he spoke, he jerked on Greg's arm. My brother whimpered.

"I'm sorry," he gasped out.

"You're not going to touch her again. Do you understand?"

"Yes!" He cried out. "Fuck! I'm sorry!"

"Clayton, please! Stop hurting him," I begged.

Clayton looked up at me, and most of the fury drained from his eyes when they met mine. He stood, releasing Greg. My brother pushed himself to his feet, wincing as he worked his arm back and forth. Despite his apologies, he was still glowering at me. He turned sharply and strode towards the door.

"Where are you going?" Anxiety made my voice high and thin. I didn't want him to leave. Not when he was so enraged. Who knew what he might do? He was probably going to use again.

He glanced back at me. "Where do you think?" He sneered. His glare briefly turned on Clayton. "And don't worry. I'll do my job. But I'm pretty sure it'll be more convincing if I'm using."

Clayton's expression was thunderous, but he made no move to stop him. "We'll be watching you," he said simply. It sounded more like a warning than a reassurance of his safety.

Greg just rolled his eyes and stalked out of the apartment, slamming the door behind him.

My legs refused to support me as a torrent of emotion overwhelmed me. I sat down heavily on my bed and buried my face in my hands, my fingers twining in my hair and pulling at it. But the resultant small, sharp pain did little to distract me from the agony that was clawing at my heart.

This was what I had always been afraid of. This was why I had never been firm with Greg about getting clean. He had turned on me, his addiction burning away any love or loyalty he had ever felt for me. But I had never imagined he would actually attack me, to try to cause me physical harm. All I had ever done was protect him, but now it seemed I was going to have to protect myself from him. Still, I knew I would never raise a hand against him. After the first time he had come to me in tears, I had taken the hits for him from too many of my mom's asshole boyfriends; the instinct to keep him from harm was so deeply ingrained in me that I would never be able to hurt him.

All I could do was pray he would keep his word and help the FBI. Then Clayton would force him to go to rehab. I would have my brother back.

If he'll ever speak to you again after what you've done.

Chapter 4

The mattress shifted as Clayton sat down beside me. His long fingers encircled my wrists and gently pulled my hands from my face so I couldn't tug at my hair. Then his arm was around my back, pulling me against his chest. He held me as I cried long and hard, his fingers stroking up and down my back in a soothing rhythm. Just as had happened with Sharon, I was again struck by the unfamiliarity of being cared for. Usually, I would have been ashamed for anyone to see this vulnerable, messed-up side of me. But Clayton knew my dark secret now, and still he was holding me. I didn't seem to disgust him.

But I had been crying far too much today for my own comfort. It was a self-indulgent act that didn't do anyone any good whatsoever. Willing myself to take control of my emotions, I drew in several deep, shaky breaths. As I centered myself, I was embarrassed to realize that Clayton's expensive suit was soaked with my tears.

"Your suit's all wet," I mumbled. "Sorry."

He hooked a finger under my chin and lifted my face to his. His soft smile helped to ease some of the tension that lingered in my chest.

"It's an occupational hazard."

"Oh?" My brows rose. "Do women often cry in your arms in your line of work?"

His smile suddenly looked a bit forced, and his eyes darkened. "Not so much lately."

A flash of irrational jealously spiked through me as I wondered what woman he had been holding. He did his best to hide it, but his expression told me she was someone he had cared about a great deal.

I shoved down my foolish reaction, suppressing the urge to pull away from him and pout. I didn't care about Clayton in that way. He seemed so sweet at times, but the fact of the matter was he was putting Greg in a dangerous situation. Even if he was just trying to help, I wished he would just put my brother through rehab and then leave him be. The FBI we coercing Greg into spying on the Kings every bit as much as the gang had coerced him into selling for them. They had given him an ultimatum: help the FBI or be murdered in prison.

I looked up at Clayton beseechingly.

"Please, don't do this to him. You don't have to arrest Greg. If you just put him in rehab, he'll be okay. He doesn't have to spy for you. You're going to get him killed."

Clayton's expression was twisted with regret, and there was something akin to anguish in his eyes. "I know this isn't easy for you, Rose," he said softly. "And I know it won't be easy for Greg either. If it were as simple as getting him clean, then that's what I would do. Believe it or not, I'm not just out to throw addicts in prison. That doesn't help anyone. But what's happening right now with the Kings is very serious. There are hundreds of other people like Greg out there right now, people who are being ruthlessly manipulated into doing the Kings' bidding. It has to stop, Rose. And Greg can help us with that."

"Why him?" I asked bitterly. "Why can't you get someone else?"

He looked at me sadly. "There are others helping us, Rose. But the Kings are split into rival factions. It only makes them more dangerous, and it means it will take more than one person to take them all down. We've been doing what we can, but it's not enough. People are suffering, Rose. People are dying. If it weren't your brother taking on this task, it would be someone else's. This gives Greg a chance to vindicate himself, to free himself from the habit that has taken over his life. In the end, he will be better for it. I'm not going to let anyone hurt him, Rose. I swear."

I still wanted to argue, to plead with him to change his mind.

"If it weren't your brother taking on this task, it would be someone else's."

A nasty little voice inside of me said I didn't care about anyone else's brother. Greg was *mine.* Some other faceless addict could take his place.

But that was wrong, and I instantly felt sickened by myself at the selfish thought. After knowing everything Greg had gone through, everything he had put me through… I wouldn't wish that on anyone. And I certainly wouldn't want to put anyone in the situation we were in now. I was terrified for my brother, and more than a little scared for myself. But Clayton was right: helping the FBI would be good for Greg. When he got clean, he would be able to see that. The good he would do would help him get past what he had become, would help him find himself again. He had always been such a sweet kid. But he was too trusting; he had believed the best in everyone to a fault. Then at seventeen he had graduated high school and moved out on his own. It only took a few months for the real world to crush that trust right out of him. Maybe if I hadn't sheltered him so carefully from bad people, he would have known how to deal with it. When it came down to it, that was the real reason why I ran myself ragged trying to look after him. I loved him fiercely and had always tried to keep him safe, but ultimately it was my fault that he had turned to the drugs. A little tough love and a healthy dose of reality were long overdue for Greg. It was time for me to step up to the plate and push him; I couldn't coddle him any longer.

Finally, I nodded, accepting the truth of what Clayton had said.

"You'll get him in rehab when this is over, right? Even if he doesn't want to go?"

"Yes. I'll make him go, Rose. He won't like me for it – and he might not like you for a while either – but you will get your brother back." He was studying me intently, and I couldn't help being captivated by his gorgeous eyes: azure shot through with cobalt and cyan. They were clear and honest, and all of the times I had cursed him as an asshole and a bastard suddenly seemed very wrong.

Those eyes darkened as he reached out and gently touched my shoulder. The feeling of his rough fingertips on my skin made me want to shiver.

"He hurt you." The thread of anger was barely discernible in his calm tone.

I was slightly bewildered to find faint bruises on my pale flesh. My puzzlement soon gave way to disgust as I realized what had caused them: Greg.

I was tired of being upset, tired of crying. My emotions were running rampant today, ruling my actions in a way I didn't usually allow. I just needed an escape. If I got away from my problems for a while they would be more manageable when I was forced to face them again.

And there was Clayton, six-feet-three-inches of the most delicious upper I could ever imagine. Sex with him was far more transcendental than a hit of Ecstasy.

My decision made, I leaned into him and boldly pressed my mouth to his. The masculine scent that was uniquely his – salt-kissed leather – enfolded me. He was as intoxicating as five Long Island Iced Teas. No. He was better than that. Because alcohol can't kiss you back.

Every tug of his lips on mine pulled me a little further away from reality and a little closer to bliss. I wanted more. I wanted to taste him, to drink him in until I was drunk. Or maybe I would even drown.

My tongue traced the line of his lower lip and made teasing forays into his mouth. He answered with the ferocity I craved. He delved into my mouth roughly as his hard body pressed me down onto my back. Between his demanding tongue and the weight of him against my chest, I could hardly draw breath. The world was falling away around me, leaving my head spinning in the most magnificent way. I *was* going to drown in him; the thought made my clit pulse with an almost painful intensity.

I ground my hips up against him in wanton abandon, and I was pleased to feel the hard length of him pressing into me. My fingers fumbled blindly at the buttons of his shirt. I longed to feel his sweat-slicked skin against mine as his body moved over me.

His hands closed around my wrists, halting my efforts. I let out a lustful moan as he pinned my arms to the bed on either side of my head, and I ground against him more frantically as my core throbbed in response to his domineering treatment.

A small whimper of protest escaped me as he tore his lips from mine. As much as I hated the loss of his mouth upon me, I thrilled at the idea of him taking control, even if it meant denying me what I wanted.

"Rose." The lust that roughened his voice when he spoke my name sent ecstatic tingles rippling across my flesh. They danced over my skin, crackling and popping like thousands of miniature fireworks. The heat of it was a delectable burn. It ignited the need within me like nothing I'd ever known, and I was desperate for him to touch me.

"Clayton," I breathed. "Please…"

His eyes glazed over with desire at the sound of my begging, and I could feel his cock harden further. But he didn't move. He was making me wait. I desperately wanted to touch him, to grab him and pull him down against me. I jerked against his grip on my wrists, but he held me fast. The reminder of my own powerlessness, of his control, made the denial of my needs a sweet torment.

He blinked hard and shook his head slightly. With a visible effort, he pulled away, releasing his hold on my wrists. I stared up at him, puzzled. What kind of game was this? His expression was difficult to read, but if anything he looked slightly abashed.

"I'm sorry," he said softly.

"What?" I felt like I had just been doused with a bucket of ice water, and I jolted up into a sitting position, suddenly uncomfortable in my vulnerable position on my back. Cutting tendrils of rejection began to slowly unfurl in my chest.

Clayton ran a hand through his hair. I refused to allow myself to appreciate how sexy he looked with it all mussed up like that.

"You're upset after everything that's happened today," he said evenly. "It was wrong of me to take advantage of you like that."

It was so absurd that I had to laugh. He looked bewildered by my reaction.

"What?" He asked, looking wary.

I smirked at him. "*I* kissed *you,* remember? Who's taking advantage of whom here?"

I had thought he might crack a smile. Or maybe even push me down again just to prove who was supposed to be in charge. That was most certainly a desirable outcome. But to my dismay, his expression remained serious.

"I'm supposed to be here to protect you. It would be unprofessional of me to touch you. Especially when you're emotionally vulnerable."

He was really killing my buzz. Didn't he understand I didn't want to be vulnerable to my emotions? This was how I took control of them.

No, this is how you suppress them, a nasty little truthful voice corrected me. But I ignored it.

"You weren't doing anything wrong," I insisted. "I wanted it. I want *you.*"

I reached out and fisted my hand in his shirt, using it as an anchor to pull my body towards his once again. He pressed his palm against my chest, stopping me short. My nipples hardened as I became aware of how close he was to touching my breasts. He seemed to realize the same thing, and he jerked his hand away as though my flesh burned him.

I made an exasperated sound and released him. "Fine," I snapped, throwing up my hands. "I get it. You're too much of a goody-two-shoes to break a few rules. I don't know what happened to the Clayton I met last night, but he was much more fun than *Agent Vaughn*." I imbued the title with as much venom as I could muster.

His brows drew together angrily. "I've made mistakes before, Rose. I don't want to make them with you."

"*Mistakes?* Is that what that kiss was? Is that what last night was? A *mistake?!*" I was suddenly livid. And more than a little hurt.

He instantly caught my hands in his, his expression contrite. "That's not what I meant at all," he said gently. "It's just... I've misread situations before. I don't want you to do something you might regret because I made a move at an inappropriate time."

He really was too good to be true. It might have been admirable if it wasn't so goddamn irritating. His sense of honor was getting in the way of my good time.

"Believe me, you haven't misread anything here," I assured him. "Besides, I fucked you before I knew my brother and I were in danger. So you can drop the 'it wouldn't be professional' bullshit."

Clayton frowned. "You've had a rough day. I don't want you to regret something that we might do right now. Besides, I don't just want to *fuck* you, Rose."

I snorted. "You wanted to last night."

His frown deepened and his eyes flashed. "I told you I don't do one-night-stands. I never would have invited you back to my place if I hadn't wanted to see you again. I certainly didn't want to meet you again under the current circumstances, but I'd be lying if I said I wasn't glad our paths crossed." He glared at me. "You weren't going to call me, were you?"

My first instinct was to scoot away from him. He looked pissed off and a little dangerous. And damn was it a good look on him.

"And why did you lie to me about your name?" He demanded when I didn't answer right away.

I tried to extricate my hands from his, suddenly uncomfortable with the turn this conversation was taking. Only a moment ago I was sure he was going to help me fuck all of my cares away, but now he was prying into painful subjects. Who was he to question my life choices? My anger flared hot and bright.

"What is this, an interrogation?" I snapped. "You might be some big-shot FBI agent, but the last time I checked there were no laws against being a slut."

Clayton's expression was livid, his eyes blazing. He stood stiffly, all of his muscles taut with his anger. "You're not a slut, Rose. But if that's how I make you feel, then I'll leave you alone. I'm sorry I forced my way onto your case. I shouldn't have imposed myself on you in that way. We'll still be keeping an eye on you, but there's no need for me to be in your personal space in order to keep you safe. You have my number. Call me if you or your brother need anything."

I was too stunned to move to stop him as he strode out of my apartment. How had I just fucked things up so epically? One minute I was close to getting the release I needed, and the next I was sitting alone on my bed, feeling like shit about myself.

"You're not a slut, Rose."

That just proved he didn't know me at all. Or maybe he envisioned me as a different person than I was. Maybe his pure-as-the-driven-snow ego couldn't allow him to see the truth of what I was, as though acknowledging my disrepute might tarnish him in some way.

It didn't matter anyway. I was just relieved he was gone. I had told myself it would be unwise to try to see Clayton again after our night of passion, and it turned out I had been right.

Chapter 5

I had to fight down the urge to spew the disgusting drink right back out of my mouth. "Ugh, that tastes like dirty woodchips or something!" My hand darted across the table to grab Penny's cosmopolitan, which I gulped down eagerly. The sugary sweetness of it helped to wash away the nasty flavor.

"Hey!" My friend cried. "That's mine! And I told you not to order that crap. It's what old men with no taste-buds left drink." Her glower was censorious as I set down the now-empty martini glass. "I believe you owe me a cocktail."

"Shit. Sorry. I'll trade you?" I asked hopefully, pushing the glass of neat whisky in her direction.

Penny just tossed her long brown hair over her shoulder and raised one eyebrow, shooting me her best *you have got to be fucking kidding me* look with those glacial blue eyes. Damn, she looked cool when she did that. I had always wished I could. Unfortunately, I looked like I was having some kind of fit if I tried to raise one eyebrow.

With a resigned sigh, I went to the bar and ordered two more cosmos, trying not to wince as I handed over my credit card. I really couldn't afford them, especially after the Glenfiddich I had ordered proved to be un-drinkable.

How the hell does Clayton drink that crap? I wondered.

A better question is: Why the hell did you order it?

It had been three days since Clayton had stormed out of my apartment, and I hadn't heard from him since. But that didn't stop my mind from constantly thinking about him. I hated how upset I had made him. Putting together a few pieces, it had become clear to me that he was dealing with some past fuck-up of his own regarding fraternization in the workplace. He was just trying to be careful not to make the same mistakes again.

Of course he was. Doing so might cost him his job.

Or maybe he really is just a decent guy.

I rolled my eyes at myself. It didn't matter if he was a knight in shining armor or a self-centered jerk. I wasn't going to see him again. I had made sure of that with my childish actions. It was for the best, really.

Plastering on a cheery, carefree smile, I headed back to my table.

"So, who's the asshole?" Penny asked perceptively.

My smile wavered slightly. I had invited her out to throw back some drinks and dance, not hash out my problems. But maybe a good bitching session would help me get my mind off of Clayton.

"Cheryl. Who else?" It took no extra effort to spit out her name like something distasteful. Penny knew all about the bitch; she used to work at Ivory too. She had gone to the same school as Cheryl had, so of course she had no trouble getting the job. It also didn't hurt that she came from a wealthy background, so somehow that made her a person of worth in Cheryl's eyes. But, much to my surprise, Penny was actually a sweet, down-to-earth person. And she knew how to keep up with me at a party. We had only worked together for six months before she found a job somewhere else. The way Cheryl treated me drove her crazy, and as much as I appreciated her show of solidarity, I asked her to keep her nose out of it. She was my only friend at work, and I didn't want to lose her. But then one day Cheryl had apparently said something so out of line that Penny couldn't stop herself from going off on her. She still wouldn't tell me what it was Cheryl had said, and a part of me was grateful for that. I didn't think I really wanted to know. In any case, her tirade had resulted in her being asked to leave Ivory. But Penny was smart and talented and she had the piece of paper that said she had the right education, so she quickly found employment elsewhere. I missed having a friend at work, but we still got together regularly for a good, long drinking session.

That imperious brow rose again. "The guy, Rose," Penny insisted. "Who's the guy?"

Shit. I didn't realize she was *that* perceptive.

"What makes you think there's a guy?"

"Well, for one thing – don't take this the wrong way – you're not looking your best today."

I couldn't help laughing at that. I could always count on Penny to bluntly cut to the chase. "How could I possibly take that the wrong way?"

She waved away my sarcastic comment. "You're still drop-dead-gorgeous. And I know not all of us are fortunate enough to not have to own foundation, but you really should invest in some if you're going to have dark circles like that. I've known you to pull an all-nighter and still show up at work the next day looking fresh as a daisy. So how much sleep have you lost over this guy?"

I touched my face self-consciously. "Damn, does it show that badly?"

"No one who didn't know you would even notice," she assured me. "But then you ordered that drink and I knew something was up. That has 'man-drink' written all over it. What really worries me is I've never seen anyone under the age of sixty order it in a bar. Please don't tell me you've fallen for some geriatric."

I rolled my eyes at her. "He's probably not even thirty."

"Ha!" She snapped her fingers and smiled triumphantly. "So it *is* a guy."

"Fine," I threw up my hands in defeat. "It's a guy."

She considered me carefully for a moment, tapping a perfectly-manicured fingernail against her full red lips. "Why, Rose Baker, I don't think I've ever known you to get your panties in a bunch over a man. You usually eat them alive, not the other way around."

"I do not!" I protested.

My friend shot me a level look. "I've seen you hunt down your quarry like a hungry lioness. And you always get your kill."

"I am not a lioness!" God, she made me sound like some sort of predator. I wanted to be the prey. But Penny didn't know about my kinks, so I kept that piece of information to myself.

"Okay, maybe a Siren, then," she conceded. "You tend to lure them in rather than tackling them to the ground. But the fact is you always get the one you want, and you always get him on your terms. Now the question is: Who has finally turned the tables on you?"

"Yeah, I definitely prefer the Siren thing," I deflected.

"You didn't answer my question," she pointed out. "Who is he, and what did he do to you?"

I pursed my lips, not up for sharing. She just cocked that damn eyebrow again. I sighed, giving in to its power.

"His name is Clayton. And he didn't do anything, exactly. It's… complicated."

I couldn't tell her about what was going on with Greg and the FBI even if I had wanted to. And I definitely didn't want to talk about Greg. I had barely seen him since he had gotten violent with me, and when I had he had been totally strung out. The one time he had been lucid I had to bully him into eating something. I tried to ask him how he was holding up, but he had just snapped at me until I gave up.

Some of my frustration and hurt must have shown in my expression, because Penny nodded sagely. "It looks like it is pretty complicated. What's wrong with him? Is he mean to you? I know you go for the rough, bad-boy type. They're hot, but they will always hurt you in the end."

Didn't I know it. Marco had taught me that lesson a long time ago. He was brawny and tattooed and mean as hell. But he was sweet to me, and I had loved him for it. The fact that he was this terrifying guy who would deny his violent urges just for me made me feel special. I thought our relationship had changed him.

But you can't change someone who doesn't want to change. And guys like that rarely want to. He turned that side of himself on me once, and I was done. It had shattered my heart, but I wasn't going to stay with a guy who thought hitting me in anger was a forgivable offense.

"No," I quickly came to Clayton's defense. "He's not like that. He's a really nice guy."

"'*Nice?*' Say no more. I totally get it. He's great, but he's a total wet blanket in the sack, right? That is a predicament."

Images of my hot night with Clayton flashed across my mind, and I blushed. "No," I said firmly. "That is most definitely not the problem."

Penny looked at me quizzically. "So let me get this straight," she said, holding up three fingers. "He's not geriatric." She ticked down one finger. "He's nice." A second finger went down. "And the sex was amazing." Now she was just holding up her fist, and she looked as though she was considering using it to knock some sense into me. "What's the problem?"

I really wanted to explain about the fucked up situation we were in with Greg in order to defend myself, but I wasn't allowed to do that. And if I was really honest with myself, Greg wasn't the problem here. Hadn't I been holding Clayton at a distance ever since I had first met him?

"Me," I admitted quietly. "I guess I'm the problem."

Penny's expression softened and she lowered her fist to rest her hand on mine reassuringly. "You're not a problem," she said gently. "But if some issue is holding you back, maybe you should talk to him about it."

I bit my lip, uncertain. "I'm not really good at talking about my issues."

"Really? I hadn't noticed," she said drily.

I had always figured Penny thought of me as her carefree, hard-partying friend. But apparently she knew me better than I realized. The thought made me uncomfortable. I didn't want her to stop hanging out with me if I became too much drama for her to handle. Because my life was loaded with more drama than an episode of *The Real Housewives of New Jersey.*

Keen as ever, Penny seemed to recognize my discomfiture and gave me an out. She picked up her martini glass and clinked it against mine. "Bottoms up. Last one to finish buys the next two rounds."

The little cheat already had her glass to her lips before I could even get my hand around mine. But as experienced a drinker as Penny was, she was no match for me. I hated to rush through a ten-dollar cocktail, but I didn't like losing. And my wallet definitely couldn't afford to take another hit. My cosmo was gone in a matter of seconds.

"Off to the bar with you then," I decreed as I slammed down my empty glass. Penny's was still half-full.

"Damn. How do you do that?"

"I just open my throat." I winked at her.

"You hear that, bro? She just opens her throat and takes it down."

"I'll bet she does."

I looked over to see two college-aged boys standing at the bar near our table. One of them was grabbing his crotch obscenely while the other high-fived him.

Penny's gorgeous features twisted into something terrifying and livid. The boys froze, and one even took a step back in the wake of her ball-shriveling glare.

"You think you can do better?" I asked them coolly as I slipped off my chair.

"What are you doing?" Penny hissed at me.

"I've got this," I assured her. The corners of my lips turned up in my most devious smirk as I sauntered over to them. Their mouths were hanging open slightly, and the one guy didn't seem to realize that he still had his hand on his dick.

If I was a lioness, then I was going to rip these boys apart with my claws. And I was going to get a few free drinks in the process.

I didn't stop walking until I had entered their personal space. The deer-in-headlights look they were both giving me was priceless. I addressed the one who was touching himself.

"Do you have herpes?" I asked bluntly.

He looked confused for a moment, but then his eyes lit up. "No, don't worry baby, I'm clean. Why? You interested?"

"Not particularly." I glanced down at his hand pointedly. "But it looks like you have an itch."

"Wha-" His face turned scarlet as my words registered, and he jerked his hand away as though his dick had morphed into a red-hot poker. The other boy laughed at his friend.

"No, baby, he was just trying to hide his boner after he saw you *open your throat* like that. Looks like you've had a lot of practice."

Inside, I bristled at the insinuation. It hit a little too close to home for my comfort. But I remained outwardly calm. Oh, I was going to make these guys pay. Literally.

Penny had come to stand beside me now. It was clear she thought I was acting crazy, but she was a good enough friend that she would stand by me even if she did think I had gone insane. Besides, getting crazy on a night out on the town was kind of my thing. She was used to it.

I just smiled at him. "And I believe I already asked you if you think you can do better?" My eyes flashed challengingly, and I was pleased to see the look of interest on the boy's face.

The one who I had embarrassed was still pissed, though. "No, baby, we don't suck dick."

His friend punched him hard on the shoulder. "Hey, don't be an ass, dude." He looked at me apologetically. "I'm Jeff," he introduced himself. "This douchebag is Sam. And he doesn't have herpes, but he does have crabs."

"Yeah," Sam agreed, rubbing his arm where Jeff had punched him. "I got them from your mom."

"Your mom" jokes? Really?

I giggled to stroke his ego, and he grinned at me. Apparently I was easily forgiven for mocking him about having herpes. What he didn't realize was that I hadn't even begun to truly fuck with him.

"This is Gloria," I hooked my thumb at Penny. "And I'm Stella." I always tried to come up with a new fake name. It was like being someone else for a night. *Rose* had a bitchy boss and a junkie brother and the FBI breathing down her neck. *Stella* could be anyone she wanted to be.

Penny rolled with it, not confused in the slightest. This wasn't her first rodeo with me.

"Are you boys up for a drinking competition?" I challenged.

Jeff puffed out his chest a little. "I don't think that would be very fair." His eyes roved over Penny and me in a way he probably thought was flattering. "You two ladies don't look like you could handle much booze."

"It's not about volume, it's about speed," I stipulated. "I couldn't help but overhear you two commenting on my skills. I asked if you thought you could do better. I still haven't gotten an answer."

I pouted slightly and put my hands on my hips in a way that thrust out my breasts. Jeff made a visible effort to maintain eye contact, but Sam's gaze riveted on my chest. God, these guys were easy to manipulate. And I had to admit, playing with them was pretty fun. Especially because they deserved it.

Jeff's smile was slightly condescending, as though he sensed an easy victory. "Okay, then. You're on. What are we drinking? Do you ladies like Bud Light?"

Penny snorted derisively. "Light beer? Where's the challenge in that? We're talking hard liquor, boys." She looked at me questioningly. "What do you think, Stella? Dirty Grey Goose martinis? You like it dirty, right?"

Oh, she was good. She was going to make them pay through the nose. The conspiratorial grin I gave her was genuine. "You know me all *too* well, Gloria." I touched her arm lightly as I spoke, the way girls do when they're trying to get attention from guys.

Jeff's and Sam's mouths were hanging open again. I was pretty sure Sam was about to start drooling. It took effort not to laugh as I stared at them expectantly. Jeff, who seemed to be quicker on his feet – if only slightly – shook himself and turned to the bartender to order the martinis. He looked a bit sick as he handed over a wad of cash for our pricey drinks, and I felt a surge of vindictive triumph. But I wasn't done with them yet. A little more humiliation was in order.

I allowed my fingers to brush his forearm as I reached for my glass, and was pleased to see lust flare in his eyes. His balls were going to be aching by the time I finished with him. Allowing my touch to linger, I leaned into him until my lips were at his ear. His breaths were warm against my neck, and they quickened as I made him wait. Smiling evilly, I finally whispered, "Go."

With that as his only warning, I pulled back from him and raised my glass. He stared at me dumbly as I raised it to my lips and poured it down my throat, never breaking eye contact with him. I finished in a matter of seconds. No one else even came close to touching me. Penny came in second, no doubt because she wasn't encumbered by a penis getting in the way of her brain. Even then, her glass was still about two-thirds of the way full. Sam had managed a swallow, but Jeff was just staring at me in awe, his drink untouched.

I wasn't sure if the rush I felt was from the alcohol or my victory. It was a shame to have downed Grey Goose rather than enjoying it, but it was either drink it or toss it in Jeff's face. I had always wanted to throw a martini at a deserving douchebag, but that wasn't the lesson I was trying to teach tonight.

"Looks like I win!" I said brightly. "What's my prize?"

Jeff's expression was almost reverential. "Anything you want, baby."

A sly grin spread across my face, and I leaned into him again, splaying my fingers across his chest this time. "Anything?" I asked huskily. He nodded enthusiastically. I touched my tongue to my lips, pretending to consider my options for a moment. "I think I'll have another martini for now," I declared. "And as the losers, you boys have to do three shots of gin. Each."

Sam had something to say about that. "Shots of *gin?!* No way. That's fucking disgusting."

I kept my attention on Jeff, making my eyes go wide and innocent. "I think as the winner it's only fair that I get to decide. Don't you?"

He hesitated, glancing over at his friend. Penny chimed in just in time to seal the deal. "Well, if you boys can't handle your liquor, then I guess we'll have to go find someone else to play with."

"No. Wait, baby. We'll do it." It seemed Sam had set his sights on Penny. She gave him a smile so dazzling he looked as though someone had slapped him across the face.

This wasn't just easy. This was *fun.* I wondered briefly if this was what it felt like to be a Dominatrix. Wielding this sort of power over men was heady.

A few minutes later, the shots were lined up on the bar and I had a fresh, expensive martini in my hand – one I intended to savor this time around.

The boys looked at each other solemnly as they lifted their glasses, apprehension etched across their features. Sam gagged and stalled out after the first shot, but Jeff took them back one after another in order to get it over with quickly. When he was finished, he grabbed his martini and gulped it down.

"Yeah, because using vodka and vermouth as a chaser is a great idea," Penny whispered, and I couldn't help laughing out loud.

We finished the last of our martinis as the boys coughed and spluttered. At one point, I thought Sam was going to be sick, but he held it together. He also decided his martini was a good chaser.

"I need the restroom, Gloria," I announced.

"Sure," she replied, hooking her arm through mine. "I'll come with you."

I smiled at Jeff. His cheeks were pink and his eyes were over-bright. Perfect. These guys were going to be too fucked up to even get themselves off tonight, much less lure some poor girl home with them. My work here was done.

"We'll be right back," I lied. "Don't go anywhere."

"We won't!" Jeff called after me, a promise in his voice.

As soon as we crossed the exit and the cool night air hit us, Penny and I erupted with laughter. It was the kind of laughter so all-consuming that it takes your breath away and makes your eyes water. By the time it subsided, I was leaning up against the brick wall outside the bar, my chest heaving as I gasped for air. My head was spinning, and I wasn't sure if it was from the lack of oxygen reaching my brain or the four cocktails I had downed in the space of an hour.

"That..." Penny gasped out. "Was awesome. Remind me never to insult you."

"You were damn good with the assists," I said seriously. "I couldn't have done it without you, Gloria."

We burst into a fit of giggles all over again. God, I had needed this. Teaching those mouthy college boys a well-deserved lesson had been exhilarating. Even better, it had gotten my mind off of Greg and Clayton for a solid hour.

Fuck. I didn't want to go home yet, didn't want to have to return to being Rose and take on all of the problems that came along with her.

"So where to next?" I asked with false enthusiasm.

"Uh-uh," Penny shook her head. "I am not up for a Rose Baker all-night adventure. I have to work tomorrow."

"Aw, c'mon. Don't be lame, Penn." My voice came out sounding more pleading than I had intended for it to. And Penny didn't miss it. She put her hand on my shoulder and squeezed lightly.

"Hey," she said gently. "If it's bothering you this much, you really should just call him."

Damn, she was perceptive. The woman should be a therapist, not a fashion designer. And I did want to call Clayton. All of the alcohol was making me horny. It heated my veins and made my pussy pulse. I could march back into the bar and find another guy easily. But I didn't want another guy.

I pulled out my phone to check the time. The numbers blurred and danced, so I blinked hard until they settled into a recognizable pattern. 10:42. That was still early enough to call, right?

"I need your opinion, Penn. Is it obviously a booty call after 10 PM?"

"That depends. *Are* you calling him for sex?"

I nodded. There was no point in lying.

She deliberated for a moment. "Maybe send a few texts to test the waters. You don't want to sound desperate if he's not up for it. It is a Thursday night, after all. Not all of us are capable of working hard all day and playing hard all night and still looking flawless," she said ruefully.

"I don't know who you're talking about. Apparently I have dark circles under my eyes," I quipped.

She made an exasperated noise and made a grab for my phone. "Are you going to text him or am I going to have to do it for you?"

My body careened to the side as I moved to jerk it out of her reach, and my shoulder collided painfully with the brick wall. Apparently I was more intoxicated than I had originally thought.

"Okay, no sex for you," Penny decreed firmly. "You're going home."

"Alright, alright." I held up my hands, capitulating. "I guess it's been enough fun for one evening."

"Do you want to share a cab?" Her eyes were filled with concern.

"Don't be ridiculous. You don't live anywhere near my apartment."

"Okay, then," she said as she hailed a cab. "You take the first one."

I shook my head. "I just spent my cab money on some pricey, disgusting whisky. I'm taking the bus."

There was a taxi waiting beside Penny now, but she still looked reluctant to leave me.

"I've been much drunker than this and gotten home just fine," I insisted. "You've seen me do it."

"Alright," she conceded. "But call me if you need me."

"Will do," I promised.

As her taxi drove away, the last vestiges of my high left me. I was alone again. And I was going to have to go home. Out of habit, I prayed I would find a lucid Greg when I got there.

But now I wasn't so sure if that was what I wanted. Recently, when Greg hadn't been high, he had been mean. And now there was the possibility he might get violent. The thought horrified me almost as much as the prospect of finding him strung out.

Hopefully he won't be there at all.

I instantly hated myself for thinking that. If he wasn't at the apartment, then he was out with the Latin Kings. They could be hurting him right now, while I was out getting drunk and toying with college boys. My little adventure with Penny suddenly soured as Rose Baker's reality settled back over me.

The idea of returning to my apartment alone was almost unbearable. With or without Greg being there, I would be alone. And I couldn't bear my own company.

As inadvisable as it might be, I pulled my phone out of my purse to compose a text. It had been hard enough to read the clock; navigating my way to my contact list and finding Clayton's name took far more effort. The final hurdle was typing the message itself. I was trying for a simple "What's up?", but random letters kept appearing on my screen. Why did the individual letter keys have to be so goddamn tiny? It didn't help that they seemed to jump away from my finger as I tried to press them.

There were some annoying jerks catcalling behind me, but I ignored them. It took a minute for their words to penetrate my fuzzy mind; I was too intent on what I was doing.

"Stella!"

"Hey, baby, where's Gloria?"

Shit.

"Go away," I ordered. Not even sparing them a backward glance, I started walking. I was pretty sure I was headed in the right direction, but I was more concerned with getting away from them. They had played their part in my little act of escapism. But I wasn't Stella anymore.

"I thought you said you were coming back. We waited for you." They were closer now. I was clearly going to have to deal with them directly in order to make them back off.

"Fuck off!" I snapped as I spun to face them. But my sense of balance was shot, and I tripped on my high heels. I let out a string of curses as my knees banged on the concrete. I was going to have a lot of self-inflicted bruises in the morning.

Two pairs of hands clasped around my upper arms and helped pull me to my feet. Jeff was laughing.

"Damn, baby. I knew you had a filthy mouth, but you cuss like a sailor."

"Hey, I don't mind, baby. You can use your mouth on me anytime." Sam's words were slurred, but his hold on my arm was firm. What had happened to the two guys who had been eating out of the palm of my hand? A sliver of fear knifed through my gut. They had been completely in my power at the bar, but now I was most definitely not the one in control.

"Take your hands off her, and walk away." His voice was calm, but it cut through the air like a cracking whip.

"Clayton," I breathed. I was both relieved and horrified to see him standing before me. Had he heard what they had said about me? About my *mouth?* One look into his blazing eyes was all the answer I needed, and my cheeks burned with shame.

"Who the fuck are you?" Jeff demanded angrily.

Clayton didn't answer him. Instead, he pulled aside his suit jacket so that his gun was visible.

"Leave. Now."

The boys released me instantly, cursing as they tripped over their feet trying to put distance between us.

I had hoped that when they had stumbled off, Clayton's fierce expression might melt into something more reassuring, but I had no such luck. Because now the furious glare that had just sent two men running away was fully turned on me. The sick thing was, it thrilled me almost as much as it terrified me.

Chapter 6

My heart fluttered against my ribcage as tense silence stretched between us. The sense of power emanating from Clayton made the hairs on the back of my neck stand on end. I wasn't afraid of his anger; I knew he would never hurt me. But the man standing before me was implacable, unbending. Nothing like the immature boys who I had so easily reduced to putty in my hands. And that challenge to my ability to control the situation was terrifying. In a decidedly arousing way.

"Do you want to explain to me what the hell you think you're doing?" I had expected him to shout at me, but when he spoke, his voice was carefully controlled.

"I…" I stammered stupidly, completely thrown off. "I was just trying to text you." I held up my phone between us like a shield. He glanced down at the severely battered device and then fixed me with a hard stare, one brow arched. Damn. Was I the only person who couldn't pull that off?

"I believe *trying* is the operative word there," he said coolly. "Allow me to re-phrase: What possessed you to get tanked and walk home alone at night when you know that the most violent gang in the city might be after you? Not to mention the fact that you just baited two drunk assholes and then dropped them cold. Are you actively trying to get yourself into trouble?"

A chunk of ice settled in the pit of my stomach. "You… You saw that?" I asked faintly.

"You're not a slut, Rose."

If he really had believed that before, he most certainly didn't anymore. How could he after witnessing my lewd little drinking game? My cheeks flamed red hot, and stupid, alcohol-enabled tears blurred my vision.

Clayton's lips twisted downward as though he had a nasty taste in his mouth. "Yes," he replied, his voice clipped. "I saw the obscene gestures they made at you. I'm not saying they didn't deserve to be knocked down a few pegs. Hell, I wanted to come give them a good punch myself." His fists clenched with suppressed anger, and I wasn't sure if it was directed at them or at me. "But what you did was reckless and dangerous. You led them on and then got them drunk. Do you even realize what they might have done to you? And then it wouldn't matter what you said; they easily could claim that you wanted it."

I dropped my eyes as the hot tears of shame spilled over. Clayton had borne witness to my promiscuity. He would never look at me the same way again. "I..." My voice wavered. "I'm sorry."

To my surprise, I felt his strong arms enfold me as he held me tightly against his chest. "I'm not judging you, Rose," he said softly. "I know you're going through a hard time. I can understand that kind of pressure can drive people to do reckless things. But I've watched too many people I care about destroy themselves that way." He suddenly sounded weary, but there was a thread of determination in his voice. "And I'm not about to stand by and watch you head down that path."

He cares about me? How could he possibly after what he had seen me do?

I laughed hollowly. "You're a little late. I've been on this path for a while." Alcohol loosened my tongue, and I couldn't seem to stop my deepest secrets from spilling forth. Especially not when he was holding me like this. I didn't deserve it. And he deserved to know who I really was. My heart twisted as I came to the realization that he would finally back away in revulsion when he did, but it would be better than the pain I felt at him forcing me to face my problems. "This is what I am, Clayton. I learned a long time ago that there was no point in fighting it. It's not your job to save me."

"Look at me, Rose," he commanded sternly. I couldn't resist his direct order, and I found myself trapped in the intensity of his piercing gaze. "That *is* my job. Not just because I've been assigned to your case, but because I care about you. I swore to protect you, and I'm not going to let you down. And nothing you do or say will make me give up on you. I'm not going anywhere, Rose. Not even if you want me to."

There it was again: he said he *cared* about me. And now he was swearing that he wouldn't abandon me. I hardly dared to believe it. I had been abandoned and shunned by too many people who should have cared about me to trust that. The only person who truly knew me who had stuck by me was Greg, and now I didn't even have him. Not really. He was just the shadow of my brother, a monster who wore his skin.

"Why?" I whispered. "Why do you care? I'm just a... a slut who's going nowhere in life."

Clayton frowned and his eyes flashed angrily. He gripped my upper arms hard, as though he wanted to shake me. "I don't ever want to hear you call yourself that word again. Whoever has made you believe that..." He stopped himself, pinching the bridge of his nose and taking a deep breath to reign in his anger. "You have every right to choose what to do with your own body. So long as you're safe about it. People have this imbalanced notion that a woman who is confident in her sexuality is a slut, but a man who does so is admired for his prowess. It's a double standard I don't believe in." He cupped my cheek tenderly, and I suddenly felt small and vulnerable in his hold. I was distantly surprised to find that it wasn't a wholly unpleasant sensation. When he spoke again, his voice was rough with emotion. "But I can't deny that seeing those guys touching you, seeing you flirt with them... It made me jealous as hell. You're free to do as you please with your own body, but I want to be the only one who touches it."

I shivered in his grasp. I had known him for such a short time, but no one had ever treated me like he did. With one piercing glance, he seemed to stare right into me, seeing the real me that no one else bothered to look for. To be fair, I had carefully hidden myself away, masking my vulnerability with a carefree exterior. That way no one could know my weaknesses; no one could hurt me. But Clayton had exposed me, and although that frightened me, I marveled at the fact that he wasn't disgusted by what he saw.

"I… I think I want that too," I admitted quietly. I wanted more of this calm reassurance, of Clayton's firm refusal to allow me to hate myself. The way he was looking at me now made me want to be the person he saw, a good person who life and shitty circumstance had driven to self-loathing and bad choices. A person who could be redeemed.

He smiled down at me gently, but there was a slightly predatory edge to the twist of his lips. "I'm glad we're on the same page, then."

He leaned into me, and my eyes closed blissfully as his lips brushed against mine. The kiss was brief but sweet, communicating his forgiveness and his faith in me. I bit back a whine of protest when he pulled away from me all too soon. The alcohol-fueled lust that had been quenched by our tense encounter came roaring back at his intimate touch.

"Come on," he said softly, "I'm taking you home."

His arm wrapped around my waist, and I was a bit embarrassed to realize I needed the support; I was still more than a little tipsy. It was no wonder I had confessed my secrets in that state.

When we got to my apartment building, I tripped over the first stair step. I let out a surprised squeak as the world spun around me, and I suddenly found myself cradled in Clayton's arms as he carried me. I couldn't help pressing my face into his chest and breathing in deeply, loving the sexy scent that was uniquely his.

"Sorry," I mumbled, a bit chagrined at my inability to put one foot in front of the other.

He just grinned down at me roguishly. "I don't mind. It gives me an excuse to hold you."

My stomach did a delighted little flip. "I guess I'm not sorry, then," I breathed. He chuckled, and I relished the way the sound seemed to rumble through me, sending warmth flooding from my chest to my fingertips.

A part of me was secretly glad to find the apartment empty. I didn't think I could handle seeing Greg right now after my emotionally tumultuous evening.

Clayton set me down on my bed, supporting my back until he was sure I could maintain a sitting position without swaying too badly. He started to pull away from me, but I caught his forearm. It tried to arch up into him, to sate the need that was coursing through my veins, making my most sensitive areas pulse. But he pressed two fingers to my lips, stopping me short.

"Not tonight, Rose," he said gently. I couldn't help pouting, and he traced the outline of my lips with the pad of his thumb. His smile was a bit regretful. "You're awfully cute when you pout, you know," he informed me. "But I won't take advantage of you when you're drunk."

I let out an annoyed huff. "*I'm* trying to take advantage of *you.*"

He laughed and tapped his finger against my nose. "I'm not that easy. But believe me, I would love to strip you and fuck you senseless. Unfortunately, that just wouldn't be right given your current state."

"Tease," I accused. "Why do you have to be so goddamn decent?"

He laughed again, and the way his warm breath fanned across my face sent my desire spiking even higher. His lips were so close to mine...

"How about we make a deal?" He proposed. "You let me take you out to dinner tomorrow, and afterward I will do some decidedly indecent things to you." His eyes glinted with a mixture of lust and amusement. He knew I would agree. I had been determined to keep my distance from him emotionally, but it seemed he had other ideas. And damn it if I didn't find his cocky determination sexy as hell.

"Fine," I agreed, throwing up my hands in defeat. I fixed him with a hard stare. "But you had better hold up your end of the bargain."

His triumphant grin was hard-edged and hungry. "Don't worry. I will. I've been doing some very interesting research, and I've found a few things I want to try." Leaving that statement hanging in the air, the bastard winked at me.

Oh, I had definitely made a mistake in drawing out his dominant side. Was it possible to die of sexual frustration? I was pretty sure I was about to explode.

"Tease," I accused again, more hotly this time.

"You're adorable when you pout like that," he informed me, clearly entertained by my frustration. Gripping my chin between his thumb and forefinger, he brushed a feather-light kiss across my cheek before whispering in my ear. "Besides, I know you like being teased."

I shuddered as another wave of lust washed through me. "You're a bastard, you know that?" I asked him shakily.

He chuckled. "I seem to recall being accused of being too *goddamn decent* a moment ago."

"I rescind that statement." The way my voice wavered ruined my attempt to sound reproachful.

"And you need to learn to watch your language," he continued on over me as though I hadn't spoken. "We can work on that."

The sensual threat elicited an audible moan from deep within me. "Fuck, Clayton. Please, just touch me already."

He was smirking at me. "Begging and more cursing? You're devious, aren't you? Unfortunately for you, I came across that in my research. It's called 'topping from the bottom,' isn't it? Well, I'm not falling for it, babe. I don't think I've told you this, but I played football in college. It made me very competitive. You should have listened to Sharon; I can be very *tenacious* when I want to win. And I don't intend to lose this game. Besides, I don't think you want me to." His expression was downright evil. But it thrilled me far more than it pissed me off. I had been right: Clayton wasn't going to let me get away with anything. The complete loss of control was terrifying in the most delicious way. The sensation was far headier than what I had felt when I had so easily manipulated Jeff and Sam.

"So you are fully aware that you're a bastard, then," I retorted weakly.

He tapped my nose again. "I'm keeping a running tally of those insults, you know. By all means, please continue with your verbal abuse." He cocked his head at me. "It will be interesting to see whether or not you enjoy the consequences."

My pulse quickened and I gasped. "I thought you said you'd never done anything like this before."

He shrugged. "I told you: I'm a fast learner. And when I find something I want, I go for it." The look he shot me was heated and full of wicked promises. "I want *you,* Rose. I've never experienced anything like what we have, and I want more of it."

What we have?

Yep, this was definitely about more than just fucking.

Clayton shook himself slightly and took a deep breath before drawing away from me reluctantly. I frowned when he turned his back on me.

"Get dressed for bed," he ordered.

"Why the sudden prudishness?" I taunted.

He didn't glance back at me. "That might not have been a curse word, but I'm adding it to the tally," he informed me coolly.

"And I'm not going to watch you because I don't want my balls to ache even more than they do already."

You want to tease me? I thought wickedly. *Two can play at that game, Mr. Big Bad Dom.*

I took my time stripping off my dress and peeling off my underwear. I decided to leave my strappy high heels on. Propping myself back on my elbows, I arched my back and spread my legs.

"Okay, all done."

When he turned to face me, Clayton's mouth dropped open slightly, and I shot him a devilish grin. Then his teeth snapped together and his jaw clenched. The glare he fixed on me promised retribution. "I guess you do like a little pain, seeing as you're practically begging me to punish you," he ground out. "You're a devious little minx, beautiful. But that's something else we can work on. Tomorrow."

Punish. When I had first met Clayton, I hadn't been sure if he was capable of such a thing. My nipples tightened to a painful degree at the prospect.

"Get dressed. Now." His forbidding glare remained fixed on me as he crossed his arms over his chest. His stance was imposing, intimidating. I obeyed with alacrity, retrieving my PJs from under my pillow and pulling them on hastily. My hands shook slightly from the adrenaline that spiked through me.

Once I was covered, a pleased, twisted smile replaced his reproving expression. He applied gentle pressure to my shoulders, pushing me down onto the mattress. The feeling of being cared for in this way was utterly foreign to me; no one had ever tucked me into bed. Clayton planted a swift, sweet kiss on my forehead and then drew away from me. I reached for him quickly, catching his hand in mine.

"Don't go," I said pleadingly. My desperation to keep him close was overwhelming. I didn't want to be alone. Clayton's presence provided a far greater release than any alcohol or drugs.

"I've told you, Rose," he said gently. "I won't do that. Not tonight."

I gripped him more tightly. "I don't want sex. Well, I do, but we don't have to do that. I just… Stay with me. Please."

His eyes softened, and he stroked his fingers across my cheek tenderly. "Now that's a brand of begging I can't resist."

"Thank you," I whispered.

I couldn't help watching him hungrily as he undressed. Even though I had done my best to memorize every contour of his gorgeous body, my mind hadn't been able to fully capture his perfection. The sound of his belt slithering against the material of his slacks as he pulled it off made me shiver. It reminded me of the punishment he had promised. He was right: I did like a little pain. I wasn't a masochist, but I found a taste of it provided a sweet release; it commanded my full attention, denying my mind the freedom to wander. My tongue darted out to wet my lips in anticipation. Tomorrow night couldn't come soon enough. Clayton's admission that he was hurting from denial as well was a small comfort.

I had hoped he would strip completely, but he kept his boxers on. That was probably best for both of us, really. I didn't think I could withstand any more sexual torment. My twin bed was almost too small for us to both fit on it, but I didn't mind. It just meant that Clayton had to hold me closer. He settled his hard body behind mine, pulling me back against his chest. I sighed when I felt his erection against my ass. But there was nothing for it; I knew Clayton wouldn't be moved, and trying to tempt him further would only land me in more trouble.

Despite the intensity of my unfulfilled lust, alcohol, exhaustion, and Clayton's comforting embrace caused me to drop off to sleep almost instantly.

■ ■

"Get the fuck off my sister!" Greg's furious roar jerked me awake. The weak light of early dawn was only just slanting through the windows, but I could clearly make out my brother's livid expression. "I knew you liked to whore around, Rose, but Jesus! You fucked this prick? In *our* apartment?!"

My mouth dropped open as my mind struggled to process the fact that the cruel, cutting words were coming from my baby brother's lips. I was used to hearing similar insults from my mom, but not him. Never him.

Clayton was on his feet in an instant, his fluid, assured movements recalling the lunge of a predatory beast. Greg's back was against the wall, Clayton's hand fisted in his shirt as he pinned him in place. "I've warned you about talking to her that way." He used the same cool tone he had turned on the drunken boys the night before. It was undeniably chilling. "I'm going to let you off this time because it *was* inappropriate for me to stay here. But know that next time I will break your arm. No matter what Rose wants. You don't deserve her protection. Do you understand me?"

Greg looked pissed, but a shadow of fear flitted across his face. He remembered how easily Clayton had taken him down before. "Yes," he hissed angrily. "But I don't want to see you in my apartment again."

Clayton pinned him with a hard stare for a long moment, allowing Greg's nervous tension to grow. "You have the right to request that," he said finally. "But if I hear that you're mistreating her, you'll find me breathing down your neck wherever you go."

He released Greg abruptly, and my brother sagged back against the wall. Clayton's threat was clearly going to be taken seriously.

To my dismay, Clayton began pulling on his slacks.

"You're leaving?" I asked, disappointment lacing my tone.

His eyes softened when they met mine. "I've agreed to honor your brother's request." He pulled on his suit jacket, looking as sharp as ever. The only sign of untidiness was his mussed hair, and that only made him look sexier.

He leaned down into me, his hand closing firmly around the nape of my neck as he crushed his lips to mine. His tongue plundered my mouth, a physical demonstration of his possession of my body. When he finally pulled away, I was gasping for breath.

"I'll pick you up at seven," he said firmly, shooting Greg a pointed glance as he spoke. Out of the corner of my eye, I saw my brother stiffen angrily, but I didn't care. Clayton's entrancing eyes commanded my attention.

"Okay," I breathed.

With that, he strode out of my apartment. I fought to ignore the sense of loss that filled me when the door closed behind him. I also ignored Greg's furious glare, schooling my expression to nonchalance as I got ready for work. Despite my years of practice, pretending to be unruffled was more difficult than it usually was. Clayton's effect on me had been sudden and intense. And even though it was a blessed release to be in his physical presence, he was causing fissures to appear in my carefree façade that had always been my protective armor.

I suddenly realized that the game we were playing was very dangerous. And I was certain that losing would prove to be just as painful as it would be blissful. Clayton had accused me of behaving recklessly, but it seemed letting him into my life was the most reckless thing I had ever done. He was going to destroy me.

But I didn't think I could bring myself to stay away from him. I was already as addicted to him as Greg was to his heroin. With that disconcerting realization, I came to a resolution.

Give him your body, Rose, not your heart.

Chapter 7

The damage Clayton had inflicted on my psyche only became more painfully apparent throughout the course of the day. Now that I was beginning to feel that I deserved better, Cheryl's haughty demeanor grated on me more than ever before, and it took all of my determination to keep a smile in place. Still, I could feel it was more of a baring of my teeth, and my obvious anger only seemed to please my bitchy boss. It was the first time I had ever visibly shown my dislike for her, and her flashing eyes practically dared me to go off on her, to give her the excuse to fire me.

I desperately wanted to bring to life my recent sketches. The sharp lines of them reflected the power of righteous fury, and creating them would have been cathartic. Unfortunately, Greg had smashed my sewing machine over a month ago while searching for his stash, so that wasn't an option.

To make matters worse, my clit had throbbed and ached all day as Clayton's lust-filled, teasing words from the night before played in my mind over and over again, tormenting me. The sweet pain of my unfulfilled arousal and the temptation of his wicked promises were almost enough to make me follow through with our agreement to meet for dinner and sex.

But I was too much of a coward to face him. I wanted him desperately, but my shitty day had just proven to me that he was just as bad for me as Greg's addiction was for him. Clayton was changing me in a way I feared would be irrevocable if I allowed myself to be near him again. The prospect was terrifying.

I was relieved to find that Greg wasn't in the apartment when I got home.

Good. If I could just release my pent-up sexual frustration on my own, then I would eliminate the strong pull to see Clayton. I quickly composed a text before I could change my mind.

I can't see you tonight. I'm sick. Sorry.

I set the phone down beside me as I laid back on my bed, choosing to ignore the chime that signaled Clayton's answering text. Instead, I pulled my dress up over my hips and slid my panties down to my knees before reaching under my mattress to retrieve my vibrator. It buzzed to life, and I touched it to my aching clit, moaning at the merciful contact. I tried to focus solely on the pleasurable sensation, but thoughts of Clayton kept flitting across my mind: his strong arms holding me down; *"Stay"*; the threatening whisper of his belt as he slowly removed it...

"You are practically begging me to punish you."

I bit my lip as a shuddering groan escaped me. After less than two minutes, I was soaking wet and close to coming.

"Rose." I jumped as the sharp knock on my door jerked me out of my fantasy. I immediately switched off my vibrator and held my breath.

Oh, no. Go away. Please go away.

He knocked again. "I know you're in there, Rose. Open up."

Shit shit shit!

There was nothing for it: I would have to let him in.

My hands were trembling as I unlocked the door. I almost shut it in his face when I saw his stern expression. But he pushed his way in, invading my personal space. He gripped my jaw firmly and studied my face.

"You seem pretty healthy to me," he said in that cool, intimidating tone. "I didn't think you looked sick, but I decided to come and check more closely."

Crap. How could I forget he was watching me? I swallowed hard.

"And if you're well enough to masturbate, then you're well enough to come to dinner with me."

My stomach dropped to the floor. "I wasn't -"

My protest turned to a shocked squeal as his arm abruptly closed around my waist, holding me in place as his other hand delved under my skirt to brush against my labia. His icy gaze speared me to my core as his fingers swirled in the wetness there. Then he raised them to his lips and slowly licked them clean. I couldn't hold back a strangled whimper at the sight of the lust that flared in his eyes as he tasted me.

"The walls are paper thin, Rose," he informed me, his voice rougher now. "Did you really think I couldn't hear you?"

"Clayton…" His name was a defeated moan as I arched up into him. God, I had never wanted anything as intensely as I craved his touch.

He pulled away from me, depriving me of the heat of his body. Our only physical contact now was his firm grip on my upper arm. Without a word, he turned to leave the apartment, pulling me along in his wake. I tried to resist, jerking against his hold.

"Wait," I practically panted. "Let's just stay here."

The look he gave me as he continued his steady progress told me I deserved my suffering. "You brought this upon yourself, Rose," he informed me. "Our bargain was that you would come to dinner with me and I would ravage you afterward. I haven't gotten any release since last night, and I'll be damned if you will."

I glared up at him. "Bastard," I spat.

"I believe that's four now," he responded calmly.

Shit. I had forgotten about his tally. *Four what?* I wondered as erotic excitement flooded me. It was only made sweeter by the little zing of fear that made my skin pebble. Clayton had promised me punishment. What did he have planned for me?

Despite my torment, I was suddenly very glad that Clayton had forced his way into my apartment.

Give him your body, not your heart, I reminded myself. I could do that. I had to. Otherwise I was going to spontaneously combust.

My discomfiture at the insistent throbbing between my legs made me cross and uncross my legs half a dozen times as Clayton drove towards the Lower East Side. I was relieved that we would be dining somewhere close to his apartment; we could get to his bedroom quickly after we ate. I half-hoped he would just take me to McDonald's so we could get in and out and on to the good stuff. Plus, that would minimize the opportunity for conversation, thereby making my new resolution easier to keep.

But I had no such luck. Clayton had made a reservation for us at a family-owned authentic Italian restaurant. The entire place smelled heavenly, and I suddenly realized I was ravenous. This would be a welcome departure from my usual diet of granola bars and ramen. Still, I was hungrier for Clayton than I was for ravioli.

"So," he began casually once we had been seated, "why did you lie to me?" The affable, sweet persona which seemed to be Clayton's default – when he wasn't being a no-bull FBI agent or a thoroughly intimidating Dom – was back.

I shifted uneasily in my chair. His demeanor might be easygoing, but already he was cutting straight to the core of me, trying to further expose my secrets. I couldn't allow that; no way could I admit to him that the way he made me feel scared me. If I told him that, he would just try to fix it. But that would only make everything that much worse for me.

"Well," I wracked my brain for a believable story. "After Greg saw us together this morning, I thought maybe being with me would cause problems for you at work. You said it's happened before, right? I figured it would be easier to nip it in the bud."

Clayton looked at me seriously. "I appreciate your concern, Rose, but I would rather you just asked me about it instead of shutting me out without consulting me. You were the one who pointed out that we got together before I was assigned to your case. Sure, it's a bit of a grey area, but Sharon and Smith – the other agents who are watching over you and Greg – aren't going to go tattling on me. So unless you were to make a complaint, then the department will look the other way. Besides, what happened before didn't get me in trouble with the FBI; I just caused my own personal shitstorm with that one."

The way his eyes clouded over with an echo of remembered pain made jealousy twist my gut. But the look was fleeting. He blinked hard, and his gaze focused on me once again. "Things are fine now, though," he assured me with a small smile. "Claudia and I actually ended up becoming really good friends."

I wasn't quite successful in concealing my discontent. He was still in touch with her?

He reached across the table and captured my hand in his. "Hey," he said gently. "That's all in the past. A certain gorgeous damsel in distress now has my full attention."

"So you fancy yourself as some sort of white knight then, huh?" I asked cuttingly. "That's rather big-headed of you, don't you think? Besides, you're far too unchivalrous to be a white knight."

His overly dramatic look of hurt was comical. I obviously hadn't succeeded in getting under his skin. "Ouch. You sure know how to knock a guy down a few pegs."

"What can I say? Your ego was getting out of control. I've clearly created a monster." My tone was teasing now, and I could feel a smile playing around my lips. He was far too charming for my own good, and I couldn't deny that his levity was catching.

Clayton laughed easily. "I can't argue with that. To be completely honest, it's a side of me I'm not all that familiar with. It's probably good if you keep it in check from time to time." His smile turned slightly predatory. "But unfortunately for you, I know you like the monster."

"Now that's something *I* can't argue with," I admitted.

"I know," he said, sounding far too smug.

I rolled my eyes at him. "There you go getting cocky again already."

"Terribly sorry. I'll try harder to be good." But his flashing eyes held no apology, only amusement. It made my pussy clench.

"Please don't," I said drily. "I wouldn't want to put you through such strain."

He shrugged agreeably. "Okay. If you insist."

He was so implacable. It was infuriating. Nothing seemed to rile him; he calmly refused to allow me to manipulate him. I was again struck by my inability to control the situation whenever I was near him. It was what made him so damn sexy, but it was also what made him scary as hell.

Even when he did get angry, he was still carefully controlled. I thought of the cool tone he used when threatening Greg and those asshole college boys. His calm assurance of his own power was far more terrifying than the aggressive attitude of the beefcake bad boys I usually went for. The only times his tight rein on his anger had slipped were the times I had pissed him off by doing something stupid and reckless. And when he turned that intensity on me, I wanted to be better than what I was.

Damn it. This was precisely why I had tried to back out on dinner. He was too intriguing for my own good. I had been getting along just fine before I had met him. Okay, so maybe I hadn't been perfectly happy, and maybe my rash behavior was self-destructive, but it worked for me. Clayton was trying to save me, to make me better. But I didn't know how to be better, and I was fairly certain that the precarious existence I had fashioned for myself would crumble if I tried. My wild little adventures helped relieve the pressure of my problems. If I gave them up, I feared I would be crushed under the weight.

But I knew Clayton's body could provide the release I sought. Unfortunately, he might rip me apart emotionally. I had always enjoyed playing with fire; the threat of getting burned was what made my adventures all the more thrilling, more all-consuming. Trusting myself to be around Clayton and not get emotionally involved was going to be the most dangerous thing I had ever done. I found the prospect too enticing to resist. Especially when he was looking at me like he was right now, his lips twisted up in a knowing smirk and his eyes flashing.

Throwing caution to the wind, I smiled at him slyly. "So you've been doing some research, huh?" I asked, deciding it was best to keep the conversation sexual. "The internet can be a pretty disgusting place. Should I be worried about what's piqued your interest? Because there are some things I am most definitely not up for."

Clayton just nodded sagely. "We can discuss hard limits if you'd like, but I don't think anything I have in mind will be out of your comfort zone. And I haven't been diving into the seedy underbelly of the internet. I have a friend who has been trying to talk to me about BDSM for years. He was only too happy to share when I asked him about it."

Hard limits? BDSM? The man had done his homework. Apparently this friend of his was pretty knowledgeable.

"If he's been talking to you about it for years, then why are you just now exploring it?" I asked, genuinely curious. "You've taken to it awfully quickly for someone who's never been all that interested."

Clayton's expression turned thoughtful. "I did experiment a little with my college girlfriend. We dated for almost two years, and you start to try out different things to spice things up after that length of time. But I suppose…" He hesitated, and I saw that flash of pain in his eyes again. "I haven't been that serious with anyone since then. And it takes a certain level of trust to venture into kinky territory."

I found it hard to believe that Clayton hadn't had any serious relationships in, what, eight years or so? He was sweet, successful, and gorgeous. Women should have been tripping over themselves to ensnare him. I wondered what had happened with his girlfriend to scar him so deeply that he had been alone for so long. Was he still in love with her or something? The thought made me cold.

"You got pretty damn kinky with me, and you didn't even know me," I pointed out.

He cocked his head at me. "I could tell it was what you wanted. You're a force of nature, Rose. You have a wild streak, but that wildness will tear you apart if it's not contained, controlled. I told you: I have a thing for damsels in distress. If taming that side of you is what I need to do in order to help you, then that's what I'll do. That's what I want. And I know it's what you want."

The truth of his earnest words made my breath catch in my throat. How could he see me so clearly?

"Besides," he added with an impish smile, "the night I met you was the hottest night of my life. Helping you isn't my only motive here; I want more of that."

"I don't think I like being considered a 'damsel in distress,' but if that's the outcome, I guess I don't mind so much," I said breathily.

Clayton flashed me a pleased smile. "So long as we're on the same page, I think we can overlook differing semantics."

I returned his grin. "I can get on board with that."

Having come to that erotic agreement, dinner passed by in a haze. I'm sure the food was delicious, but I barely registered the flavors. I was hungry for something else. Our conversation was pleasant, but I wasn't really engaged in what was being said. I mostly allowed Clayton to talk while I made noises of agreement and occasionally prompted him to continue carrying the conversation. He tried to ask me a few personal questions, but I deflected him with practiced ease. When I did so, he frowned slightly, but I was relieved when he didn't push me.

I barely stifled a thankful sigh when we finally left the restaurant. It took less than ten minutes to walk to his apartment, but the wait became more and more agonizing as my pussy pulsed in time with my every step. Our only contact was Clayton's arm around my waist, but even that barest touch through my clothes made my skin tingle after being denied for so long. I felt as though I had been enduring this sexual torment for weeks rather than less than twenty-four hours. Clayton had said he intended to *tame* me. The thought sent pleasurable trepidation coursing through me.

He physically demonstrated his intent to control me as soon as we entered his apartment. Gripping me firmly by the waist, he bent and lifted me effortlessly. The world blurred around me and I found myself thrown over his shoulder in a fireman's lift.

"Hey!" I cried, surprised and slightly indignant. My eyes widened with shock and I gasped in a sharp breath when his hand came down hard on my ass. Had sweet, easygoing Clayton really just *spanked* me? He had promised me punishment, and it seemed he was going to make good on that promise.

"Quiet." His voice had the cool, controlled quality that communicated his confidence in his complete power over me. The sound of it made me shudder delightedly.

All of the wind was knocked out of me as he flung me down on the bed unceremoniously. I was momentarily disoriented, and he took advantage. He flipped me onto my front and straddled my hips, pinning me down with his weight as he swiftly wrapped something silky around my wrists, securing them behind my back. The material was soft, but when I pulled against the restraints I found that I was securely bound. I twisted my head back, and I realized he had used his necktie to restrain me. This had barely registered when he shifted me again, easily manhandling my body. Already he was eliciting feelings of vulnerability as he demonstrated my helplessness to his physical strength. It made my nipples tighten and my core throb.

He draped me across his knees where he sat at the edge of the bed. My ass was thrust upward, and my long hair fell around my face, obscuring my vision. Oh, god. I knew what was coming next; I had been in this position before. I gasped at the shock of cool air hitting my sex as he flipped up my skirt and roughly yanked my panties down to my knees. Clayton gently touched his fingers to my inner thigh, swirling in the wet evidence of my intense arousal. His soft laugh was slightly evil as I squirmed in his lap. The movement made me acutely aware of his own desire for me as his erection pressed into my stomach.

When he spoke, his tone was matter-of-fact, almost detached. "I believe I gave you fair warning that I was going to punish you." A lustful groan escaped me as he traced the curve of my ass with a feather-light touch. I arched my back, offering myself up to him.

"More," I begged, half-delirious with need. "Please, Clayton."

"Not yet," he told me softly. "You have to earn it."

I whined and ground my hips against him, trying desperately to achieve some kind of release. His hand instantly fisted in my hair, pulling my head back so I had no choice but to look into his eyes. They were glinting with amusement.

"And that's not the way to go about it," he informed me dispassionately.

"I'm not so sure I like this friend of yours who's taught you these tricks," I declared irritably, my frustration getting the better of me.

His fingers stroked my ass again, and I shuddered. "But you like it," he informed me. "You can protest all you want, but your body tells me everything I need to know." His grin was wicked.

"God damn it, Clayton!" I snapped. "Touch me already!"

He tutted at me. "If you insist." His palm came down on me hard, hitting the sensitive flesh where my ass met my thighs.

My shocked cry was laced with pain, and I stared up at him, wide-eyed and panting. His pupils dilated at the sight of my visceral reaction, and I could tell he was quickly learning that doling out punishment could be just as pleasurable for him as receiving it was for me.

"I've been told that I'm supposed to inform you of why I'm doing this to you. Otherwise, how will you know what behavior to correct?"

I swallowed hard as I realized that I was completely at his mercy now. He was firmly asserting his control over me, his dominance, and he wasn't going to give me an inch. No one had ever made me feel so utterly defenseless before. And no one had ever aroused me this intensely.

"Your actions at the bar last night were foolish and rash," he continued. "You put yourself in a dangerous situation. I won't allow that kind of behavior." His hand came down on me again, and my traitorous body responded lustfully despite the panic that suddenly spiked though my chest.

"No!" I protested, trying to ignore the way my inner muscles contracted. "Clayton, that happened outside the bedroom. You can't punish me sexually for something like that."

He tenderly stroked his palm over my stinging flesh, eliciting both an erotic tingling and a sense of comfort. His expression was gentle, but he still maintained his grip on my hair so I didn't have the option of looking away. "I can understand if this is too much for you. What's your safe word?"

"Red," I said quietly.

"Do you want to use it now?"

I bit my lip, torn between desire and fear of what giving Clayton that kind of control might do to me emotionally. I had promised myself that I would give him nothing more than my body, but this was moving into a grey area. But Clayton had already overcome my impulses to deny him, and my last vestiges of willpower left me as I ceded myself to him.

"No. I don't want to use my safe word." My voice was a defeated whisper, and all of the tension left me as my resistance was shattered. My body and my mind were in Clayton's hands now; I had entrusted them to him. The sensation was incredibly freeing.

With my consent, my punishment resumed. The blows were sharp, and each resultant *crack* that echoed around the room was an audible reinforcement of Clayton's lesson. He wasn't gentle with me, but I didn't want him to be. This wasn't a sensual spanking; it was a reprimand. I had hated myself for making a fool of myself in front of Clayton by toying with those college boys, and I had been ashamed of the fact that he had witnessed my promiscuous behavior. The pain he gave me now was cleansing, and as I earned his forgiveness through enduring it, I began to forgive myself. All of the years of acting rashly, of running from my problems by indulging in lust, had only resulted in the destruction of my own sense of self-worth. And Clayton wasn't going to allow me to continue down that path any longer. The fact that he believed I could change, that he demanded I do so, gave me hope that I *could* be the person who was reflected in his eyes whenever he looked at me.

The tears that spilled down my cheeks weren't from the pain, but from an overwhelming flood of relief. When Clayton saw them, he stopped immediately. His fingers untwined from my hair so he could gently wipe away my tears. He was looking at me with concern.

"Did I hurt you that badly?" He asked, his worry evident in his tone.

I gave him a small, watery smile. "No. I'm not hurt. Not really. I'm... happy. Thank you."

Clayton's eyes widened in amazement. "I have to admit I wasn't expecting that," he said, smiling at me softly. "But I'm glad to hear it."

He stroked my enflamed skin to soothe away the burn, and his gentle touch reignited the need that had been pulsing just below the surface as he had punished me. The complete surrender that the pain had brought forth had only stoked my desire as I reveled in the heady release.

"Please, Clayton," I begged desperately. "I'm sorry for what I did. Will you please touch me now? I need to feel you inside of me."

He groaned softly. "You don't know how badly I've wanted to hear you say that." As he spoke, his hard cock twitched beneath me, and I couldn't hold back my smirk as I writhed against him.

"I think I have a pretty good idea," I teased.

With a low growl as my only warning, he swiftly maneuvered me off of his lap and positioned my body on the bed so that I was on my knees. The bindings on my wrists prevented me from supporting myself with my hands, so my face pressed into the mattress. I was still wearing my dress, but it stayed bunched up around my waist from where he had exposed me for my spanking. I licked my lips as I heard hip unzip his slacks and tear open a condom wrapper. We were frenzied in our need for one another. We had waited for this for a full day; we weren't going to wait for one minute longer.

I cried out in bliss as Clayton drove into me in one hard thrust. His movements were harsh, almost brutal, as he was completely consumed by the passion that he had so determinedly held at bay for long hours. I gloried in it. Despite his ferocity, I was so wet and ready for him that there was hardly any pain. His fingers dug into the tender flesh at my waist as he held me with almost bruising force, keeping me firmly in place as he pounded into me, taking his pleasure from my body. Sharp cries escaped me at his every demanding thrust as I was driven towards the precipice. Clayton's raw ferociousness drew out the primal hunger in me, and I jerked against my restraints, longing to dig my nails into his skin and hold him to me tightly. But the reminder of my complete helplessness was what drove me over the edge, sending me spiraling into the fiery abyss. My core rippled around him as I screamed out my orgasm, the intensity of my release so acute that it ripped viciously through my body, tearing me asunder in the most ecstatically brutal way. Rose Baker had been replaced by a being of pure pleasure, and there was nothing but the bliss coursing through me and the feel of Clayton's cock pumping inside of me as he reached his own completion.

I was a quivering, boneless mass beneath the weight of him as his body collapsed atop mine. I don't know how long we lay there, but eventually I became vaguely aware of an emptiness inside of me. Time passed slowly as my mind gradually coalesced, returning me to some semblance of myself. Clayton's body was entwined with mine. As I clutched him to me, I realized I had been released from my bonds and he had removed our clothes. The feeling of his heated flesh against mine was delicious. I snuggled closer to him, and he tenderly kissed the top of my head.

For the first time in I didn't know how long, I felt truly happy and safe. What had just happened between us hadn't been a cheap thrill. It had been real.

"Thanks for trusting me, Rose," I heard him murmur.

Of course I trust you.

I was distantly shocked at the fervor of the words that ran across my mind. But I was too exhausted to worry about my reaction, and in the morning I didn't remember it anyway.

Chapter 8

I gently trailed my fingertips over the hard planes of Clayton's body, taking my time exploring him. Every time I had seen him naked I had either been too consumed by lust or too dazed from being fucked senseless to fully study him. As my touch raked across his rippling abs, I noticed a small, circular inconsistency in his smooth flesh. Peeking under the sheets, I saw that the skin there was slightly puckered.

Clayton groaned softly as my touch roused him from sleep. I looked up to find him smiling at me languorously. He reached for me and tenderly cupped my cheek in his large hand, tracing the line of my cheekbone with the pad of his thumb. "Good morning, beautiful."

I closed my eyes and leaned into his touch. It felt good. Too good. I was acutely aware of the fact that I was failing miserably at keeping my resolution to guard my heart. "How did you get this?" I asked softly as I touched his scar, deciding that allowing myself to fall into his arms right now was not a good idea.

"I was shot," he said simply, as though it wasn't a big deal. I had never fully appreciated just how dangerous Clayton's job was until that moment.

All the more reason not to get involved with him, I thought. Too many people had abandoned me over the course of my life, and I didn't want to have to go through that again.

"What happened?" My curiosity got the best of me.

"My friend Claudia was in trouble with the Irish Mob. Someone tried to hurt her, and I stopped him."

I turned this disconcerting information over in my mind. *Claudia?* Wasn't that the name of the woman who he had a thing for? He had taken a bullet for her. Had he been in love with her?

I hated the sharp tang of jealousy that arose in the back of my throat, and I did my best to hide my unease.

Wanting to put distance between us, I rolled off of him. "I should get back to my place. I have to get ready for work."

Clayton grabbed my wrist and pressed my hand against his erection. "Are you sure you don't have a little time to spare?" His voice was rough with lust. The sound of his desire and the feel of his hard cock made my mouth water, but I stood my ground, pulling my hand away.

"Sorry, but I really don't have time." My voice was breathier than I would have liked, but Clayton relented, releasing me. I was careful not to look at his tempting body as I hastily pulled on my clothes, and I was relieved to hear the rustle of fabric that told me he was doing the same. But he looked damn sexy in boxers and a white t-shirt, his hair untidy from our night together.

He walked me to the door, his hand on the small of my back. The gentlemanly action contrasted sharply with the decidedly ungentlemanly things he had done to me last night.

He leaned into me slowly, and I found myself torn between the desire to bolt and my intense craving to feel his lips on mine. A knock on the door saved me from my dilemma. Clayton frowned and then cursed softly when he looked through the peephole.

A deep, masculine voice drifted through the door. "Come on, Vaughn. Your shift was supposed to end ten hours ago."

Clayton jerked the door open irritably. "What are you doing here, James?"

The man standing in the hallway was gorgeous. Even though he was a little shorter than Clayton, his broader shoulders made him every bit as imposing. He was dressed in a sharp suit like the ones Clayton wore, but his appearance was a little rougher around the edges. His dark, wavy hair curled around his strong jaw, which was covered with stubble. When he turned his eyes on me, my heart skipped a beat. They were such a light blue that they were almost silver. They reminded me of a wolf's eyes. I was sure I had seen those eyes somewhere before.

"Do I know you?" I blurted out.

His smile was enigmatic. "I don't believe we've met properly." He extended his hand for me to shake. "I'm Agent Smith James. I'm supposed to be part of your security detail, but Vaughn seems to be determined to keep me chained to my desk." He eyed Clayton significantly. "It's time for my shift. *You* can spend the day in the office."

Clayton glowered at him. "Fine. But you don't have to be so hands-on. You're supposed to be running surveillance from a distance."

Smith shrugged. "So are you. And if stickler Agent Vaughn gets to break the rules, then no one can bitch at me about it this time. Cheer up. I brought you coffee." He picked a cup from the cardboard tray he was holding and offered it to Clayton. He winked at me as he handed one to me too. "He gets pissy if he doesn't get his fix."

Clayton took a sip and then grinned ruefully, allowing the taunt to roll off of him. "The offering of coffee doesn't excuse your nosiness, but it does help your case."

"What can I say? I was curious. You've been keeping her all to yourself." He turned his attention back on me. "How would you like to come to a party at my place tonight?"

"Smith!" Clayton said sharply, his tone imbued with warning.

"Oh, calm down, Clayton. You're invited too."

"We're supposed to be working," Clayton reminded him sternly.

"We will be," he insisted smoothly. "Our job is to watch over Rose. If we're all together, then we'll both be watching her. Besides, you don't seem to mind mixing work and play these days." His eyes glittered, and he smirked at Clayton.

"I would love to come," I interjected before Clayton could say something snappish. It didn't seem he was going to leave me alone anytime soon, and being in a group setting would help me keep him at arm's length. And I liked parties. Having fun would keep my mind off of Greg and off of the tangled situation I had gotten myself into with Clayton.

Smith beamed at me. "Excellent."

Clayton sighed, resigned. "I guess I'm coming too, then."

Smith clapped him on the shoulder. "Try not to sound so miserable. You might even have fun." He tugged his sleeve back and glanced at his watch. "Sorry to tear her away from you, Clayton, but we should probably get going."

Clayton took me by the shoulders and turned me so that I was facing him. His expression was regretful, and I couldn't deny that I felt a pang of unhappiness at the prospect of leaving him.

"Meet me at Blue Café for lunch." It wasn't a request.

I had fallen into his azure eyes, and I spoke before I could think. "Okay."

He smiled down at me before planting a swift kiss on my forehead. I was grateful he didn't try to take my lips in front of Smith. When he drew away from me, he forcibly turned my body and pushed me towards his friend.

"Get going. I wouldn't want you to be late for work." My eyes widened and I yelped in shock when his hand cracked against my ass. My cheeks burned as I heard Smith laugh. The nerve of him! I had just been relieved that he hadn't kissed me in front of his friend, but he thought it was okay to *spank* me?! We were going to have to have a serious talk about boundaries later. I needed to put the monster back in check.

"Bye, gorgeous!" He called after me.

I was still too mortified to speak, so I flipped him my middle finger as I stalked away from his apartment, not looking at either man. Smith just laughed harder.

The fact that my pussy was now burning even hotter than my cheeks did nothing to improve my mood.

. . . .

I still hadn't forgiven Clayton by the time I got to Blue early that afternoon. Not only was I irritated by the fact that he had spanked me in front of his friend, but I was even more maddened by the arousal he had awoken within me that just wouldn't seem to dissipate. The soreness of my ass against my desk chair served as a constant erotic reminder of his harsh discipline that had brought me such intense pleasure. Every time I shifted in my seat, a blush colored my cheeks, and it took all of my willpower to keep my head down and my mouth shut when Cheryl commented on it.

"What's his name?" She had asked chattily, as though we were best gal-pals. I bit my tongue to hold back the stream of vitriol I wanted to release, but my silence only goaded her on. "Or don't you remember? I guess it gets hard to keep track after a while." Her voice was snide.

It was almost painfully difficult to force my lips into some semblance of a smile. "Did you want me to do the alterations on Miss DeLuca's dress next?" Ignoring her poisonous words was my only option.

Now I found myself sitting alone at Blue; Clayton had texted to let me know he was stuck in traffic and running late. My fingers were itching to sketch, to let some of my pent-up anger and frustration flow out through my pencil. I gave in to the urge and pulled out my journal, deciding to indulge myself until Clayton arrived. I fell into my task, allowing the rest of the world to fade around me as I became completely absorbed in the creative process.

"That's incredible, Rose." Clayton's voice jerked me back to reality, and snapped my journal closed, hiding my drawing from view.

"Hey," I said quickly. "What's up?" I wanted to divert the conversation away from my sketches. I never shared my work with anyone.

"I knew you worked at Ivory, but I didn't realize you designed some of the clothes there," he remarked as he settled down across from me.

"I don't," I said sharply. "I just do alterations."

I was relieved when a waitress interrupted us to take our order, hoping we would move on to a different topic once she left. But I had no such luck. Clayton was nothing if not tenacious.

"Why?" He pressed.

I could feel myself frowning at him. "Because my bitchy boss would die before she let me design anything for her shop."

"Then why don't you quit? You should be working somewhere where your talent will be appreciated." He said it as though it was the simplest thing in the world. It became clear to me then that he had no concept of being trapped in the lower-class.

"Because I couldn't afford the fancy degree that would grant me the luxury." I was almost snapping at him now. "Not all of us were handed everything we could ever want on a silver platter." I couldn't hold back the bitter words.

He folded his arms across his chest and fixed me with a stern stare. "I can't deny that my parents were able to provide for me. But I won't apologize for that, Rose. And I haven't had everything handed to me; I've made my own way since high school. A football scholarship paid for my college education, and after I graduated I went to work for the FBI. I started out at the bottom and worked my way up, just like everyone else. You don't get anywhere without working hard and paying your dues. Not everyone has to face the problems you've had to, Rose, but no one's life is all sunshine and roses." Something flickered in the depths of his eyes that made my heart ache. "And just because I've never lived in poverty that doesn't mean I haven't been through my own personal version of hell."

"Clayton, I…" I hesitated, unsure of what to say. I suddenly felt like a self-absorbed brat with a chip on my shoulder. "I'm sorry. It was wrong of me to assume…"

To my great relief, he didn't look angry; he was as imperturbable as ever. Instead, he reached out and took my hand in his. "I know life has dealt you a pretty shitty hand, Rose," he said earnestly. "But you have the talent, brains, and spirit to do anything you put your mind to. You just have to let yourself believe that."

No one had ever said anything like that to me before. My mother had always told me I was useless, a disappointment. But, trapped in Clayton's sincere gaze, I almost *could* believe that I had the power to change my own destiny.

Our intimate moment was interrupted by the arrival of our food. I shook myself slightly and tucked Clayton's words away at the back of my mind. Maybe I could give them further consideration at a later date, but right now I was in no position to be making any changes in my life. When this mess with the Latin Kings was over and Greg was out of rehab, maybe I would allow myself to contemplate it.

"So," I said firmly, heralding a subject change. "Two questions: Why does Smith James have a first name as a last name and a last name as a first name? And why the hell do you think it's okay for you to spank me in front of him?"

Clayton shot me a playful smile. "Sorry, I didn't quite understand that first question."

I glared at him. "I'm really more interested in the answer to the second question, and you know it."

He held up his hands in a show of capitulation, but he didn't look at all contrite. "I told you I have a friend who's into BDSM. Smith gets it. I didn't mention your name when I started asking him questions about it, but I don't think it was too difficult for him to put two and two together. Besides, he recognized you when he saw your photo in Greg's file. It seems he already knew all about your proclivities."

What?! How could he know that? Oh, God, I hadn't slept with Smith on a drunken night out and then forgotten him, had I? That was impossible; I wouldn't have forgotten a man who looked that divine. But this morning, I had thought there was something familiar about him...

Those eyes. I *had* seen them before. Only they had been peering at me out of a black mask that concealed the Dom's face.

No. Way.

"Smith is Master S?! Like, *the* Master S?!" Everyone on the kink scene in New York knew Master S. He was the expert, aloof, unattainable Dom that every unattached submissive salivated over.

Clayton arched an eyebrow at me. "Please try not to look so excited. You're really crushing my ego here."

I just laughed. "I think we've already established that your ego could use some serious downsizing. But don't worry," I reassured him, "I don't think he's all that interested in me." I had tried to flirt with Master S – Smith – a few times in the past, but he had never taken the bait.

Clayton frowned. "So that means *you're* interested in him?"

I grinned at him. "You're awfully cute when you're jealous."

To my surprise, he returned my smile, unflappable as ever. "I think I'm going to add that show of impertinence to our running tally. With the obscene gesture you gave me this morning, I believe that puts you at six."

"Six what?" My voice was somewhat shaky as a delicious sense of erotic trepidation began to stir within me.

"That's for me to know, and you to find out," he taunted. His eyes glowed with triumph, satisfied that he had reasserted his control of the situation.

And damn it if he hadn't.

"But not right now," he added a touch regretfully. "You had better get back to work or you'll tick off your bitchy boss. Sorry I was so late getting here."

I glanced at the time on Clayton's watch and jumped to my feet. "Crap." My sandwich was untouched; I would have to scarf it down while I jogged the three blocks back to Ivory.

"I'll pick you up at eight and we'll head over to Smith's place." His habit of informing me what our plans were rather than asking me was infuriating. And somewhat sexy.

Damn it.

Chapter 9

"You're good for him, you know," Smith informed me casually as he sat down in the armchair across from me.

"What?" I asked, bewildered.

Clayton had just left my side for the first time in over three hours, and Smith had swooped in as soon as I was isolated. We had engaged in a few group conversations since I had arrived at his apartment, but now the small gathering was thinning. And Smith seemed content to leave the few guests left to their own devices so that he could corner me. I glanced nervously towards the kitchen to see if Clayton was coming back with our drinks. The prospect of being left alone with Smith without some kind of social buffer was nerve-wracking. Now that I knew who he was – Master S – I couldn't help but find him intimidating. He looked so casual in his dark-wash jeans and grey t-shirt, but I knew how he looked in black leather with a mask concealing half of his face and a whip in his hand. And that man was kind of terrifying, in a wonderful way.

"Clayton," he clarified. "You're good for him." The kindness in his eyes made some of my anxiety ease. The man sitting beside me was Clayton's friend, not a predatory Dom.

But I was still puzzled by his words. "Why do you say that?" If anything, it was Clayton who was good for me.

He's not good for me. He's too good for me, I mentally corrected myself. Clayton might sometimes make me feel like I could be a better person, but I would never be able to change my past. And Clayton deserved someone better than who I had been, than who I was now.

"He needs to loosen up," Smith explained. "And I know you'll be able to help him with that." He winked at me.

"Clayton seems pretty loosened up to me," I countered. "Nothing gets a rise out of him. Believe me, I've tried."

"That's his problem: he tries so hard to be the good guy all the time. He carefully adheres to all of the rules and never has any fun. He feels like he fucked up in a big way and now he lives his whole life trying to atone for it." Smith's gaze turned inward as he frowned slightly. "But it's been almost ten years now and the guy hasn't really been living."

"Just because I've never lived in poverty that doesn't mean I haven't been through my own personal version of hell."

"What did he do?" I asked softly. I couldn't imagine Clayton doing anything wrong. Especially not something so bad that he would spend a decade of his life trying to make up for it.

"He didn't do anything," Smith said firmly. "But we have differing opinions on that."

"Smith doesn't have opinions," Clayton said jokingly as he approached us. "He has facts. At least, that's the way he sees it."

Smith shrugged. "My opinions are always right. That makes them facts. I don't see what you don't understand about this."

Clayton rolled his eyes and then directed his gaze at me. "I'm sure you can imagine what a joy it is to work with James here."

"As much of a joy as it is to work with you, I'd imagine," I retorted coolly. "I don't think I've ever known you to be wrong. In your opinion."

Smith laughed. "I knew you were good for him," he declared. "My opinion has once again been proven as fact."

It was my turn to roll my eyes. "I can't imagine anyone enjoys working with the two of you if all you do is try to one-up each other all day. Would you like for me to keep a running tally so we know who's winning?"

The amused grin Clayton turned on me had a vicious edge to it. "No, but I believe *I'll* keep running a tally. And according to my records, I'm winning." His hand moved from where it had been resting on my knee to squeeze my upper thigh. He was touching me through my jeans, but his fingers were obscenely close to my sex. Heat pooled low in my belly as desire stirred within me, and I couldn't help glancing around nervously to see if anyone noticed.

Mercifully, the few people still remaining in the apartment were chatting in the kitchen; we were completely alone in our little corner. Then my darting gaze met a pair of keen silver eyes, and my heart faltered. We were completely alone except for Smith. The light in those eyes was knowing. And hungry. He was a wolf that had caught the scent of running prey, and he was ready to join the hunt.

I jumped to my feet, automatically acting on a fight-or-flight impulse in the wake of that stare. And I was choosing flight. "I, um… I need the restroom. Excuse me."

I heard Smith chuckle softly behind me as I fled. He sounded far too pleased with himself, and I was tempted to turn on my heel and knock him down a few pegs. But I was too much of a coward, so I continued walking quickly towards the bathroom. Even though Clayton was just getting in touch with his inner Dom, he was intimidating enough on his own. Now that Smith had given me a glimpse of his own Dominant side, the aura of power that surged in our little corner of the room was stifling.

Once I was locked in the safety of the bathroom, I splashed my face with cold water in an effort to cool my heated skin. When I looked at myself in the mirror, I was chagrined to find that my cheeks were pink and my eyes were wide and over-bright. Ever since Clayton had walked into my life, I had completely lost control of my own body. In the past, I had sought release through kinky games and a little pain, but ultimately I had played on my own terms. I had always been a sexual creature, but now Clayton was ruthlessly manipulating that part of me. Once again, I found that the realization frightened me. But ultimately I still couldn't resist the pull of walking that knife's edge of pushing myself to a new sexual extreme without losing myself.

Taking a few deep breaths, I decided to engage in the challenge. Although a part of me knew I *was* losing myself, another part thrilled at the idea that Clayton was helping me change for the better. And he wasn't changing *me;* he was changing my behavior so I could finally be a version of myself that wasn't miserable and self-destructive.

When I re-emerged into the living room, I was dismayed to find that Smith was saying goodbye to the last of his friends as they left the apartment. I walked to Clayton and looped my arm through his.

"This was really fun, Smith. Thanks for inviting me."

But the two Doms shared a conspiratorial look as Smith closed the door. The sound of the lock sliding home was ominous.

"We're not leaving just yet," Clayton informed me in that cool, controlled tone that told me I was in trouble.

Oh, shit. What had I done wrong?

I swallowed hard and glanced from one stony expression to the other. Smith had his arms folded over his chest, his stance making him appear suddenly larger.

"Clayton tells me that you've been insulting him." His tone was reproving. "I know you've been on the BDSM scene for long enough to know that's unacceptable."

I tried to take a step back, but Clayton's hand was suddenly vice-like on my upper arm. His grin was positively evil. "Smith has been kind enough to offer to help show me how to deal with your infractions. Now would be the time to use your safe word if you want to get out of this."

My fearful shudder was visible, and Clayton's expression softened slightly, a hint of his usual kindness shining out of his eyes.

"If you consent, we will both touch you, Rose. But it won't go any further than that," he promised.

An undeniably enticing image of both of these strong, gorgeous men penetrating me flitted across my mind, and I licked my lips unconsciously. I wasn't sure if I was ready for that; I had never been with two men before. But the prospect of being utterly helpless in the hands of the two Doms was too tempting for me to refuse.

I closed my lips firmly and managed a small nod, letting Clayton know that I didn't want to use my safe word. Lust flared in his eyes and his fingers tangled in my hair as he tilted my head back so he could crush his lips to mine. His tongue swept into my mouth without preamble, claiming me with hot, demanding strokes. I moaned up into him as I melted for him, practically quivering in his arms in ecstatic anticipation of what was about to happen to me.

There was a sudden warmth at my back, and then I was being touched by two pairs of hands. I jerked in shock as I gasped into Clayton's mouth, but he held me firmly, refusing to allow me the opportunity to run. Even if he hadn't been holding me, escaping them would have been impossible. The heat of them engulfed me, sending flames of desire licking across my flesh.

Smith's fingers dipped beneath the hem of my shirt, his hands gliding up my sides as he slowly exposed me. After he had peeled off my tank top, his lips grazed my neck. All of my nerve endings jumped to life, and my skin pebbled. I trembled as pleasure washed over me, rippling from his lips to my core.

My fingers were digging into Clayton's arms through his shirt, clinging onto him for support. He began to unbutton my jeans, finally releasing my mouth to trail soft kisses down my chest and stomach as he bent to slide my pants down my legs. As he did so, Smith bit down on the sensitive flesh where my neck met my shoulder. His hand dipped into my bra at the same time, and he pinched my aching nipple viciously. The contrast of the sharp pain he gave me with Clayton's tender touches was nearly enough to send me over the edge. I sagged back against Smith as my muscles turned to jelly.

Clayton pressed a soft kiss against my clit through my lacy panties as Smith ruthlessly twisted my nipple. My harsh cry filled the space around us, and I could feel Smith's hardening cock jerk against my ass.

"So sensitive," he rumbled in my ear. "You're a lucky man, Clayton. Thanks for sharing."

The way he talked about me as though I was nothing more than their plaything made my inner muscles clench as my need spiraled impossibly higher.

"I'd be luckier if she was more polite," Clayton remarked. "I believe you said you would help me with that."

I had a brief moment to register the smell of hemp before Smith forced my wrists together in front of me, ensnaring them with rope.

"This is your most basic tie," he informed Clayton as he looped more rope between my wrists, fashioning makeshift handcuffs. He slipped one finger through the small gap between my skin and the rope. "There needs to be enough room so that you won't cut off her circulation, but not so much that she can get free." He abruptly grasped the length of rope that was attached to my cuffs and jerked it upward. My arms were forced over my head, and my elbows bent to relieve some of the pressure. Smith pulled the length of it taut down the center of my back, and my hands fisted as they came to rest at the nape of my neck. The position thrust out my breasts so that they were offered up to Clayton. Even though I was still wearing my bra, my cheeks flamed in embarrassment at my flagrant exposure.

"Isn't that beautiful?" Smith asked.

Clayton trailed his fingers over the tops of my breasts, and I shivered under his touch as he nodded his agreement.

Smith drew the rope around my chest so that it encircled my body before he looped it back through itself at my spine. He pulled it tight, and the feeling of the rough material sliding across my skin elicited a moan from deep in my chest.

"This is called a *karada*. It's a basic chest harness," he explained to Clayton as he continued to wind the rope around my chest in a complicated tie, wrapping it around the back of my neck and drawing it between my breasts. As he worked, I could feel my blood flow being restricted and redirected, making my breasts swell. My tender flesh became so hyper-sensitive that even the slightest brush of Clayton's breath over it made me ache.

"*Shibari* is a form of Japanese bondage. It can take a while to learn, but I would be more than happy to provide you with more demonstrations." Although I couldn't see his face, I could practically feel Smith's wicked grin behind me.

My shout was strangled and animalistic when Clayton touched my breasts again. Even though he stroked them lightly, the intense pleasure he brought forth made my head spin.

I found myself trapped in his hungry eyes, and my lips parted as my breath came in sharp, shallow gasps. His smile was twisted. "I would like that," he told Smith.

Satisfied with his tie, Smith gripped my waist and roughly directed my body where he wanted me to go. I stumbled as I fought to remember how to move my legs. His hand pressed between my shoulder blades, and he shoved me hard. The wind was knocked out of me as my stomach hit the back of the couch. Unable to catch myself on my hands, I was helpless to stop myself from bending forward, leaving my ass exposed. My only scrap of modesty was my skimpy thong, and that did nothing to hide my body from them.

"Now," Smith said softly to Clayton as his finger traced the line of my spine, running downward from my neck until he reached the little dip where my lower back met my ass. I moaned and writhed beneath him as he traced a circular pattern there, making the little secret bundle of nerves jump to life in the most delicious way. "I believe you said you've been keeping a tally of her infractions. Just how much trouble is she in?"

"The count currently stands at six," Clayton informed his friend. But he was looking at me, and the steely glint in his eye made a sliver of fear knife through my gut.

I dropped my gaze, as though I could hide from his retribution so long as I didn't look at him directly. But that was a mistake. My eyes instantly fell on his crotch, and his evident arousal made my tongue dart out to wet my suddenly dry lips.

Don't look there, I ordered myself. I averted my gaze again, but this time it riveted on his belt. How was he going to punish me? Oh, god, would he…?

Clayton addressed me personally for the first time since we had begun to play, and my eyes snapped back to his. "I couldn't help but notice that you have a certain fascination with my belt." His smile as he unbuckled it was positively vicious. "I wonder why that is?"

"Please." My voice was a strangled whisper, and I wasn't sure if I was pleading for mercy or if I was begging him to strike me.

My heart was racing. It beat madly against my ribcage as I watched Clayton fold over his belt before he disappeared behind me. I tried to crane my head back so I could see him, but my bindings prevented me from doing so. My breasts throbbed delectably where they pressed into the couch cushions. The men were silent behind me, and the sound of my rapid breaths seemed to echo around the room.

When they finally did touch me, I jumped at the shock of the sudden contact. The supple leather of Clayton's belt glided across my ass. Despite the gentleness of its touch, it communicated a silent threat of what was to come. In contrast, Smith's fingernails raked down my back, confusing my senses and jumbling my ability to think as the men inflicted two diametrically opposed sensations on me simultaneously.

My hips ground against the couch as my body instinctively sought the release I so desperately needed. I heard the *snap* of the belt just before the pain registered. God, it *hurt.* A stripe of searing heat bloomed deep within my flesh. It spread rapidly to the surface and made my skin sting something fierce. But at the same time, the heat raced to my pussy, and I could feel wetness trickling onto my thighs. My body's visceral reaction to the pain was so shocking that I couldn't even cry out; all I could do was draw in a ragged gasp.

"Don't move." Clayton's cold command drifted down to me through the fog that was beginning to roll over my mind, stifling my ability to think. "This is a punishment. You won't receive pleasure until I decide to give it to you. That was a warning. You still have six more."

I whimpered, torn between fear and carnal hunger.

"Don't worry," Smith said to Clayton. "My neighbors are accustomed to hearing screams coming from my apartment." I heard his soft laugh just before the sound was drowned out by the second *snap* of the belt. The hits came in rapid, merciless succession, and the world fell away as the pleasure/pain consumed me. I desperately wanted it to stop, and I never wanted it to end.

When the blows ceased, the pain lingered as my ass throbbed and burned. My sense of sight was obscured by a red haze, but I could still hear Smith's command.

"Apologize."

"I'm…" I struggled to find my voice. "I'm sorry, Clayton." Despite my pain – or perhaps because of it – I was still burning with desperate desire. "Please," I begged. "I need… I'm sorry."

"That's a good girl," Smith rumbled his approval. I gasped and my back arched as his nails gently raked across my enflamed skin.

Yes! Touch me. Please…

Clayton responded to my silent pleading, and he roughly drove two fingers between my desire-slicked folds. At the same time, he pinched my clit sharply as Smith continued to stroke me.

My orgasm hit me with the force of a mac truck, and I screamed as my inner walls contracted. It went on and on, Clayton's fingers continuing to pump in and out of me until he had wrung every last drop of pleasure from me.

I was trembling as Smith released me from my bonds. Clayton gathered me up in his arms and cradled me to his chest as I floated in my bliss-filled haze.

"Thank you," I whispered mindlessly as I snuggled into him. He kissed the top of my head affectionately, and I relished the feeling of being warm and safe and cared for.

Chapter 10

I was a nervous wreck. Three days had passed since my incredibly hot night with Clayton and Smith, and Clayton was falling into his new Dominant persona far too quickly for my comfort levels. Every night, passion would cloud my judgment and I would find myself in his arms, cherishing the heady release and the feeling of being cared for.

But during the day, my mind would backpedal, making me question the prudence of my actions. I was rapidly becoming addicted to him, becoming dependent on him. That was disconcerting. I had taken care of myself for my entire life and had taken on the responsibility of caring for my kid brother as well. If I lost my independence, would I be capable of looking after Greg? He had been my whole life for so long, and I didn't know how to function without him. I felt guilty for spending so much time with Clayton. Greg was twisted and cruel right now, but he didn't deserve my abandonment.

Selfishly, I tried to push him from my mind. He would need me again when he quit the drugs, but right now my presence in his life only seemed to make him more crazed. And that was Clayton's fault as well. Greg felt like I had betrayed him by taking up a relationship with the FBI agent who was going to force him to get clean.

But no, it wasn't Clayton's fault. It was *my* fault for giving in to his advances.

Tonight I found myself callously surrendering to my lusts once again. Smith had suggested that Clayton try out a BDSM club, and to my surprise, he had been game for it. It was one thing to engage in kinky acts in the privacy of his friend's apartment, but another thing entirely to step out in public.

He was examining our surroundings with open curiosity as we stepped into Decadence, my favorite BDSM club. Smith had said he hadn't been there in a while, but I had requested that we come here. The rules had gotten a little looser at Decadence in the last few months; I knew I would be able to throw back a few shots if I needed them in order to calm my nerves. Most clubs had a three drink maximum, and they didn't serve shots.

Clayton looked powerful and sexy in his usual sharp black suit. Smith's leather pants and tight black t-shirt were a little more on the fetish-wear side, and he wore his customary mask. He had told me that because he worked for the government, he had felt the need to conceal his identity. Clayton asked if he should do the same, but Smith just laughed, saying it was no longer necessary.

"Women read *Fifty Shades of Grey* on the subway these days. Kink is 'in,' and the negative social stigma is fading. I just keep this up because everyone knows me as 'Master S' now. And I rather like my reputation." The man was cocky, but I couldn't deny that he had earned the right to be that way.

"Rose!" The man's pleased voice called me back to the present. "It's great to see you again."

I grinned at Derek, the sexy owner of Decadence. His reputation as a skilled Dominant rivaled Smith's, but he rarely played with submissives these days. Not that it would have been difficult for him to ensnare one. The guy was a former Marine, and he had stayed fit since his term of service had ended five years ago. His method of barking orders militarily had brought dozens of subs oh-so-willingly to their knees. Plus, the man was *hot*. His light brown hair was always mussed in a rough-and-tumble way that made him look like he had just enjoyed a good fuck, and his caramel-colored eyes often sparked with a playful light that put his customers at ease.

"It's good to see you too," I replied truthfully as I hugged him with easy familiarity.

"Master S," he nodded respectfully at Smith. "I haven't seen you in a while. It's good to have you back."

Smith's expression was difficult to read with half of his face hidden, but he seemed genial enough. "Always a pleasure, Derek."

I turned to Clayton. "This is Derek Carter. He owns Decadence," I introduced. "Derek, this is my friend Clayton."

Derek smiled warmly and shook Clayton's hand. "Any friend of Rose's is more than welcome here. Thanks for coming. Here, have a drink on the house." He waved down a bartender, and I ordered a double rum and coke. Clayton gave me a disapproving look, but he didn't say anything. He and Smith ordered non-alcoholic beverages. I knew Smith didn't believe in drinking and playing; he said it was irresponsible and clouded a Dom's senses. But he hadn't said anything about submissives not being allowed to drink, so I chose to ignore his censorious look.

"Would you like for me to show you around?" Derek asked, ever the gracious host.

Clayton returned his smile, but he declined. "I think Rose knows her way around."

Derek laughed. "That's true. Just let me know if you have any questions."

"Talk to you later, Derek," I promised as Clayton led me away.

"You had better!" He called after me.

I had always liked Derek, but I had never done anything sexual with him. I didn't want to make a mess of things so that I couldn't come back to my favorite club. Even I wasn't that reckless. Maybe that was why I hadn't seen Derek play with anyone for a while. He might be playing it safe for the sake of his business.

Smith led the way from the bar to the main dungeon. It was well-equipped, with several different apparatuses for bondage so a Dom could put his sub on display. Some found the humiliating experience arousing. And I had to admit that I was one of them.

Clayton seemed interested too. He paused near the St. Andrew's Cross, watching a Dom flog his sub. She was covered in red stripes from her shoulders to her thighs, but she moaned pleasurably as the wicked implement thudded against her skin in rapid, figure-of-eight strokes.

My sex pulsed at the sight, and I couldn't help imagining what it would be like to have Clayton do that to me. His arm snaked around my waist, pulling me tightly against his body as he bent to whisper in my ear. "See something you like?" He asked.

I drew in a shuddering breath. "Yes," I admitted quietly, my voice tinged with longing. I craved to feel the touch of his skin against mine as he held me, but my burgundy corset was a thick barrier between us. He seemed to feel the same need, because his hand slipped beneath my tight leather skirt to roughly grab my ass. The feeling of his fingers digging into the fading bruises inflicted by his belt made me wet, and I pushed back into his hold.

"I think another demonstration from Smith might be in order." As he spoke, his warm breath fanned across my neck, and I shivered in delight.

Smith grinned at me. "I heard that. And I would be more than happy to oblige." He looked at Clayton questioningly. "Are you up for it now?"

Clayton considered for a moment, but then he shook his head. "I think I'd like to have her to myself tonight." He squeezed my ass harder, and I yelped at the zing of pain.

"I understand. We'll arrange another time," Smith replied easily. "I'll show you the private rooms, if you'd be interested in that?"

"Definitely."

Clayton maintained his grip on me as he guided me along in Smith's wake. But as we neared the private rooms, my nervousness came creeping back. Going into that room with

Clayton would be tantamount to a public declaration that I was his sub; I never played in the private rooms. And I wasn't ready for that. As much as I relished the sexual dynamic I shared with Clayton, accepting him as *my* Dom would be a big step. Too big. It was a commitment I wasn't ready to make.

But the insistent throbbing between my legs told me I wanted him so badly…

I needed a moment to myself in order to sort out my tangled thoughts. And I needed some liquid courage if I was going to see this through.

I stopped dead in my tracks. "Um, I need the restroom," I told Clayton.

He released me instantly. "Okay," he agreed. He planted a swift, sweet kiss on my lips. "Hurry back."

I nodded, desperate to get away.

"You should use Room 3," Smith advised. "I think it'll best suit your needs."

"I'll meet you there," I promised Clayton quickly. It took effort to walk away casually so as not to betray my anxiety.

Peeking over my shoulder to make sure they weren't watching me, I changed my course and headed for the bar.

"A double shot of Cuervo and another rum and coke, please," I requested. The bartender poured without question, but I was glad Derek wasn't around to see me. Even though the rules were more lax lately, I had a feeling he might have something to say about me getting plastered in his club. I grimaced slightly as the tequila burned its way down my throat, but the harsh bite was comforting in its own way. I needed it to relax.

Grabbing up my rum and coke, I headed for the bathroom. If I chugged it in front of the bartender, he might be less willing to look the other way. I was thin, so most people assumed I couldn't handle my liquor. But I had been drinking like a fish for years, so I knew I would be able to hold it together.

As soon as I had reached my refuge, I tipped the plastic cup back and poured the sweet drink down my throat with practiced ease. Just as I was polishing it off, a woman emerged from one of the stalls. I was relieved to realize she was someone I knew. We weren't anything more than acquaintances, but I had seen Gemma at Decadence before with her Dom, Garrett. I had also seen her trip her way tipsily across the dungeon. She wasn't going to judge me for my drinking.

"Hi," she said brightly. "It's Rose, isn't it?"

"Yeah," I replied, trying to summon up a smile and failing miserably. I was practically shaking with nerves now. The alcohol just wasn't doing the trick.

She looked at me sympathetically. "Man trouble?" She asked. "Who's the big bad Dom?"

"He's not bad," I admitted, the alcohol loosening my tongue. "He's too damn good. That's the problem."

She nodded in understanding. "Those are always the scariest ones. But they're also the most fun if you can get past the fear."

I sighed miserably. "I know." Clayton had ensnared me with sexual ecstasy; his erotic pull bound me to him more cruelly than any chains ever could.

Gemma gave me a little conspiratorial smile as she reached into the top of her corset. "I think I have just what you need, honey," she said, pinching a little plastic bag between her thumb and forefinger as she held it up for me to see. It was filled with a white powder that I wasn't unfamiliar with. "You want to do a line? I promise it'll make you feel better. It's good shit."

Oh, I knew it would make me feel better. It would make me feel like I was on top of the world. I didn't do coke often, but the few times I had experienced the high had been incredible. It had made me feel powerful, like I could do anything. And sex had felt amazing.

I bit my lip, unsure. If Clayton realized that I was high, he would be pissed as hell. But on the other hand… I remembered how incredible I had felt when he had spanked me for my reckless behavior. Even if he did figure out that I had used, it would only result in something decidedly delectable. And I wanted release. I wanted release from my anxiety and the release that I would achieve when Clayton punished me.

I knew this was exactly the kind of self-destructive behavior that Clayton was trying to put an end to, but I couldn't resist the tempting outcome. Besides, I could get serious about being a better person once Greg went through rehab. Having convinced myself that I had formulated a reasonable plan of action, I held out my hand to accept the drug.

"Thanks." This time, my smile was genuine. I put down a paper towel over the counter and tipped out a line onto it. One should be just enough to give me the buzz I wanted without getting me completely fucked up.

Almost as soon as I inhaled the cocaine, the high hit me. I closed my eyes in bliss as the intoxicating sensation coursed through me. My confidence spiked; I felt like I could do anything. Facing Clayton suddenly didn't seem at all intimidating. I was eager for him to touch me. All of my qualms about taking the drug disappeared. This was the best decision I had made in a long time.

"God, that's good," I practically groaned. I looked at Gemma questioningly. "Do you want to do a line?"

She beamed as she shook her head. "Already did some." She stroked her hand down my arm intimately. The contact felt delicious. "Could I tempt you away from your big bad Dom? I know Garrett would love to get to know you better."

I knew what she was asking, but as good as her touch felt, I didn't want anyone other than Clayton. For a change, that thought didn't bother me at all. I stepped away from Gemma. "Maybe some other time," I hedged. "Thanks for the hit. I owe you one."

I thought I saw annoyance flit across her features, but a moment later I was sure I had imagined it. She was smiling at me sweetly. "I'll be sure to hold you to that."

A distant part of me registered that her words should have made me uncomfortable, but I chose to ignore it. Clayton had been waiting for me for a while now. I almost hoped he was angry.

Feeling more self-assured than I had in months, I boldly stepped into Room 3. Clayton had taken off his jacket and loosened his tie. His roguish smile made warmth pool between my legs.

"I thought you had gotten lost," he commented drily.

"Sorry. I ran into a girlfriend in the bathroom and couldn't get away." It wasn't a total lie.

I approached Clayton confidently, swaying my hips seductively as I usually did when I was trying to lure in a man. His eyes widened slightly, surprised, but I didn't give him a chance to ask questions. I straddled his lap where he sat on the edge of the wrought iron bed, twining my arms around the back of his neck as I hungrily took his lips with mine.

The low, rumbling sound that issued from him was disapproving, and he quickly grabbed my waist, flipping me onto my back and trapping me under his weight. I moaned when his fingers encircled my wrists, pressing them into the mattress. I could feel the blood pumping through my veins as my heart fluttered at a thousand beats per minute. My skin was enflamed and *alive,* sparking with pleasure everywhere Clayton's body touched mine. My head was spinning from the intensity of my bliss.

As soon as he had me pinned, Clayton tore his mouth from mine. My vision blurred and I momentarily saw two Claytons hovering above me. I blinked hard until he coalesced back into one frowning Dom.

"You haven't acted like this since the night we first met. What's wrong, Rose?"

"Nothing," I panted, squinting my eyes in an effort to keep him in focus. "Everything is perfect." I jerked in his hold and tried to lean up into him so that I could claim his lips once again, but he pulled back further. His frown deepened as he studied me carefully.

"Tell me what you've done, Rose," he demanded.

I knew I should feel fear in the wake of that look, but I just grinned widely. "Tequila shots. You like them too, remember?"

His grip on my wrists tightened. "Don't lie to me. I've seen you drunk before. This is something different. What did you do, Rose?"

I rolled my eyes at him. "Chill out, Clayton. It was just a little coke."

He pulled away from me instantly, his expression furious and a little repulsed. "Are you serious, Rose?!" He half-shouted. "What the fuck? You know what my job is. My whole life is about putting an end to drug abuse. And after seeing what your brother is going through, how could you possibly think taking cocaine isn't a big deal?"

His tight control over his anger was slipping for the first time, and my own fury rose to meet his as his words cut at me like a whip. He was killing my buzz. "It's *not* a big deal, Clayton," I informed him hotly. "People do it all the time. Smith told me you needed to loosen up. Stop being such a goddamn prude and learn to live a little."

Clayton stood, grabbing my arm and pulling me up with him. "We'll discuss this later when you're not being such a fucking idiot," he snapped as he dragged me toward the door.

But I dug in my heels, refusing to budge. "What do you think you're doing?" I demanded.

"I'm taking you home," he informed me coldly.

"No!" I said staunchly. No way was I leaving with him when he was being such a mean asshole. Adrenaline was coursing through me, and I wanted to continue riding my high. "I came here to have some fun, and that's what I'm going to do."

Looking disgusted, Clayton released me. "Is that really what I am to you? Just someone you use for *fun?* I thought this was something more than that. I thought I was helping you put a stop to that kind of behavior. But clearly I'm just enabling it."

His words pushed threateningly against my bubble of happiness, a dozen little pins that were going to make it burst. I folded my arms across my chest in a show of defiance, but the stance also made me feel more protected from him. "I want you to leave now, Clayton."

He glowered at me. "Yes," he snapped. "I can see that. In fact, I'm beginning to see a lot of things clearly. You'll have to find someone else to entertain you in the future. I'll be keeping my distance from now on."

Clayton split into two again as he stormed from the room, and I collapsed back onto the bed as the world tilted around me. I shoved him from my mind and closed my eyes so I could more easily focus on the pleasurable tingles that were sparking over my skin. Besides, the way the room was spinning was making me feel a little sick. Blocking off my sense of sight would help to alleviate that. But it didn't help much; the bed felt like it was rocking beneath me. I was getting a wicked case of the spins.

Shit. I guess my alcohol tolerance isn't as high as I thought.

"Hey, honey. Are you okay?" Gemma's voice floated down to me. I also registered the sound of the door closing and the lock clicking into place, but I couldn't summon up any concern over what that meant.

"I'm not sure," I whispered. "I don't think so."

I suddenly wished Clayton hadn't left. He should be here to take care of me. But I had driven him away.

My eyes snapped open when I felt a pair of rough hands grasp my arms and pull them over my head. I could hardly make out the man who was hovering above me, but his leer was clear enough. Something hard and cold closed around my wrists, and I heard the familiar sound of cuffs clicking into place. I tried to tug my hands free, and alarm shot through me as I realized how much effort it took to move my arms.

"What are you doing?" My words were slurred as my heavy tongue refused to function normally. He lightly touched the upper swell of my breasts where they were pushed up by my corset, and I couldn't hold back a pleasurable moan. My flesh had never felt so sensitive, so responsive.

"Don't worry, sweetheart," he said. "You'll enjoy this."

My moan turned to a terrified whimper as fear finally penetrated my little bubble of happiness.

Chapter 11

A second pair of hands was touching me. They were smaller and softer, but they induced just as much terror as they slowly began to pull at my clothes, unsnapping the front of my corset and tugging my skirt and panties down my legs. I hated how the cool air on my exposed flesh made my skin dance.

This was all wrong. I had no control over my body; it reacted instinctively and without my consent, and my leaden limbs refused to move, to fight.

Gemma's lips closed around my hardened nipple as the man's fingers trailed through the traitorous moisture on my thighs.

"Please," I forced out. "Don't."

The man pressed his moistened finger to my lips, and I could taste my desire on his skin. It made my stomach turn. "Shhh," he said softly. "You're going to help Gemma live out her fantasy. She's been very good lately, so she's earned it. She's always wanted to watch me take an unwilling submissive. You should be grateful; her ideas were much more violent than this. Just relax and enjoy. The drugs will make it feel good." To prove his point, he brushed his thumb over my painfully engorged clit, and I shuddered beneath him. "And if it makes you feel any better, you won't remember this in the morning."

No. God, please no.

Bile was rising at the back of my throat, and tears leaked from the corners of my eyes.

There was a loud banging on the door. "Rose! Rose, open this door now."

Clayton! He had come back for me. I had to let him know I was here; I couldn't let him leave me again. With a great effort, I opened my mouth to scream for help. But the man's hand was already covering it, his fingers digging into my cheek as he smothered the sound.

"Rose!" The lock rattled as he tried to turn the doorknob. He cursed loudly, and then there was a deafening bang as the door crashed open.

My eyes were sliding in and out of focus, but I could make out Clayton's shocked expression from where he stood in the now-open doorway.

"You're interrupting our scene," my molester said angrily, keeping his hand firmly over my mouth so I couldn't protest.

No! Clayton couldn't believe him. *Don't leave me. Don't leave me.*

My strangled whine slipped through the man's fingers, and Clayton's uncertain expression darkened.

"Let her speak," he ordered in his most dangerous voice.

The man hesitated, but after a moment he seemed to decide that it was worth the risk to do as Clayton said. He knew I was unable to move, and the hopeful light in his eyes let me know he was banking on that.

At first, I couldn't do more than force a strangled sound from my throat. But I willed my tongue to cooperate. I couldn't allow Clayton to leave me here at the mercy of these terrible people.

"Red." The word was soft and slurred, but the flash of Clayton's eyes let me know he understood.

"That's her safe word," Clayton informed my tormenter. "Get your hands off of her now."

The man looked desperate, and he made a last-ditch effort to save himself. "It's just a game," he insisted. "She likes it." He brushed his thumb over my clit again, and my moan mingled with a sob.

Clayton moved faster than my eyes could follow, and suddenly the man's back was against the wall, Clayton's forearm pressed against his throat. He writhed in Clayton's grip as he struggled to draw in air. "Please," he gasped out, his eyes wide with fear.

Clayton just pressed harder against his windpipe, his expression twisted into something rictus and terrifying. "Did you show her any mercy when she begged?" He seethed.

"What the fuck, Clayton?!" Smith tore his friend away from the man he was choking, and he slid to the ground, clutching at his throat as he drew in ragged breaths.

"What's going on here?" Derek was in the room now.

I was naked, exposed. My skin crawled, and I wanted so badly to cover myself. But I couldn't move. I let out a high, keening cry of distress.

Clayton jerked himself out of Smith's grip and was at my side in an instant. He covered my body with the bedspread, and I drew in a shaky, relieved breath. His hand was cupping my face, and all I could see was the intense blue of his gorgeous eyes.

"You're okay now," he reassured me gently.

Safe. Clayton would take care of me. With that knowledge, I let go of my mental struggle, surrendering to the soporific haze that had been pressing at the edges of my mind. I allowed my eyes to close, shutting out the spinning world.

"Rose? Rose!" There was a thread of fear in Clayton's voice, and he shook me hard. "Look at me," he demanded. But I couldn't open my eyes now even if I wanted to. "What did you do to her?" I heard him growl.

"She..." Gemma's voice was high and fearful. "She wanted to take the coke. And she had been drinking. We didn't know that she didn't want to have a scene with us. We thought she liked it."

"Bullshit!" Clayton snarled. "Cocaine doesn't do this. Tell me what you gave her."

Gemma was silent for a long moment. "Tell him now, or I'll make you talk." The threat in Smith's voice made me want to shudder.

"Rohypnol," Gemma squeaked. "I laced the coke with rohypnol."

"Fuck!" Clayton barked out. "Call an ambulance."

"Already on it," Derek said.

"And somebody get me the keys to these goddamn handcuffs." Clayton's fingers were running through my hair. "You're going to be okay, Rose. You hear me? You're going to be okay."

It sounded more like an order than a reassurance.

Something was very wrong. My head was pounding, and my whole body felt strangely heavy. I was terrified, but I couldn't remember why. I sucked in a deep breath to try to calm myself, but I inhaled the sharp scent of antiseptic, and my panic spiked higher. Where was I? And how had I gotten here?

I cast my mind back, searching for my most recent memories, anything that would give me a clue as to what was going on. Everything was hazy, but I could remember the way I had felt: sick, dirty, and violated. Those feelings still echoed within me, making me shudder.

Don't. Please, don't...

The hand that squeezed mine was warm and familiar. "It's okay, Rose," Clayton assured me gently. "You're in the hospital. You're alright."

My eyes fluttered open to find him sitting beside my bed, holding my hand tightly in his.

"Why am I here?" I asked, my voice tremulous. "I don't remember..."

"The cocaine you took was laced with rohypnol," he informed me calmly, as though he didn't want to spook me. But his eyes tightened at the mention of the cocaine. I couldn't focus on that now. All I could think about was the feeling of a stranger's hands upon me, eliciting the most disturbing reactions from my body.

"Did he…?" I trailed off, unable to say the words aloud. *Did he rape me?*

"No, Rose. I got there in time." Clayton's tone was still gentle, but his muscles tensed in a visible effort of contain his anger. "If you want to press charges, I'll help you. But I won't lie to you: the fact that you chose to abuse an illegal substance won't cast you in the best light. And there is the possibility that your whereabouts and your choices will affect your professional life if what happened becomes public knowledge. That's why I decided not to contact the police until I could ask you what you wanted to do."

My gut twisted as I realized the truth of his words. My position at Ivory was already precarious enough; I couldn't risk losing my job. And if Cheryl ever found out about this it would be all the excuse she needed to fire and blacklist me. Plus, how would my indiscretion affect Clayton if the FBI found out? He was on the anti-narcotics task force, for God's sake.

"No," I said quietly. "I don't want to press charges."

Clayton nodded in understanding. "I thought you probably wouldn't. That's why I looked the other way when Smith beat the shit out of that guy. And Derek promised to make sure no club will ever allow the two of them through their doors ever again."

It wasn't enough to erase the feeling of violation, but it was something.

"I'm so sorry, Clayton," I whispered. "For everything. What I did, the things I said to you… You were right. I *am* a fucking idiot."

"No," he said quickly. "I'm sorry, Rose. I never should have left you. As soon as I came to my senses and realized it was the drugs talking, not you, I came back so I could drag your ass home." He ran a hand through his hair in frustration. "God, how many times can I fuck up in the same way?" He muttered to himself, his gaze turning inward. When his eyes re-focused on me, they were filled with anguish. "I need to tell you something, Rose.

I told you about my girlfriend in college, the one who I experimented with sexually? Her name was Jen, and she was my first love. I thought she was the girl I was going to marry. But I fucked everything up. I was on a football scholarship, so I couldn't really drink a lot or do any hard partying; I had to stay fit. But Jen was a social butterfly, and she loved to have a good time. When she first started smoking pot, I didn't approve, but I didn't say anything. After all, it wasn't a big deal. Half of the people on campus smoked casually every now and then. Only, it wasn't every now and then for Jen, and when she started to do harder drugs, our relationship started falling apart. I broke up with her, hoping it would be the wake-up call she needed to set her life straight again." Clayton's expression was twisted with remembered pain. "That backfired. She took too much acid to try to numb the pain. She lost her mind, Rose. I had thought pushing her away would bring back the girl I loved, but instead I lost her forever." His eyes blazed with a ferocious, determined light. "And I'm not going to lose you, Rose."

My mind spun as I tried to absorb the enormity of what Clayton had just admitted. Everything Smith had said about him suddenly made perfect, awful sense. Clayton really believed it was his fault that he had lost her. That was what he was trying to atone for.

"You're not responsible for what happened to her, Clayton," I said softly. "She made her own choices."

He fixed me with a hard stare. "Like you make your own choices, Rose?" He challenged. "Do you really expect me to stand idly by and watch someone I care about destroy herself? I won't do that again."

Someone he cares about. A horrible realization made my gut twist and my heart ache. I thought about how Clayton looked at me as though he saw someone standing before him who I didn't recognize as myself. He hadn't been seeing the good in me; he had been seeing *her.*

"I'm not Jen, Clayton," I said quietly. "And saving me won't bring her back."

His brows drew together, and his grip on my hand tightened. "I know that, Rose."

"Do you?" I whispered. "You said you have a thing for 'damsels in distress'. I don't want to be just another woman who you've fixated on because you want to save her. Helping me won't change what happened to Jen."

"No," he agreed. "But I can change what might happen to you if you stay on this path. And you're not just some woman I've become fixated on. I haven't felt this way about anyone in a long time. Not since…" He trailed off, catching his mistake.

"Not since Jen," I finished for him hollowly.

Clayton made a low, frustrated sound. "You're looking at this all wrong, Rose. Why won't you just listen to what I'm saying? I want to help *you* because I care about you. You're more than just an assignment to me. I would think that would be obvious by now."

"You're not helping me!" I burst out. "You're *hurting* me. Maybe my life wasn't perfect before you came along, and maybe I made shitty choices, but I managed just fine. Now I'm an emotional wreck and every day is an uphill battle. When you look at me… All of my shortcomings, my fuck-ups, become painfully clear to me. Being around you makes me feel like crap about myself all the time. I just can't take that anymore."

And it was true. I had reached my breaking point. My life had been a struggle before, but Clayton had come along and made it impossibly more difficult. I was constantly conflicted about my decision to be with him, fearing the loss of my independence and feeling guilty about my abandonment of my kid brother. The high that I got from being with Clayton sexually just wasn't worth it. Especially not now that I realized I was some sort of project to him, a hurdle he had to overcome to get one step further on his road to personal redemption. He said he cared about me, but I knew that was just an illusion. He saw *her* reflected in me, and she was the one he truly cared about.

"I want you to leave me alone, Clayton," I said in a broken whisper.

He was silent for so long that I thought he might not say anything at all. When he did finally speak, his voice was hoarse with emotion, his iron control gone. "I'm sorry, Rose. I didn't know. If that's what I'm putting you through…" He stood abruptly, and the loss of the warmth of his hand on mine made me want to cry out. "I'll transfer someone else to your case. I'll leave you alone." He bent to kiss my forehead sweetly, the touch of his lips feather-light and all too fleeting. "Goodbye, Rose."

Watching him walk away almost broke me. I wanted to call him back, to throw myself at his feet and beg for forgiveness, to promise him that I would be anyone he wanted me to be if only he would stay.

I had given him my body, and I had failed miserably at keeping my heart.

Chapter 12

"I'm not trying to be a bitch, but you look like crap, girl. What the hell did Clayton do to you?"

I tossed back my tequila shot, and I wasn't sure if my grimace was from the burn of the alcohol or from her pointed question. Just the sound of his name made my heart twist painfully in my chest. "I really don't want to talk about it, Penny. And thanks for the confidence booster. It's always nice to hear that you look like crap."

Penny gave me a no-nonsense look, refusing to allow my acerbic tone to affect her. "Hey, I'm just trying to help. And I've found a blunt approach is the best way to get through to you."

"I don't want anyone's help, Penn," I informed her irritably. "I just want to be me. I just want to have fun."

She studied me for a long moment, clearly debating whether or not she should push the issue. Finally, she sighed, deciding to be supportive rather than starting an inquisition. And I loved her for that. "Okay, then. We'll have fun. But feel free to let me know where he lives and I'll go give him a good kick in the balls for you."

"Thanks," I said tersely, my tone letting her know that any further mentions of Clayton would be unwelcome.

"This round's on me," she said brightly. "And I'm getting us the good shit." Penny didn't let me down. The pomegranate martinis were heavenly. They were also fifteen dollars a pop. I would have to owe her one.

"I owe you one."

"I'll be sure to hold you to that."

I shied away from the memory of my encounter with Gemma, of my stupid decision to take drugs from someone I barely knew. What they would have done to me if Clayton hadn't gotten there in time made me want to be sick. It wouldn't be the first time this week that I had gone running to the bathroom to heave up the contents of my stomach. I forced down the bile that was rising in the back of my throat by taking several large gulps of my martini.

"Hey, slow down there," Penny advised. "I'm not buying you another one of those, so you had better take your time and enjoy it."

I made a show of taking the tiniest of sips. "Happy?" I asked.

Penny put a hand on her hip and cocked that eyebrow at me. "If you're going to be snippy all night, then we aren't going to have much fun," she informed me.

She was right. I needed to pull my shit together. The week that had passed since Clayton had left me in that hospital room had been agonizingly long as the stress of constant fear ate away at me. I hadn't seen a single FBI agent, but I knew someone was watching me from a distance. Still, without Clayton constantly by my side to protect me, I had taken precautions. I now kept a loaded gun stashed under my bed, just in case.

My traumatic experience at Decadence had made me reluctant to go out and seek my usual hedonistic releases. But being cooped up in my tiny apartment with Greg was wearing on me, and tonight I just had to get out. I wasn't about to screw up the opportunity to lose myself in the buzz of alcohol and sex by acting pissy.

"Right," I muttered to Penny. "Sorry." I plastered on a glowing smile and clinked my glass against hers. "To the hunt," I toasted. "I feel like being a lioness this evening."

"I thought you preferred the term 'Siren'," Penny pointed out.

"Nope. 'Lioness' is definitely growing on me. Let's go find some unsuspecting prey."

"S.L.A.P.," Penny agreed. *Sounds Like A Plan.* "Pick a target. First one to get a drink bought for her wins."

"Since when is this a competition?" I asked. "And what will I get for my prize?"

"You're a cocky bitch, you know?" But it wasn't a real insult. Penny was laughing. "And no prizes, just bragging rights. And the free drink, obviously."

"Deal," I grinned. This was going to be fun. I liked a good competition. Just like Clayton, I enjoyed winning.

Only when I'm with him, losing is pretty amazing.

Stop it! I reprimanded myself. I refused to spend any more time pining over Clayton. He was out of my life for good. I had made sure of that.

Mentally shaking myself, I turned my attention on my task. No way was I going to let Penny beat me. My eyes roved over the various man-candy in the bar, and my interest was instantly sparked when an impressively ripped guy raised his glass at me when he noticed me looking at him. He was totally my type: his bulging muscles were obvious under his tattered, low-slung jeans and tight black t-shirt. Intricately colored tattoos twined their way up his corded arms, and his features were angular and slightly mean. He was every inch the bad-boy type I usually went for. He was powerful enough to hold me down and fuck me hard, and he looked like the kind of guy who wouldn't give a shit if I left in the morning and never saw him again.

But I found myself frowning at him as the thought made me profoundly sad. He frowned right back and then shrugged, his gaze roving elsewhere. Yep. He was definitely a callous bastard.

I noticed Penny had already moved in on a target, and I hastily continued my search. My eyes were drawn to a guy who couldn't have looked more different than the tattooed asshole. He was wearing a well-fitted suit, and his demeanor gave off the impression that he was a man who was used to success. His blond hair was a few shades lighter than Clayton's, but he had blue eyes.

A part of me recognized that I was totally fucked up; it was a terrible idea to sleep with a man who reminded me of Clayton. But a yearning rose up within me, and I knew this guy was my best shot at finding some modicum of pleasure in a man's arms tonight. His eyes met mine, and I gave him a slow, sly smile before taking a sip of my drink. As I did so, I allowed myself to think of sexual pleasures so he could see the lust in my eyes.

Unfortunately, images of Clayton dominating my body flooded my mind. I gulped down the rest of my martini in order to mask my anguished expression. My tactic must have worked, because the guy grinned at me and slipped off his barstool so that he could join me where I was leaning casually on the bar.

"Hi, gorgeous," he said as he sidled in next to me. "What's your name?"

"Sarah," I lied. *Rose* wouldn't be sleeping with this man; Sarah would. Somehow, that would help me get through this.

He smiled at me warmly and extended his hand so I could shake it. "I'm John," he introduced himself. But instead of shaking my hand, he gripped it gently and raised it to his lips, kissing it softly.

Shit. Another white knight.

I took a deep breath. *This is good. You like this now. Just go with it.*

"Can I buy you a drink, Sarah?" He asked, noticing my now-empty martini glass.

"Sure," I forced myself to smile at him. "I'll have a Long Island Iced Tea, please."

I would like to get completely fucked up, please. Getting drunk always lowered my inhibitions and made me horny. I needed that desperately.

As John handed me my drink, I glanced over to see that Penny's man was just ordering one for her. I had beaten her by less than a minute. She grinned at me a touch regretfully before raising her glass to toast me in congratulations, conceding her defeat. But the victory felt hollow, and I didn't feel any sense of triumph. Somehow, I managed a smirk and toasted her back.

"Friend of yours?" John asked.

"Yeah," I replied. "We just had a little bet going. I won."

"Oh? And what was the bet?"

I touched his arm lightly, the slight contact full of promises that I wasn't at all sure I could keep. "That I could snare a hotter guy than she could," I lied to stroke his ego.

His brows rose in flattered surprise. "Well, she can join us if she wants," he said, his smile a lustful invitation.

"I wouldn't have a problem with that," I purred. "But unfortunately I don't think she would be comfortable with it." That last part was true, and my first statement was half-true. I was interested in involving another woman in my sexual play, but I would never be comfortable introducing my vanilla friend into the mix. That would be too weird.

The interest in John's eyes didn't waver. "I'm cool with that, baby. I'm sure you'll be hard enough to handle that you'll need my full attention."

The indication that he might be a little controlling in the bedroom should arouse me, but I just felt cold. It bothered me that he assumed sleeping with me was a foregone conclusion. Did I scream *slut* that loudly?

Yes. Yes I did. And it wasn't fair for me to resent John for making the assumption. I had come onto him strong, after all, and within a few minutes I had basically promised him I was a sure thing.

God, I hated myself. I felt dirty and desperate and worthless.

I took long draws of my Long Island Iced Tea through my straw, drinking almost half of it without pausing for breath. The buzz of the ridiculous amount of alcohol went to my head almost instantly.

"Damn, baby, you in a hurry or something?" John asked. "Because I don't mind that."

Well I *did* mind. My behavior sickened me. I had always been able to shove down my discomfiture at my reckless actions. But Clayton had made me acutely aware of the fact that I was destroying my own sense of self-worth.

God, why couldn't I stop thinking of him? I had come here to escape the pain of losing him, but it was futile. He had ruined me.

I felt stupid, drunken tears sting at the corners of my eyes. John's cocky expression instantly shifted to one of concern, and he took my hand in his.

"Hey, baby, what's wrong? Was it something I said? I didn't mean to insult you."

It was his kindness that broke me. I let out a sob, and the tears spilled freely down my face.

John looked alarmed and utterly bewildered at my total 180°.

"I'm- sorry," I gasped out as I fought to heave in air between the sobs that now wracked through my chest. "You didn't do- anything. It's- me." I turned from him quickly, jerking my hand out of his. I hated that I had allowed him to touch me even in that innocent way.

I fled from the bar, oblivious to the stares I was attracting with my erratic behavior.

"Rose!" Penny called after me as I crossed the threshold and stepped out onto the sidewalk. "Rose, wait!"

I spun to face her. "Please, Penny," I begged. "Don't ask me about it. I can't... I won't talk about it. I just want to go home."

But I didn't want to go home. I wanted to go to Clayton. I wanted him to hold me and comfort me; I wanted him to take care of me. He made me feel cherished, like I was someone better than who I really was. And even if I knew deep down that he wasn't really seeing *me* when he looked at me like that, I almost didn't care.

"Hey, Rose." I blinked hard to clear away the tears that blurred my vision, and I saw that Sharon had arrived out of nowhere. "Why don't you let me take you home?" She asked gently.

Penny folded her arms across her chest distrustfully. "Who the hell are you?" She asked. She sounded a little rude, but I knew she was just being protective of me.

"This is Sharon," I said, my voice ragged from crying. "She's a friend of mine."

I wasn't quite sure if that was true; I didn't really know the FBI agent, and I still resented her slightly for arresting Greg. But she had been kind to me, and I knew she wouldn't let me come to any harm. I also knew it was safer to let her escort me back to my apartment so that I didn't give in to the foolish temptation to go running to Clayton.

"Come on," Sharon urged. "I have my car here, so it'll save you the cab fare."

"Okay," I breathed. "I'll see you later, Penn. Thanks for trying to cheer me up. I'm sorry I'm such a mess."

My friend's arms closed around me, and she hugged me to her tightly. "Anytime, Rose. I'm here for you. You can talk to me. Call me if you need me, day or night."

Her words brought on a new flood of tears. She was a better friend than I had ever given her credit for. "Thanks, Penn," I whispered. "I will."

Sharon didn't press me to talk about my problems as she drove me back to my apartment, and I was thankful for that. Greg was home, but he was unmoving on his bed. I wasn't sure if he was high out of his mind or just sleeping. I was grateful he didn't wake up when I came in. If he wasn't high and I disturbed him, he might go off on me. He had such a short fuse now during his brief periods of sobriety. He was using more often than ever now that he knew he was going to be forced to quit. All I could do was hope this mess would soon be over and I could finally get him the help he needed.

I buried my face in my pillow to muffle the sound of my sobs. It was soaked with my tears when I finally fell into sleep, utterly exhausted from my emotional turmoil.

"Baker! Where are you, you little shit? You think you can just take our drugs and then skip out on your part of the deal?" The man's shout as he pounded on the door jerked me out of my fitful slumber. I ran to the door to see who was there; Greg stayed frozen on his bed, his eyes wide. He looked too terrified to move.

My stomach clenched in fear when I looked through the peephole. Two Latino guys were standing in the hallway. They were big and heavily muscled. And they looked *pissed.* If they got in, they would tear my brother apart.

I dashed to my bed and grabbed my gun from underneath it and my cellphone from my bedside table. I went back to the door and trained the gun on the men through the wood, steeling myself to use it if I had to. With my free hand, I dialed Clayton's number, knowing I could get help from him more quickly than I could if I dialed 911.

"Go away!" I yelled, my voice high and thin. "I'm calling the cops."

"*Puta!*" One of them cursed before he kicked in our flimsy door. As it banged open, it smacked into my forehead, sending me reeling backwards. The impact made my head spin, but I forced myself to stay on my feet. My cell phone had slipped from my fingers, but I determinedly kept my grip on my gun. I cocked it and pointed it directly at the two men who had come for Greg.

"Get out of here," I demanded, trying to keep my hand from trembling. "Leave my brother alone." I could feel something warm and wet trickling down the side of my face.

The men paused, looking wary as they stared down the barrel of the gun. But they didn't leave.

"Look, guys, I'm sorry," Greg choked out. "I just made a mistake. I got too fucked up last night. I swear I'll make it up to you. I'll sell double tonight."

"I know you will," one of them said menacingly. "We're going to make sure you're motivated."

He started to advance on Greg. But I wasn't about to let him lay a hand on my baby brother. Grasping the gun in both hands to steady it, I aimed at the floor and fired a warning shot right in front of the guy's feet. He cursed and jumped back, glaring at me.

"Get out!" I shrieked.

"Crazy bitch!" He stood his ground for a moment, and I cocked the gun again.

"I won't tell you again," I threatened.

He glowered at me and spat on the floor. But mercifully he decided it wasn't worth risking it, and the two men backed slowly out of our apartment before running for the stairs.

As soon as I was sure they were gone, I sat down hard on my bed, shaking madly and pressing my palms against my aching head to help alleviate the throbbing where the door had hit me. It didn't help much.

"Rose!" Sharon's voice was alarmed as her footsteps quickly approached me. She gently grasped my hands and pulled them away from my face. "Shit," she cursed under her breath. "Clayton is going to murder me." She raised her voice, addressing me again. "Don't move, Rose. I'm calling the paramedics."

Concern shot through me. "Why? Is Greg okay?" I knew the Kings hadn't attacked him, but the sharp pounding in my head was making me fuzzy.

Sharon eyed me carefully as she dialed. "You're bleeding, Rose," she informed me. "It doesn't look bad, but you might have a concussion."

I looked down at my hands as she ordered an ambulance to come to my apartment. They were smeared with something crimson. God, my head hurt. I closed my eyes and lay back on my bed, trying to shut out the pain.

Sharon shook me insistently. "Open your eyes, Rose," she commanded. "Don't pass out on me."

The hint of fear in her voice made me do as she said, but the way the room spun around me made me feel sick.

"Rose!" I recognized his voice instantly, and I blinked hard to sharpen my vision so I could look at him. It was the first time I had laid eyes on Clayton in over a week, and I drank in the sight hungrily. He knelt beside my bed and took my hand in his before lightly brushing his fingers over my forehead to check my injury. The slight pain it elicited should have made me wince, but I was so thrilled to feel his skin brush against mine that I barely registered it.

He turned a terrifying glare on Sharon. "What happened?"

"A couple of the Kings got in here. I heard a gunshot and came running, but by the time I got here, they were already gone."

"That was me," I admitted. "But I just shot the floor to scare them off."

Clayton continued to scowl at his partner. "Well it's a good thing Rose is more competent than the goddamn FBI. How the hell did you let this happen, Silverman?"

Her brows drew together, and her eyes narrowed. "Look, *Vaughn*," she said hotly as she came to her own defense. "We don't have records of those guys in our files. I can't just go stopping every Latino male who enters this building. That's called racial profiling. I'm sorry Rose got hurt, and I'm sorry I didn't get here sooner. You can file a report against me at the office if you want to, and I'll understand. But don't you dare talk down to me like that."

Their raised voices were making my head hurt, and I closed my eyes again.

Clayton cursed softly. "Keep your eyes open, Rose," he ordered.

I obeyed, focusing on his perfect face to help keep my vision from blurring. I never wanted to lose sight of him again.

Chapter 13

It didn't take long for the paramedics to patch me up. I didn't have to go to the hospital, and I didn't have a concussion. They closed up the cut on my forehead with some glue and said I wouldn't even have a scar. Head wounds bled a lot and usually looked scarier than they actually were. After giving me some extra-strength Advil to help with the pain, they left my apartment.

Sharon had gone back to the office a while ago. Clayton hadn't chewed her out any more since she had told him off, but he still looked furious. I didn't blame her for wanting to get away from him when he was seething with that kind of anger. I was just grateful it wasn't turned on me. Clayton hadn't left my side since he had arrived, and he held my hand through the whole thing, tracing little circles over my palm with the pad of his thumb. It was incredibly soothing. A truly sick part of me was almost glad that the Kings had hurt me. It had brought Clayton back to me, and he was taking care of me again. A huge weight was lifted off my shoulders as I leaned into him, relieved that someone else was taking responsibility for me so I didn't have to be responsible for myself. I needed Clayton to guide me, to center me. And I needed him to be hard on me when I was tempted to do something reckless. I trusted him completely.

"I'm so sorry, Rose." It was the first time Greg had spoken. I had almost forgotten he was there. When I looked at him, my heart twisted to see that it was my sweet brother who was looking at me with agonized concern.

"'Sorry' just isn't going to cut it, Greg," Clayton said harshly. "Rose might have coddled you for years, but you're not a child anymore. It's time you started acting like a man and took responsibility for your actions. Those men might have killed your sister. And after she's spent her entire life trying to protect you,

you did nothing to help defend her when they broke in here." Clayton's mouth was twisted in disgust. "This is *your* fault. Rose has put up with your behavior because she didn't want to lose you if she challenged you. Do you even care about the fact that you could have lost *her* today?"

"Of course I care!" Greg cried out, sounding alarmed. All the blood had drained from his face, and his usually-tanned skin looked almost as pale as mine.

"She has proven she would give her life to keep you safe, and what have you ever given her? Nothing but heartache and a shit-ton of problems that she doesn't deserve. You just take and take, and now you've gotten greedy enough that you would let the Kings take her life just so you could get your next fix."

Greg's mouth was hanging open in shock; no one had ever talked to him like this before. Certainly not me. Tears of shame glistened on his cheeks. They made my heart twist, but I knew he needed to hear this. I didn't think I would ever have been capable of delivering these hard truths to my brother, and I was thankful Clayton was doing it for me.

Greg tore his eyes from Clayton's so that I was caught up in his pained gaze. "Rosie, I... I'm sorry." He shook his head. "No. He's right: that's not enough. Nothing I can say will ever be enough." His anguished expression nearly broke my heart. "I don't know when I became this person, Rose. But I don't want to be him anymore. I won't lose you. I'm going to get clean, and I'm going to be there for you from now on."

Overwhelmed with emotion, I leapt to my feet so that I could go to my brother. The movement made my head pound, and Clayton steadied me when I swayed. I gently extricated myself from his hold so I could get to Greg. He met me halfway, and I wanted to cry with joy when he wrapped his arms around me.

"I love you so much, Rosie," he whispered fervently. "I'm not going to let anything happen to you. I promise."

I clutched him to me more tightly. "I love you too, Greg. More than anything. I'm not going to let anything happen to you, either. You're not going to do this anymore, Greg. It's too dangerous for you to keep spying on them. You're going to go to rehab. Today." I turned my face to look at Clayton questioningly. "The FBI will let him out of this deal now, right? It's obvious that the Kings are going to hurt him. You swore to me that you wouldn't let them hurt him."

Clayton suddenly looked weary, but he nodded. "No. He doesn't have to do it anymore. The last thing we want is for more people to be hurt by the Kings. That's what we're trying to put a stop to."

Greg pulled away from me. Holding me at arm's length, he addressed me solemnly. "No. I'm not going to back out. I need to do this. I need to make things right."

Panic speared through me. "Don't be stupid, Greg!" My voice was colored with alarm. "They could kill you!"

"If we don't bring them down, they might kill *you.* Those men who came here today…" He swallowed hard. "They know you now. And they won't forget what you did." He turned his gaze on Clayton. "That's true, isn't it? She won't be safe until they all get taken out, will she?"

Clayton nodded somberly. "Yes. That's true."

"Clayton!" I cried, unable to believe that he was really considering allowing Greg to go through with this. "You can't let him do this!"

He looked at me sadly. "It's his choice, Rose. If this is what he wants, I won't stop him."

"No!" I gripped Greg's forearms. His skin felt paper-thin beneath my fingers, and I could feel that his pulse was anemic. He was so weak. He wouldn't survive this.

Greg looked at Clayton beseechingly. "Help me, please."

Clayton's arms closed around me from behind, pinning my arms to my sides as he locked his own around my waist.

"I'm going now, Rosie." Greg's voice broke on my name. God, he sounded so scared...

"No! You're not going to leave me, Greg! I'm not going to let you!" I gripped him harder, my fingernails digging into his skin in an effort to keep him with me. He winced as he ripped his arms away, and I could see long red gouges in his skin from where I had clung to him.

His eyes were agonized as he paused to look at me one last time. "I love you, Rosie."

"NO!" I screamed as he turned his back on me. "Clayton, stop him! Stop him!" I writhed in his arms, desperate to break free and run after Greg, but he held me firmly. His hold on me restricted my movements, but I clawed at his exposed hands in an effort to get him to release me. He just grabbed my wrists, keeping me restrained. I couldn't see my brother anymore. "Please! God, Clayton, please let me go! They're going to kill him! Help me!" I shrieked as I twisted madly in his grip. He said nothing. I don't know how long I fought him, but he was just too strong. Eventually, my exhausted muscles gave out, and I sagged against him as broken sobs ripped their way out of my chest.

Clayton shifted me in his arms, lifting me up so I was cradled against his chest. I buried my face against him, my hands fisting in his shirt. I was so mad at him, but his strong arms and his warm scent were reassuring. He was implacable, unbending. And he wasn't going to let me go until my sanity returned. I cried and cried until I didn't have any more tears to shed. I went quiet, trembling against him.

"I'm sorry, Rose," he whispered, finally breaking his silence. "We will have agents watching him. We'll protect him as best we can. But it's time to let your brother make his own choices. I won't deny him a chance at redemption."

"What good is redemption if he's dead?" I asked brokenly.

Clayton's fingertips were under my chin, tilting my head up so that I was looking into his eyes. "Do you really think Greg could live with himself if anything happened to you because of his actions? He would spend the rest of his life hating himself, consumed by the knowledge that he was responsible for losing his sister." The pain etched across his features made me realize that he knew the burden of that kind of responsibility all too well.

"It wasn't your fault, Clayton," I said quietly. "You're not responsible for what happened to Jen."

"Aren't I?" He breathed, his voice laced with anguish.

"No," I said firmly, putting my own problems aside for the moment. Clayton needed to hear this, needed to believe it. I couldn't bear the thought of him going on one more day carrying the weight of this undeserved guilt.

"People are responsible for their own actions. I can see that now. *You've* helped me to see it. I've spent the last year of my life feeling responsible for Greg, hating myself for what I had allowed him to become. But it didn't matter what I said or did; once the drugs got hold of him, he wasn't going to change. It took the threat of me being murdered for him to finally be convinced to give it up." I took a deep breath. "And I'm responsible for the shitty choices I've made. I can't blame my reckless behavior on Greg. I could have forced him into rehab at any time. I could have gone to the police and made them get a court order to get him clean. But instead I selfishly allowed it to continue because I didn't want to lose him. Every stupid, self-destructive thing I did to escape the pain he put me through was ultimately my own fault. People don't change until they're ready to, and you can't force them to be the person that you want them to be. No matter how badly you might want to."

Clayton looked uncertain, but there was a longing in his eyes that let me know he was desperate to believe me. "But I'm helping *you* change, Rose," he said. "At least, I thought I was. I could have done that for Jen. If I had just been harder on her…"

"You *are* helping me, Clayton. But I think I've wanted to change for a long time. Hell, I never wanted to be this person. But

I let myself get buried under my problems, and I excused my behavior by blaming my circumstances. Before I met you, I couldn't see a way out. I didn't *know* how to be better. I didn't even think it was possible for me to be better. But I want that, Clayton. Desperately. I'm *asking* for your help because I'm ready. When you punish me, when you correct my behavior, you're not beating me into submission and forcing me to change. The pain you give me helps me to forgive myself so I can move on. I need that, Clayton. I need *you*."

"Rose," his voice shook slightly, and his eyes glistened with unshed tears. "I... Thank you. I've never seen it that way before."

He leaned into me slowly, and I quickly closed the distance between us. Our kiss was desperate and fierce. It was full of pain and forgiveness and our intense need for one another, body and soul. Clayton eased me down onto the bed, settling himself over me. The weight of him, the delicious heat of him, was everything I craved.

When he finally took his lips from mine to gasp for breath, he was looking down at me as though I was the most precious thing in the world. And I felt the same about him. He was the key to my redemption, and I had helped him to finally accept that he didn't need to be redeemed at all.

"I need you too, Rose," he said raggedly, his voice rough with emotion.

I reached out to tenderly cup his cheek with my hand. "Then take me," I whispered. "Please."

He touched my forehead lightly, looking regretful. "We can't. You're hurt."

Now that he called my attention to it, I became aware of the soft, insistent throbbing just inside my skull. But my need for him was more acute than my discomfort. "I don't care," I declared. "I forgot it was even hurting until you mentioned it." I ground my hips up against his. "You help me forget about it when you touch me."

He still looked hesitant, but his hard cock let me know how badly he wanted me. "Are you sure?"

I smiled up at him softly. "You're a far better painkiller than Advil is."

He chuckled. "That's the strangest compliment I've ever received. But I'll take it." He stroked my hair tenderly. "I'll be gentle with you," he reassured me.

"I don't want you to be gentle," I huffed petulantly.

He grinned down at me. "How can I resist you when you're pouting like that? I shouldn't have told you my weakness. You're not trying to manipulate me, are you?"

"That depends," I said teasingly. "How much trouble would I be in if I was manipulating you?"

His expression turned stern, but the playful light in his eyes told me he was enjoying our little game. "Loads," he told me. "I thought I warned you not to try topping from the bottom."

"In that case: yes. I am trying to manipulate you." I pouted again to drive home my point.

Clayton laughed. "You little minx. If I punish you now for topping from the bottom, then I'll just be giving you what you want, thereby allowing you to top from the bottom. That leaves me with a bit of a dilemma now, doesn't it?"

"Why do you have to be so goddamn clever?" I asked sulkily.

"And now you're cursing at me again. Does your deviousness know no bounds? I think I'm going to have to have a long talk with Smith about what we should do with you." His tone was musing, but his words held a clear threat. My shiver was a result of both fear and a spike of pleasure at the thought of being at the mercy of both Dominant men once again. How far would they push me...?

Clayton lowered himself so his lips were at my ear, his hot breath playing over my sensitive neck. "I think someone likes that idea," he remarked, his voice low and hungry. I whimpered beneath him as my erogenous zones throbbed to life, my desire enflamed by the promise in his tone.

"Touch me," I begged. "Please, I'll be good. Just touch me."

Clayton nipped lightly at my earlobe. "Now that's the proper way to get what you want," he told me, his pleasure evident in his voice. "No tricks." He trailed his tongue in a hot line from my ear to the nape of my neck. "And no backtalk." He brushed his lips across my collarbone. "Just be my sweet and obedient sub." His teeth bit into the sensitive flesh where my neck met my shoulder, and I cried out as the sharp pain sent searing lines of pleasure shooting to my sex.

"My" sub. His.

"Yes, Clayton," I moaned. "I'm yours."

He drew back slightly so he could stare down at me. His eyes were blazing with a desire that was more than just lust; it was yearning.

"Say it again," he ordered. "Who do you belong to?"

"You. I'm yours, Clayton." My voice shook with erotic longing as I made the confession.

His expression twisted in triumph as his primal side took over, drawn out by my admission of his complete ownership of my body and soul. He tore at my clothes, his movements rough and almost frenzied, as though he couldn't strip me fast enough. I met him with equal passion, my lips finding his as I undressed him, my fingers roving greedily over every inch of flesh I exposed. When my touch found his hard cock, he growled into my mouth, a low, warning sound. He jerked away from me, briefly depriving me of his heat so that he could grab a condom from his pants pocket. I licked my lips in anticipation as I watched him roll it on. He noticed, and he leered down at me.

"Tell me how badly you want my cock inside you."

"Oh, God," I groaned as his crude command washed over me, making my ache for him even more painfully acute. "I want you to fuck me, Clayton. I *need* you to fuck me. I want you to slam your cock into my pussy so hard that my teeth rattle. And I don't want you to ever stop."

"Fuck, Rose!" He barked out as he impaled me. My fingers twisted in the sheets and my toes curled at the raw ferocity of it.

"Yes! Clayton!" I cried. "Just like that. Just like that. Thank you thank you thank you…" The words dripped from my tongue in tandem with every hard, rapid thrust, but I was hardly aware I was even speaking. The intensity of my pleasure overwhelmed all other thoughts as Clayton's cock hit my g-spot over and over again. The friction of his body's movements against my clit only stimulated me further.

My eyes were half-closed in my delirium, but they flew open when I felt Clayton's hand wrap around the front of my throat. He gripped me firmly, but he didn't squeeze. I automatically surrendered to the primitive part of my brain that was hardwired to capitulate when threatened in this way. My body went limp beneath him as I surrendered to the Alpha, giving in to his physical declaration of his dominance.

"Who do you belong to?" He gritted out through clenched teeth. His face was contorted into something fierce with the effort of holding himself back. We were both so close…

"You, Master. I belong to you." I had never called anyone that before, but the title came to my lips naturally. Clayton owned me in every way possible, and I reveled in it.

"Rose," he groaned, and I felt his cock begin to pump inside me as his orgasm hit him. I finally let myself go, not even realizing until that moment that I had been forcing myself to wait for him. I came hard and long, and Clayton continued to thrust into me as I rode out the aftershocks that crackled within me like little lightning strikes.

As I came down, I found us gasping in each other's arms. When Clayton had finally caught his breath, he lightly touched his fingers to the side of my cheek, turning my face so I was forced to look into his eyes. They were filled with wonder.

"I wasn't expecting that," he said softly. "Thank you. Are you really comfortable calling me 'Master'? I would never ask you to do that, Rose. Not unless you wanted to."

"I've never wanted to before," I admitted. "But it just felt right. You're only my Master in the bedroom, though," I stipulated.

He grinned at me mischievously. "What if we're somewhere more interesting than the bedroom?"

"Okay," I conceded. "I will call you 'Master' outside the bedroom, if we happen to be fucking elsewhere."

He tapped his finger against the tip of my nose in reprimand. "You really should learn to watch your language. All of this cussing isn't very lady-like."

"I seem to recall that you rather enjoyed my dirty mouth when I begged you to slam your cock into my pussy," I retorted.

He grinned. "Alright. From now on, try to keep the cussing inside the bedroom. Or outside, if we happen to be fucking elsewhere." I fought back a smile as he mimicked my words.

"Agreed." I tried to sound solemn, but I couldn't stop a giggle from escaping. Clayton laughed with me, the warm sound wrapping around me like rich velvet. I savored the feeling. I didn't ever want to lose this.

Chapter 14

Clayton and I had been officially dating for a little over a week, and – despite my worry for Greg – I was happier than I had ever been in my entire life. Mercifully, the Kings hadn't hurt him. I wasn't sure if it was my threat that had kept them from doing so. I really doubted that was the case, but I decided not to question it. The relief at having my baby brother back and finding him unharmed after he had bravely returned to them filled me with hope. He was going to get through this.

Clayton had intimated that the FBI would have enough information soon to move in on the tribe of Kings that Greg had been spying on, known as *Los Furiosos*. It was all going to be over, and Greg was going to get his life back on track. He was still using, but not to the degree he had been. It would be physically dangerous for him if he stopped cold turkey without the medical care he would receive in rehab. His body might just shut down because his dependence had become so acute. It bothered me that he wasn't fully clean yet, but I accepted Clayton's rational explanation that this was actually what was best for Greg. Still, the drastic reduction in his consumption meant he was lucid more often, and my heart swelled near to bursting every time I was able to see my real brother again. Even when he was hurting with want and on edge, he was never cruel to me like he had been. It was a vast improvement, and it made me believe he really could recover, and our relationship would remain intact.

Even Cheryl's enduring haughtiness couldn't penetrate my bubble of joy. Her bitchiness had only spiked when she had seen my head injury, and I had had to lie and say I fell. I couldn't tell her that I had gotten hurt trying to save my brother from the wrath of the Latin Kings. She loudly speculated about why I had fallen, her favorite theory being that I had gotten drunk off my face and smashed into a wall. But I didn't let it get to me. It was as though the high from the endorphins that pumped through me when Clayton dominated my body was so potent that it lingered in my bloodstream long after he was done fucking me.

Even though I wasn't out of the woods yet, my life had never been more perfect. The joy Clayton gave me was pure and lasting, fulfilling in a way the cheap highs from alcohol and drugs had never been. He was the best thing that had ever happened to me, and – incredibly – it seemed he felt the same way about me.

"Where are you taking me?" I asked, curious and a touch worried.

Clayton shot me a slightly twisted smile as he glanced at me out of the corner of his eye. "You'll see." He had told me this morning that he had a surprise waiting for me after work, and excitement and trepidation had warred within me all day as I wondered what he could possibly have planned for me. He had taken to the responsibility of being my Master beautifully, as though it was the most natural thing in the world for him. It felt right to me too, but I couldn't deny that it was a bit alarming how quickly he had embraced his role. If I thought he had been ruthless and thoroughly domineering before, what he had now become was all-consuming, claiming my body and mind so deeply that I knew I would never be able to go back to who I was before I had known submission at his hands. And I didn't want to go back.

It wasn't until we had parked and were about to enter a high-rise building that I realized where we were: Smith's apartment. I stopped in my tracks, suddenly nervous.

"I think I'm going to have to have a long talk with Smith about what we should do with you."

I had forgotten his erotic threat until that moment, and now fear shot through me. It made my panties wet. "Master," I whispered, automatically falling into my submissive role. "Please…"

I wasn't sure if I was begging him to take me home or to drag me up to Smith's apartment.

Clayton paused beside me, turning my body so he could look into my eyes. His expression was soft, caring. He touched his fingertips to my face, tracing the line of my jaw. Even that gentle contact made me want to shiver. "I think you know what's coming, Rose," he said quietly, his tone calm and even. "If you don't want it, you can use your safe word now or at any time if you feel uncomfortable."

But it wasn't the idea of both men taking me that was really worrying me. "You don't mind… sharing me?" I asked.

He ran the pad of his thumb over my lower lip. "At one time, I would have thought that," he admitted. "But after seeing your reactions when we were both touching you… You've never been more beautiful, Rose. I want to see that again; I want to give you more of that. Making you happy makes me happy." He shot me a wolfish grin. "And I know the prospect makes Smith more than happy."

I shuddered in his grasp, overcome with lust and the intensity of his words. "I want to make you happy too, Clayton," I whispered. "More than anything."

He bent to brush his lips against mine. "I assure you this will make me happy, little sub." His hot breath tickled across my skin at his proximity, heightening my lustful anticipation. "One we go up, I expect you to be on your best behavior."

"I won't let you down, Master," I promised, my voice barely audible.

He kissed my lips lightly again. "Good girl. You're going to enjoy this."

I nodded jerkily in agreement, my erotic trepidation choking off my ability to speak.

When Smith opened his door, he was smiling at me predatorily. "Hello, sub," he said, his pleasure evident in his tone. "I'm so glad you've decided to join us."

Us. A small, strangled sound issued from my throat, and Smith laughed softly, his grin turning slightly evil as he stood aside so we could enter. Clayton guided me in on shaking legs with his hand at the small of my back.

Without sparing me so much as a backward glance, Smith led us through the living room and into his bedroom. I should have expected it, but my eyes still widened at how blatantly kinky the space was. It was clear Smith had been doing this for years, and he knew exactly what he wanted. The idea that he would show Clayton what to do with me when it came to using these sort of devices made me quiver with fearful excitement. Clayton couldn't have asked for a more experienced guide.

When Clayton pulled away from me, I almost fell to my knees with the loss of his support. And his suddenly cool, controlled expression didn't help my efforts to resist the impulse.

"Strip," he ordered. When he spoke the word, his voice was low and calm, but the power imbued in it made me obey instantly. I could feel Smith watching me with hungry curiosity as I began to bare myself to him completely for the first time. When he had seen me at clubs, I had always been clothed to a certain extent, and when we had played with Clayton my bra and panties had at least granted me some modicum of modesty. I hesitated when I was down to my lingerie, nervous at the prospect of fully exposing myself, of making myself utterly vulnerable to the two of them.

"I believe Clayton gave you an order, sub," Smith said coldly, threateningly.

I swallowed hard, but I hastily removed the scraps of lace. I had promised Clayton I wouldn't let him down, and I didn't intend to.

As soon as I was exposed, lust flared in Clayton's eyes, and he was on me in an instant. He grabbed me, wrapping one arm firmly around my lower back and tangling his other hand in my hair as he sharply pulled my head back. My lips parted as I gasped at the small pain of it, and he thrust his tongue into my open mouth, his stokes demanding and possessive. I melted for him, my hands fisting in his shirt to keep myself upright.

When he finally pulled away from me, my head was spinning as I gasped for air. Looking up at him, I was consumed by the flames of desire that danced in the depths of his entrancing eyes.

"You are so goddamn beautiful," he said roughly.

He grasped my shoulders and turned me so that I was facing the bed. It was a four-poster crafted of black wrought iron that was wickedly beautiful. I could see that there were well over a dozen points where restraints could be clipped in. I wondered which ones they might use for me, and my pulse quickened.

Clayton held me firmly from behind, his body trapping mine against the footboard as he gripped my forearms, holding them out so that they were offered to Smith, my vulnerable wrists exposed as he turned them upward. Clayton alternated soft kisses and sharp nips of his teeth on my shoulder, making the hairs on the back of my neck stand on end as all of my nerve endings came to life. Smith took my wrists, wrapping leather cuffs around them before pulling the buckles tight. I whimpered at the feeling of them ensnaring me. Smith's grin was hard-edged as he clipped chains to the rings on the cuffs before looping them through a restraint point directly above my head. He pulled slowly, raising my arms inexorably. The clanking sound of metal sliding against metal made me shudder. When my body was finally stretched upward so that I was forced onto my tiptoes, Smith anchored the chain on another tie point.

I was burning with need, and it was only further enflamed as Clayton splayed his hand across my abdomen, pulling me back against him so that I could feel his erection pressing into my ass. I closed my eyes and moaned as my head dropped back on his chest, loving the feeling of his arousal.

But my eyes snapped open and I cried out in shock as something hard and cold closed around my nipple, pinching it cruelly. Smith had attached a clover clamp to it. There were little pads of rubber separating my flesh from the harsh bite of the metal, but that did little to shield me from the pain. I saw him lift a clamp to my other nipple, and I realized they were attached to one another by a short chain.

"Please," I begged. "Don't. It hurts."

He showed me no mercy, catching my nipple in the other clamp. Smith lightly traced the undersides of my breasts, and the pleasurable contact only made my nipples tighten further, increasing my torment. "Shhh," he soothed me. "Accept the pain. Embrace it. Let it take you."

I whined as I struggled to do as he instructed, taking in deep breaths as I tried to absorb the cruel sensation. After a few long moments, I was shocked to find a feeling of euphoria rolling over my mind. The pain was undiminished, but as I learned to welcome it, it turned to a sweet torture.

Just when I had learned to handle the torment, Smith pulled on the chain that connected the clamps. He didn't jerk it hard, but his steady, relentless pull made my back arch as I struggled to lessen the tension that drew my breasts away from my body, making my nipples stretch. The wicked design of the clover clamps made their pinch tighten impossibly harder.

The shout that clawed its way out of my chest was strangled, but the shock of the increased pain only sent me spiraling higher as I accepted it.

"Exquisite," Clayton breathed at my ear, his admiration evident in his voice. He was stroking my breasts, tracing around them in a spiraling pattern that slowly progressed to my nipples. When he reached them, he flicked the clamps. White lights popped behind my eyes as I screamed. The chains holding me upright rattled as my knees gave out with the brutal force of the pain. Clayton caught me around my waist, preventing my weight from falling on my wrists.

My world was awash with a red haze, but Smith's voice drifted down to me.

"If we push her further, she'll hit subspace," he remarked casually. "But I'm not going to give her that. I want her to be completely lucid for what we're going to do to her."

I moaned at his words, my legs quivering with the intensity of my desire. "Please, Clayton," I panted. "Please, Master. I need…"

Clayton kissed my neck and stroked my hair. "Not yet, little sub."

I almost sobbed at his refusal. My whole body was on fire. The clamps on my nipples were white-hot, as though they had just been removed from a forge fire. It awoke an answering conflagration deep within me, and flames roared under my skin, consuming me from the inside out. I was almost delirious from the pleasure/pain. I craved more, and I was desperate for it to stop.

Mercifully, Smith released the chain, alleviating the tension on my nipples. But the weight of it as it swayed beneath my breasts caused the clamps to tug slightly, eliciting sharp little sparks with every breath I took. The heat of him before me let me know he had drawn closer, and as Clayton's hands explored my desire-slicked inner thighs, Smith's caressed my ass. His fingers brushed across my labia, gathering up the moisture there. I jerked when they moved slowly upward, pressing into my cleft insistently as he neared my dark entrance. When he reached it, he moved his index finger in a circular pattern. I cried out as the taboo bundle of nerves jumped to life. This wasn't my first time being touched there, but it was most certainly the most erotic. He pressed insistently, and his lubricated finger penetrated me.

"Have you taken her ass yet, Clayton?" He asked conversationally as he slowly slid into me.

Clayton's touch traced around my clit, teasing. "I haven't had the pleasure," he rumbled.

"Then I'll let you do the honors." Although my eyes were closed, I could practically feel Smith's wicked grin as he slipped a second finger in, stretching me as he began to pump in and out, preparing me. I was making soft, mewling noises that I didn't even recognize as my own. The pleasure was building within me like a gathering storm. Even though Clayton refused to touch my sex directly, just the sensation of Smith inside my ass was going to make me come.

Just as I thought I was about to explode, Smith popped out of me, and Clayton's touch disappeared as the heat of both of them retreated from me.

"No!" My eyes snapped open as anguish flooded me at the cruel denial. "Please, Master. Please!"

They ignored my agonized begging, saying nothing. I heard the rustle of clothing falling to the floor, and when they entered my line of sight again, both men were naked. Clayton was glorious as ever, but it was the first time Smith's body had been revealed to me. He was just as impressively fit as Clayton, but where my Dom was tall and lean, Smith was broad and brawny. A dark dusting of hair covered his chest. My eyes followed its trail down his abdomen and came to rest on his impressive cock. I swallowed hard. While he wasn't quite as long as Clayton, he was wider. If they both took me at the same time, they were going to tear me apart. I craved it.

When Smith turned to unhook the chain that held me upright, I saw that his back was covered with an intricate black tattoo that started at the top of his sculpted ass and spread upward to curl around his shoulders. The lines of it were harsh and beautiful, but I didn't get a chance to study it carefully. I was too maddened with need to really take it in anyway.

I had thought Smith would unclip the chain from my cuffs, but instead he tugged on the length of it, pulling me forward. I would have fallen face-first onto the bed if Clayton hadn't gripped my hips and lifted me up onto it so that I was on my knees in the center of the mattress. Smith looped the chain through another tie point on the canopy where iron bars crisscrossed directly above my head. He left the chain loose enough that I could sit back on my heels, but other than that my freedom of movement was effectively restricted.

Smith slipped on a condom and lay on his back. Clayton lifted me up briefly so that his friend could position himself under me, and when he set me back down I was hovering just over Smith's erect cock. I started to lower myself onto it, but Clayton held my waist firmly.

"Not yet," he said roughly. "I'm the one who owns you, and you're going to take me first."

As I groaned at his words, Smith's hands roughly gripped my cheeks, pulling them wide so that I was offered to Clayton. I didn't hear him tear open a condom, but I didn't mind. I knew we were both clean, and there was no risk of pregnancy with him fucking me this way.

He coated himself in my wetness, and then I could feel him pressing against me. I clenched automatically at the fear that shot through me at the size of him.

"Easy, sub," he cooed. "Relax. Let me in." As he spoke, he brushed his thumb over my clit. I shuddered as the pleasure that had been denied so many times came roaring back to the fore, desperate to be released. "Don't you dare come," Clayton growled in my ear.

"No," I pleaded raggedly. "I have to. I can't stop it."

"If I even think you're about to come, everything will stop," he threatened.

No! I couldn't let them stop. If I didn't achieve release soon, I was sure I was going to die from the exquisite agony of my need. I drew breath in short, shallow gasps as I fought to control my insistent urges. Somehow, I managed to restrain myself.

"That's it," Clayton said softly, approvingly. "Just relax."

With that, he began pressing into me insistently. I struggled to comply with his command to relax, trying to welcome him into me. But he was so big, and it *burned.* I whimpered, and he touched my clit again.

"Almost there," he reassured me gently. Moments later, I felt his hips sit flush with my ass; he was fully in me. He paused there, letting me get used to the size of him.

Smith's fingers dug into my flesh where he still held me, calling my attention to him. "Take a deep breath," he ordered. "Accept your Master's cock."

I did as he commanded, and I slowly loosened to accommodate him. The stinging burn began to turn to hot tingling, and I found myself pushing back into him, communicating my submission.

But just as I was getting used to the huge intrusion, Smith pulled me forward, guiding me down onto his own erection. My cry was harsh as he slowly, inexorably, pushed into me, and I could hear my chains rattling as I jerked against them, longing to dig my curling fingers into the men's flesh. But I was utterly vulnerable, helpless to stop them taking me. Smith was sheathed within me now. I felt so *full*, and I suddenly froze, hardly daring to breathe lest my movements cause them to rip me asunder.

They showed me no mercy. Clayton began to move inside me first in small, shallow pumping motions. Then Smith ground his hips up against mine in a circular motion. I could feel the friction of their cocks against my inner walls, and the sensation made me drop my head back in ecstasy as I fully surrendered my body to them.

Smith released one of my ass cheeks to reach up and grab the chain between my nipple clamps. I had almost forgotten about the throbbing pain there, but I screamed as it came clawing back when Smith pulled the chain ruthlessly, forcing me to bend at my waist as I again fought to alleviate the tension. He grinned evilly at the sound of my beautiful pain, and he thrust into me roughly. Clayton mirrored his motion, no more than a heartbeat behind him. His weight pressed against my back, and his hand curled around my throat, applying pressure so that I was pulled into him. Torn between his hold and Smith's grip on my chain, my vision went white.

They began to drive in and out of me in earnest, roughly alternating so that I was forced to accept one and then the other. My screams were ragged and endless until Clayton increased the pressure on my throat. I was silenced as all of my effort shifted to drawing air through my restricted airway in little gasps. The curb of oxygen to my brain made my head spin in the most delicious way. My Master had complete control of my body, from my carnal holes to my very breath.

Their rhythm altered, and they were both thrusting into me at the same time, filling me brutally. Agony lashed at my nipples as Smith abruptly removed the clamps, the surge of blood returning to them searing me. But his hot mouth was upon them instantly, his tongue licking and soothing away the pain.

There was a roaring in my ears as my head spun, overwhelmed by the intensity of the sensations assaulting my body and the diminishment of the air that reached my lungs.

I felt Clayton's cock twitch, and his grip on my throat eased. The world dropped out from under me as I rocketed upward, propelled by the sweet high of the oxygen returning to my brain. "Come with me," he ground out before shouting out his orgasm. The feeling of his burning seed lashing at me for the first time pushed me over the edge; I couldn't have stopped myself even if I had wanted to. My inner muscles contracted around both men. Smith grunted as it triggered his own release.

Nothing was real anymore, nothing but the feeling of them inside me and the sweet, agonizing pleasure they wrung from my body. Tears wet my face as I wept at the intensity of it. When the final ecstatic shudders wracked my body, everything went black as my overwhelmed brain short-circuited, unable to take any more.

I came back to reality slowly. I could smell Clayton's addictive scent and feel his strong arms around me as he stroked my hair tenderly. His words held no real meaning for me, but his soft, rumbling voice was reassuring. I don't know how long I lay there, savoring Clayton's comforting warmth, but eventually I opened my eyes so I could see his gorgeous face.

He was smiling down at me gently, and I leaned my face into his palm where it cupped my cheek. "Welcome back, little sub."

My heart leapt at the possessive endearment. "Hi," I whispered.

Although most of my attention was focused on Clayton, I realized that we were no longer in Smith's bedroom. We were sitting on a different bed, Clayton's back propped up against the headboard with me draped across his lap. I was wrapped in a soft blanket, but Clayton's skin was still bare; he only wore his boxers now.

"Where are we?" I asked, my voice a little ragged from my screaming.

"You're in my guest room," came Smith's voice. He was sitting on the edge of the bed wearing a robe, and he was smiling at me fondly. "The two of you can stay here tonight."

"Thanks," Clayton accepted, laughter in his voice. "I really didn't want to have to carry her down to the car like this. The porter might suspect me of drugging her."

I shook my head. "That was way better than any drug," I said fervently, looking up into Clayton's breathtaking eyes. "Thank you, Master," I said softly. I hadn't thought it possible to experience such extreme, earth-shattering ecstasy. It had made me pass out, for God's sake.

He tapped his finger against the tip of my nose. "Isn't there someone else you'd like to thank?" He asked pointedly.

"Yes. Thank you, Smith. That was incredible."

"Anytime," he said, his wolfish grin letting me know he meant that literally. He cocked his head at me, considering. "You know, I was surprised to hear you say 'Master'. After watching you at the clubs for a few years, I didn't think that was possible for you. Do you know why I never accepted your advances, Rose?" He asked. "It certainly wasn't because you're not beautiful. Believe me, I was tempted a few times. And the way you tried to lure me in with that self-assured attitude made me want to put you in your place. But I could see it was just an act, a way of protecting yourself. And trying to break you of that would have been cruel and traumatic." His eyes flicked to Clayton and then back to me. "I knew you would be good for Clayton, but it seems like he's been good for you as well." His smile was warm and genuine. "I'm really happy for the two of you."

I shifted against Clayton, suddenly slightly uncomfortable. Smith had just voiced what I had only barely been allowing myself to think at the back of my mind. Hearing him lay it all out on the table like that made me feel just as exposed as I was when I had been stripped naked before them.

But even my slight movements made my body ache in the most delicious ways, a sweet reminder of the joy Clayton had given me tonight.

"Making you happy makes me happy."

Deciding not to let Smith's words bother me, I closed my eyes and snuggled into Clayton, basking in my post-orgasmic glow.

Chapter 15

When I came home from work the next day, my lingering elation was instantly doused by the sound of low, pained whimpering.

"Greg!" I cried as I rushed to join him in the bathroom. He was lying on the floor, curled up into himself and rocking back and forth. A sheen of sweat covered his skin, and I could see that he had emptied the meager contents of his stomach before I had arrived. Oh, God, how long had he been like this?

"Greg." I fought to make my voice calm and soothing, and I tenderly pushed his sweat-soaked hair back off his brow. When he opened his eyes at my touch, my own stomach clenched at the sight of the desperate pain that filled them. "You're going into withdrawal. How long has it been since you last used?"

"Almost two days," he panted out. "Oh, God, Rosie." He shuddered beneath my hand. "It *hurts.*"

"That's not good, Greg." I hated myself for saying it, but he still needed some of the drugs in his system or he might die. "I know you want to quit, and I'm proud of you. But unless you're going to go into rehab you can't just stop like this. Where's your stash?" I felt sick at the idea that I was offering to help my brother get high, but I didn't have a choice.

"I don't have any," he groaned. "And they won't give me any more. The FBI moved in on one of the other tribes. The Kings don't trust the new recruits anymore. They've turned us all away, Rose, and I can't afford to pay them."

"It's okay, Greg," I assured him. "That's okay. Clayton will understand. You've done all you can. Come on. I'm taking you to the hospital."

Greg's eyes went wide with panic, and he jerked out of my reach. "No! I…" He licked his lips nervously and ran his hand up and down over the crook of his elbow. "I can't quit. I mean, I can't stop. If I don't go to the Kings, then I can't help the FBI anymore. I won't be able to get back at them for what they tried to do to you, and you won't be safe." His eyes were feverish with need, and his voice shook. He looked as though he was barely clinging onto his sanity.

My brows drew together, and I looked at him sternly, ready to give him some tough love. "I appreciate that you want to protect me, baby brother, but I'll be fine. Clayton won't let anything happen to me. He'll understand that -"

"Clayton!" Greg growled, suddenly looking feral. "It's always 'Clayton' with you now! What about me, Rose?! I'm your goddamn brother!"

"Greg, calm down," I tried to make the order steady, but my tone was laced with panic. I could see him slipping away from me as his monstrous addiction dug its cruel claws into him. He wrenched out of my grasp, jumping to his feet and putting distance between us. I followed him into the living room, my movements slow and careful as I held up my hands before me as though to ward off a rabid animal. "Come to the hospital with me. I know this is hard, but you'll feel better."

"You don't know *anything!*" He bellowed. "You don't know what this feels like! I'm fucking dying, Rose! Are you just going to let me die, or are you going to help me?"

Okay, now I was pissed. He was trying to manipulate me into buying him drugs? No fucking way. I put my hands on my hips, making my body larger so that I could block his way to the door. "You're going to die if you don't quit, Greg," I said sharply. "So yes, I am going to help you. But not in the way you want."

I pulled my cell phone out of my pocket and started to dial Clayton's number.

"What are you doing?" Greg asked, sounding scared and angry.

"I'm calling Clayton," I informed him. "You won't seem to listen to me, but maybe he can talk some sense into you."

Despite his unsteadiness on his feet, Greg moved quickly, and the phone was suddenly flying out of my hand. My back was against the wall, and his forearm was pressing ruthlessly against my windpipe. His mouth was twisted in a snarl and his nostrils flared, insane fury etched in every twisted line of his face. He was physically weakened since his addiction had caused him to start wasting away, but now a desperate, starved beast was lending him strength. My hands were on his arm, struggling to pull him away from me. But he just pressed harder, blocking off my air entirely.

"You love him," he accused. "You love him, and you don't love me anymore. Well I'm not going to quit. *He* can't make me."

My heels drummed against the wall where Greg had lifted me from the floor with his grip on my throat. My lungs were burning, and my fingertips were starting to go numb. I was no longer fighting, but my body was convulsing in his hold as dark spots began to dance before my eyes.

Just as I began to go limp, my clawing hands dropping from his arm, I saw Greg's expression melt from one of mindless fury to horrified anguish. He stepped back and released me abruptly, and I collapsed to the floor, clutching my throat as the harsh gulps of air that I managed to draw in burned their way down into my lungs. When I looked up, I could hardly make out my brother through my watering eyes.

"I'm so sorry, Rosie. I'm so sorry." His voice was trembling; he sounded terrified. I heard the pounding of his footsteps moving further and further away as he fled the apartment.

"Greg!" I tried to cry out, to call him back to me. But all that came out was a harsh rattle, and I began coughing painfully.

I had to get help. Someone had to stop him before he did something that got himself killed. With a great effort, I forced my limbs to move, and I somehow managed to drag my body across the room to get to my phone.

"Hi, beautiful," he answered sweetly.

"Clayton," I forced out raggedly.

"Rose? What's wrong?" His voice was calm, but I knew him well enough now to detect the hint of fear in it.

"It's Greg. Please. Someone has to go get him. He's out of his mind, Clayton. He…" I tripped over the words, hardly able to believe them even though I had experienced it firsthand. "He almost killed me."

"Where are you now, Rose? Where is Greg?" He sounded truly panicked now.

"I'm okay, Clayton," I assured him. "But Greg isn't. He needs help. He just ran out of our apartment, and I couldn't stop him. Please send someone after him."

"I'm going to have to hang up now Rose so I can call Sharon and Smith. Sharon will come right up, and Smith will go after Greg. I'll be there in ten minutes."

"Okay," I breathed. "Thank you."

I ended the call so that Clayton could get on with it. Having done what I could, I allowed my body to relax, pressing my face against the cool floorboards as I struggled to return my breathing to some modicum of normalcy. By the time Sharon appeared in the doorway, I was starting to feel in control of my muscles again. If only I weren't shaking so hard, I might have been able to stand.

"God damn it," Sharon cursed as she came and knelt beside me. "I just keep fucking up, don't I? I'm sorry I'm so shitty at my job, Rose." She sounded weary, defeated.

"It's not your fault, Sharon," I insisted. "You weren't supposed to be in our apartment. You're supposed to be protecting me from the Kings, not…" I swallowed hard to hold back the tears. "Not my own brother," I finished softly.

She pursed her lips together, saying nothing as she put a supporting arm around my back to help me to my feet. She guided me to my bed and then crouched before me. Her fingers gripped my chin gently, urging me to lift my face so that she could examine my throat.

"You might have some bruising," she informed me. "Did you hit your head?"

"No," I assured her. I didn't want any paramedics, and I didn't want to go to the hospital.

Sharon nodded, seeming to understand without me having to say anything. "You're going to be fine. Your throat is wicked red right now, and you'll probably be sore tomorrow, but you don't need to go the hospital."

"Thanks," I whispered.

She reached out and took my trembling hand in hers, providing me with silent, steady comfort.

"You should leave now, Sharon." Clayton's voice was clipped, and all of his muscles were taut with suppressed anger. I knew he would never physically hurt his friend, but the daggers he was glaring at her clearly communicated that staying was not in her best interest.

Sharon sighed and hung her head, looking crestfallen as she stood to leave. I thought about telling Clayton that she wasn't at fault and she didn't deserve his anger, but one look at his livid expression told me it was best if I didn't get involved.

She paused for a moment as she passed Clayton. "I really am sorry, Clayton," she said, her voice barely audible. "For Rose, for Claudia. And you almost died…" Her eyes were haunted. "I'm sorry."

Clayton's eyes softened slightly, but his jaw was still clenched. He didn't look at her as she walked away, her shoulders slumped.

"She didn't mean to let me down, Clayton," I said gently as he sat beside me.

He grimaced. "That doesn't change the fact that she did."

I decided it was best not to say anything more on the matter just now, but I tucked it away for later. Sharon had looked like she could use a friend, and she certainly didn't need to lose one right now. Clayton would come around once he accepted that I really was okay.

He touched his fingers gently to my throat, tracing the line of the bright red stripe Greg's arm had left behind. His hand that wasn't touching me was clenched into a fist at his side.

"I can't believe he did this to you," he ground out. "When I find him…"

"What?!" I asked alarmed. "You mean you don't know where he is? I thought you had people following him!"

Clayton looked slightly pained. "That's the problem, Rose. He *knew* we were following him. Apparently he's sharper than we gave him credit for. He figured out how to evade us. We gave him a cell phone with GPS tracking, but he's ditched it. Smith is looking for him now." He squeezed my hand, trying to reassure me. "We know he's going to go looking for a fix, and we know where he's been meeting the Kings. We'll stake out the area and see if he goes there. In the meantime, Smith is going to be checking elsewhere. We're not going to give up on him, Rose." His expression hardened. "Not that I'm not tempted to after what he's done to you, but I swore to you that I would protect him. I'm not going to back out on that."

I hadn't wanted to cry – I was sick to death of crying – but Clayton's solemn promise made me break down. He wrapped his arms around me, tucking my head under his chin as I pressed my face into his chest.

"I'm scared, Clayton," I admitted, my voice wavering.

His arms tightened around me as his muscles tensed. "We'll get a restraining order against him until he's gotten clean, Rose. I won't let him come near you again. You're not leaving my sight until this whole mess is behind us."

"No," I clarified. "I'm not afraid of Greg. I know he didn't mean to hurt me. I'm afraid he's going to die."

Clayton pulled back from me slightly so my eyes could meet his. When he spoke, his voice was tight with suppressed violence. "I don't care if he meant to or not. I'm not letting him anywhere near you."

I sighed heavily, accepting that Clayton's protection was probably the best thing for me right now. "Greg will be angry with you for keeping me away from him. He'll be angry with me for choosing to be with you. He accused me of loving you more than I love him. That's not true." A sudden realization struck me, an absolute truth that had been hiding in the recesses of my mind until that moment. "But I... I do think I love you, Clayton."

He took my face in both of his hands, and his eyes burned down into mine with a raw ferocity that took my breath away. "I *know* I love you, Rose."

I gasped as the power of the words washed over me. They had never felt so right when spoken from anyone else's lips. "I love you too," I said fervently, fully committing to my declaration. "It's a different love than what I have for Greg, but it's just as strong. I don't think I could live without either of you. Hell, I was barely functioning when I met you. But you saw something in me that I had never been able to see." My smile was lopsided. "And you were every bit as ruthless as I needed you to be in forcing me to acknowledge it."

Something sparked in Clayton's eyes. "Speaking of my ruthlessness, I think you're ready to hear something. I've been putting off telling you because I was worried you would get scared and pull away from me. Here." He reached into his jacket and pulled out a slightly crumpled envelope.

Having no clue as to what was going on, I took it from him with slightly trembling fingers. If he thought this was something scary enough that it would make me want to run from him, then I wasn't sure I wanted to see it. When I unfolded the envelope, I saw my name on it, but it had been sent to Clayton's address. I looked at him quizzically. What the hell had he done?

"Open it," he ordered.

The seal had already been broken, and I shot him a reproving look. He was changing my address *and* opening my mail? It seemed we needed to have another talk about boundaries.

As soon as I pulled out the letter that was inside, my heart stopped when my eyes fell on the first few lines.

Dear Miss Baker,

Congratulations! You have been accepted at the Fashion Institute of Technology!

A part of me was thrilled, overawed at the fact that FIT would ever accept me. But mostly I was crestfallen. And a little angry. This was just too cruel.

"What is this, Clayton?" I demanded stormily. "You know I could never afford the tuition. Are you trying to hurt me?"

To my amazement, he smiled at me. "Keep reading."

I glared at him for a moment longer before doing as he said. As my eyes devoured the rest of the letter, my mouth fell open in shock.

"They..." I began disbelievingly. "They want to offer me a scholarship? Why? My grades were never all that stellar." I glanced down at the letter again. "Wait. It says here that they were impressed by my sketches." I fixed Clayton with a hard look. "Explain," I demanded tersely.

"Working for the FBI allowed me full access to your academic records and your social security number. And I took pictures of your sketches one night after I fucked you senseless. That was all the information I needed to submit your application."

"Aren't there some kind of laws against that?" I demanded.

"Against fucking your brains out? Not that I'm aware of. And I'm pretty well-versed on the law."

I rolled my eyes at him. "Against accessing my information like that without my consent!" I clarified hotly.

He shrugged, not looking apologetic in the slightest. "Homeland Security gives me a lot of free rein. I do believe Sharon warned you early on that I'm not above using underhanded tactics when it comes to getting what I want. And what I want is for you to be happy." He was looking at me more seriously now. "You shouldn't have to put up with that haughty bitch at Ivory. You deserve so much better than that, Rose. You're passionate and you're talented."

I bit my lip, hesitant to admit my fears. "But what if I fail?" I asked, my voice small.

Worthless, useless. A disappointment.

My whole life, everyone had told me that I would never amount to anything. The desire to try to succeed had been stamped out of me a long time ago.

Clayton tenderly brushed a stray lock of hair back from my face. "Take the chance, Rose," he urged. "If you did fail, I would be there to catch you. But you're not going to. I believe in you, Rose. And it's time you started believing in yourself."

I looked at the letter again, longingly. It was then that I noticed the stipulation. "It says I have to come for an interview before they'll award me the scholarship."

"I know," Clayton said. "And I've already informed them that you'll be there."

"But… What if they don't like me? What if I've gotten so close and then this gets ripped away from me?" That horrible prospect was too much for me to bear. "I don't want to go," I said quietly.

Clayton gripped my chin firmly, and his eyes bored into mine, pinning me to the spot. "You're going, Rose. Even if I have to drag you there kicking and screaming. Although I'm pretty sure they won't be so keen to accept you if you make a scene like that." He cocked his head, considering. "But who knows? Creative types can get away with being eccentric."

I couldn't believe he was joking about this. Was he really not going to give me the option of refusing?

No. No, he wasn't. He wasn't going to let me give up on myself. And I loved him for that. Suddenly, I saw a whole future opening up before me that I had never even dared to dream up. I could have a job I loved and a comfortable lifestyle. And I could have Clayton. It was better than anything I could have ever imagined before I had met him.

"I'll go," I whispered. "Thank you."

He shot me a cocky smile. "I knew you'd come around to my way of thinking. I'm always right, after all."

I shot him a cutting look, but there was no real malice in it. "In your opinion," I amended for him. "But I will concede that you were right this time," I allowed.

He laughed. "I can work with that. For now."

His grin was positively devilish as he brought his lips down on mine. My mouth clashed with his fiercely as I poured all of my gratitude and my love for him into the kiss. He responded in kind, the possessive strokes of his tongue communicating his devotion to me.

I loved Clayton Vaughn. And he loved me. Nothing had ever been so right.

Chapter 16

I sighed happily into Clayton's mouth as he gently pushed me back onto his mattress. The feel of his skin against my naked body was delicious. He had said he wasn't going to let me out of his sight, and he meant it. I didn't mind one bit.

He gently brushed his lips across my injured throat, dulling the soft throbbing by awakening a wonderful tingling on my skin.

"How are you feeling?" He asked, his voice filled with concern but his eyes clouded with lust.

I smiled up at him and twined my hands around the back of his neck. "Terrible," I answered. "I think I need a good painkiller."

He laughed softly. "How can I deny you if you're hurting?"

"You can't," I teased. "You want to make me happy, remember?"

His grin turned hard-edged, but his eyes were sparkling with amusement. "You really are a devious little minx," he accused. "But I'm willing to let it slide for now, given your current condition. In fact, I fully intend to make you so far gone that you're incapable of feeling any pain. Of course, getting you there will require me to inflict some pain. But I think Smith helped you learn how to accept it." His voice turned low and rough. "Would you like for me to push you, Rose? If you agree now, know that I won't hold back, and I won't stop unless you use your safe word."

I shuddered beneath him. Yes, I wanted that more than anything. Clayton had brought me mind-blowing pleasure, but I had never been pushed over the edge into subspace, that elusive, bliss-filled state I had yearned to reach for years. I found I craved the pain he would give me if he could take me to that place.

"Yes," I whispered my consent. "I want that. Please."

"Address me properly," he ordered.

"Please, Master." The honorific was a lustful moan as it sunk in that he really would show me no mercy. He was in full Dom mode, and he was going to force me to take the pain, to embrace it as I fully surrendered my body and mind to his control.

At my pleading words, he was on me instantly, grabbing my shoulders and roughly flipping me over. I heard his bedside drawer slide open, and I inhaled the scent of hemp just before the rope looped around my wrists, drawing tight and securing them at the small of my back. Clayton's fingers dug into my hips, pulling me up into a kneeling position, my ass in the air and my face pressed into the mattress. Something clanked metallically, and Clayton forced my knees apart. Cool air danced across my heated sex as he ensnared my ankles in leather cuffs. Automatically, I tried to bring my legs back together in order to protect my most sensitive flesh, but the unyielding spreader bar that Clayton had secured to my ankles kept me fully exposed to him.

"Looks like someone's been shopping," I panted.

His rumbling chuckle drifted down to me and rippled lusciously across my skin. "Yes," he said. "Smith helped me pick out a few things we thought would be good for you."

Oh, God. What had the experienced Dom convinced Clayton to purchase? I squirmed uncomfortably, but I was thoroughly restrained.

Clayton's actions answered my silent question. Something hard was pressing against my lips, the pressure insistent and unyielding. My mouth opened automatically, and the ball gag forced my jaw open as he buckled it firmly at the nape of my neck. In the next instant, the world went black when he slipped a blindfold over my eyes.

I was completely powerless. I couldn't see, couldn't speak, couldn't move. All I could do was feel and listen to Clayton's matter-of fact words.

"I'm going to hurt you now, Rose. I want you to welcome the pain I give you because it's my will that you do so. You don't have any say in what's going to happen to you; you have no choice but to accept it. You are free from any responsibility because I am in control. And there's nothing you can do about it."

My moan was half-frightened and half-lustful. The sound of it being muffled by the gag only further stoked my desire.

I jumped slightly as I heard the sound of something heavy cutting through the air with an ominous *whooshing* noise. The sound was familiar to me, and I whimpered as I realized that he was going to flog me. And it was going to hurt.

The first punishing stroke drew a harsh, shocked cry from my throat as the leather tendrils slapped heavily across my ass. My mind barely had time to process the throbbing it elicited, inflicting a dull but insistent pain deep below the surface of my flesh. But my lustful reaction was visceral and fierce as my inner muscles contracted in response, reveling in his dominance of my body.

The next blow came down almost immediately on the heels of the first, landing on my other cheek. My core began to pound in answer to every throbbing pain that the flogger inflicted as Clayton thoroughly punished all of my exposed flesh until my ass was burning.

I was torn between my focus on the pain and my concentration on drawing in enough breath through my nose so I didn't suffocate. I couldn't draw air through my lips; the gag restricted my ability to gasp in the oxygen I needed. Panic began to grip me, and all of my muscles tensed as I tugged against my restraints. But Clayton didn't stop.

"Accept it, Rose," he commanded, giving me no quarter.

Struggling to obey, I tried to recall how I had managed to take the pain Smith had inflicted upon me with the cruel nipple clamps.

Embrace it. Absorb it.

I allowed the pain to wash over me, and it caught me up in its raging torrent, claiming my body in its ruthless rapids. I was drowning in it, but I gratefully gulped it down, allowing it to fill my lungs and send my head spinning into black oblivion.

But just when I thought I had learned to handle it, Clayton altered his tactic. I screamed into the gag as just the stinging tips of the flogger raked across my skin, sending lines of fire searing across the surface of my flesh.

Just as he had promised, Clayton pushed me relentlessly, driving home my utter vulnerability at his hands with every harsh stroke. The realization made my clit throb with an answering pain.

It wasn't the waters that took me this time, but the stifling sense of power that radiated out from Clayton in palpable waves. In that moment, I gave my mind to him just as completely as I had ceded my body to him long ago. The steady, rhythmic *whooshing* of the flogger cutting through the air as he deftly wielded it in swift figure-of-eight movements was suddenly soothing rather than terrifying. My entire body relaxed, and my cries of pain ceased. My mind went completely blank, taken to a blissfully calm place where I didn't have any worries or cares. I was safe in Clayton's hands, and nothing could hurt me. My breathing came in slow, deep draws of air as I entered that glorious state.

The hits stopped, but I was barely aware of it; the sensation of pain had faded so completely that it had become almost imperceptible.

A strangled shout was torn from my chest when my Master raked his fingernails across my abused flesh. Sparks of pleasure flew out from his touch and tingled their way up my spine, going to straight to my head. I fell further into that blank space, rocketing down through an endless white tunnel. Then I reached free fall, and I wasn't falling anymore; I was floating.

His cock impaling me and his rough hands upon me became my entire reality. I was unaware of the endless, soft mewling that was issuing from my throat. I came immediately, the intense ecstasy of my Master finally taking my enflamed body enfolding me where I existed in my exquisitely empty world. The bliss went on and on as he pumped into me, the raw brutality of his movements seeming tender and loving.

I was dimly aware of him roaring out my name as he came, but I was so far gone I barely heard it; the pleasure I felt at having given him that ecstasy was what communicated his completion to my foggy mind.

My body was limp, completely sated as he removed my bonds. I couldn't have moved even if I wanted to. My brain didn't remember how to make my limbs cooperate.

I stayed in that state for a long time, completely content as I rested my head against my Master's chest, loving the feel of his fingers trailing across my hyper-sensitive skin as he stroked my back.

When I did finally open my eyes, I found him smiling down at me, his eyes filled with wonder.

"Do you have any idea how breathtaking you are, Rose?" He asked softly.

I grinned. "You're not so bad yourself."

He laughed. "If you keep complimenting me like that, you'll make me blush," he joked at the disparity between his intense words and my flippant ones.

I reached up and lightly touched my fingers to his cheek, my expression turning serious. "I love you so much, Master," I said fervently. "And I love Clayton, too. I never imagined anything could be this good. I never thought I would have this. Thank you."

He brushed a kiss against my forehead. "And I love my sub and my Rose," he answered. "I never conceived of having something this wonderful, either. And I'm not ever going to let it go, Rose. I'm not going to let *you* go."

My eyes widened at his implication. "I'm not going to let you go either," I breathed.

Our kiss was sweet and full of promises I fully intended to keep. I was never going to leave him.

· ·

The following afternoon, I found myself smiling as I walked around the FIT campus. It was a good thing Clayton had given me the acceptance letter when he had, or I would have missed my interview date. He told me he would have just applied for me again the next semester if the moment hadn't been right in time, but I was ecstatic that I wasn't going to have to endure Cheryl for an extra four months. If I got this scholarship, I was quitting the next day. I couldn't wait to see her shocked expression; *she* hadn't gotten a scholarship. I felt a surge of vindictive pleasure.

Clayton hadn't wanted to leave my side, but I had put my foot down and made him go wait in the café across the street from campus. He wasn't too pleased with my demanding tone, but he had capitulated, finally agreeing that it would look ridiculous if he came to my interview with me.

I had been nervous at the beginning of the interview, but as soon as Professor Coker had started going over my sketches with me, I relaxed as my passion for my work wiped away my anxiety. If I was accepted into the scholarship program, I would be able to attend workshops with renowned designers such as Nina Garcia and Calvin Klein. The prospect was so wonderful that I could hardly conceive of it.

After talking for nearly an hour, Professor Coker was smiling at me, and she offered to give me a tour of the campus. I took it as a good sign.

FIT was beautiful, with greenery breaking up the harsh lines of the severe buildings. I was amazed and flattered when Professor Coker even took the time to show me the fashion museum that was on campus, asking for my commentary on several of the designs.

"Well, I think that about covers it," she said when we finally arrived at the edge of the campus.

"Thanks so much for showing me around, Professor Coker," I said gratefully.

"You can call me Erika," she offered. "And I'm really looking forward to working with you in the Fall." She gave me a conspiratorial wink. She was on the head of the board that awarded the scholarships, and she had as much as just told me I was going to get it. My heart swelled in my chest as an ecstatic smile spread across my face.

"I can't wait," I said ardently. "Thank you so much."

She smiled at me again before turning to go back to her office. If the dull, throbbing pain of my bruised ass hadn't been very real, I would have thought I was dreaming.

I was still grinning as I waited for the "Walk" sign to appear so I could cross 7th Avenue and join Clayton. I could see him through the window at the front of the café, sipping a ridiculously large coffee. The man was an addict, but I supposed caffeine wasn't such a terrible vice. He didn't see me where I was practically bouncing on the balls of my feet as I eagerly anticipated giving him the good news, but I watched him hungrily, drinking in the sight of his perfect profile.

Then he was abruptly hidden from view. The world turned to chaos around me as everything happened too quickly for me to comprehend. There was the screeching of tires and the sound of the door on the side of the black van sliding open. I screamed as strong arms closed around me, jerking me off my feet. I had a moment to register the shocked expressions of the people around me as terror consumed me. Then the door was sliding closed again, trapping me inside the van, and I was fighting my captors madly as adrenaline took over. I clawed at the face of the man who held me, my fingernails raking crimson lines across his cheek. His fist was a blur, and I only had a moment to register the sickening crack as it collided with the side of my head. I was out before my body hit the floor.

∎∎∎

"Rosie?! Oh, God, Rosie!" Greg's high-pitched cry made my head throb, and I groaned. The concrete floor was hard and cold beneath my body. I tried to push myself up, to go to my frightened baby brother, but the thick, unyielding plastic of a cable tie bit into my wrists.

No. Oh, no.

I forced my eyes open, squinting against the searing pain of the harsh light as I searched for my brother. He was sitting with his knees drawn up to his chest, his back pressed up against a concrete block wall. His hands seemed to be secured behind him as well, and his eyes were wide and terrified.

His gaze shifted to focus on something above me, and I looked up to find a huge, heavily-muscled man looming over me. Red lines marred his cheek where I had clawed at him, and I now recognized him as the man who I had shot at when he had come to my apartment for Greg. I drew my knees up to my chest protectively as I took in his leer.

"Please," Greg begged. "Let my sister go. She's not involved in this." He was rocking back and forth, and the sweat that was beaded on his brow let me know he hadn't gotten a fix since I had last seen him. He had to be in agony.

The man didn't take his cruel eyes off of me. "Oh, but she is. You told me the FBI agent who's handling your case is fucking her. You told me the reason you wanted to come clean to us was because you hated the fucker." He sneered. "But you just wanted a fix, you pathetic junkie. Since you can't give us the names of the other snitches, we're going to have to get Clayton Vaughn to surrender the information. In exchange for her life."

Terror shot through me, stealing my breath away and leaving my body trembling.

"No," Greg moaned. "Let her go. I'll find a way to get the names for you. Please…"

Another brawny man entered my line of vision, and he kicked Greg viciously in the side. "You don't get to cut a deal with us, you fucking narc," he spat. Greg sucked in a breath as the pain consumed him, and he fell onto his side, curling in on himself.

"Stop!" I shouted. "Don't hurt him!"

The man standing over me was still smiling down at me cruelly. "That's enough, Jorje," he commanded. "He needs to be in one piece so he can deliver our message to Vaughn."

He reached down and grabbed my arm, jerking me to my feet. I cried out as the action caused the cable tie to tear the delicate skin at my wrists.

"Rosie!" Greg gasped out, still catching his breath after having the air kicked out of him.

My tormentor held me from behind, his arm wrapped firmly around my waist so that my back was pressed against his chest. The other man – Jorje – left Greg's side to stand in front of me. He pulled out a camera phone and directed the lens at me.

"You're going to scream for me, bitch," my captor growled in my ear as the light on the front of the camera turned on.

Chapter 17

Instinct urged me to scream out my fear, to give voice to the terror that was clawing at my insides. Ruthlessly, I shoved down the impulse. If these men wanted me to scream, then I wasn't going to give them the satisfaction. Especially if this recording might end up in Clayton's hands. I knew how much it would hurt him to see me in pain. I couldn't bear that.

My captor's Spanish accent was thick, but his demanding words rang out loud and clear. "We have your whore, Vaughn," he addressed the camera. "And unless you want her blood on your hands, you're going to turn over the names of the little worms who have been spying on us. In a short while, Baker will bring you this recording. Give him the information we need, and then send him back to us."

"NO!" I cried. I looked beseechingly into the camera. "Don't you dare send him back to them, Clayton. You swore you would keep him safe. Don't you -"

My words were cut off as the back of Jorje's hand cracked across my face. I tasted the metallic tang of blood in my mouth as the inside of my cheek tore against my teeth. It made my stomach turn.

"Quiet, whore," my tormentor ordered as my head spun. "Baker's going to meet us at Coney Island with the information, and then we'll leave her there in his place," he continued on, addressing the camera again. "If we even get a whiff of an agent or a cop, the deal's off, and her pretty little brains will be splattered all over the pavement."

I shuddered at the horrific mental image that his words conjured up with cruel, sharp clarity.

"And you had better work quickly," he threatened. "Every minute we have to wait, she will suffer."

No! No no no no no …

"Leave her alone!" Greg shouted, his voice high with panic. "Don't hurt my sister! I'll do what you want. I'll get you the information. Just, please, God, don't hurt her."

Jorje looked at him coldly. "We already told you: narcs don't get to cut deals."

"And just to let you know I mean what I'm saying, Vaughn…" The man behind me began menacingly, and I knew pain was coming. I braced myself for it. I wasn't going to scream. If I did, Clayton would break and give in to their demands. He would send Greg back to them, and they would kill him. I couldn't allow him to trade my brother's life for mine.

The man's fingers delved under the hem of my shirt, his hand gliding slowly up over my abdomen. My eyes flew wide as I began to tremble in his grasp.

No. I had been ready for pain, but not violation. I bit my lip hard to hold in my terrified whimper. But then his calloused palm was slipping under my bra, and I could feel him harden against my hip.

"Don't," I whispered desperately, losing some ground. Memories of being touched by strangers' hands, of being violated against my will as I was unable to fight, danced across my mind.

Not again, not again. "Please, don't…"

His soft laugh was cold and pitiless at my ear as his fingers closed hard on my nipple. I sucked in a ragged breath, clinging to my determination not to scream. I had endured worse pain than this. I had experienced worse pain than this and enjoyed it.

But no matter what I told myself, this was infinitely, inconceivably, more agonizing. I was being hurt against my will, and that made this horribly different from Clayton's carnal torment.

The man wasn't satisfied. He had told me he was going to make me scream, and he wasn't going to relent until I did. The realization made my blood freeze in my veins.

No, Rose, I ordered myself. *Don't give in. Don't scream, don't scream, don't scream...*

His fingernails dug viciously into my tender flesh, but I gulped back the sound of my pain. The loud, strangled sound that did manage to escape me seemed to goad my tormenter on.

"You can do better than that." The way his hot breath played across my neck in a perverse, twisted echo of what Clayton did to me made my stomach turn. I felt traitorous tears stinging at the corners of my eyes.

He dug in his fingernails harder, breaking the skin as he twisted ruthlessly. My agonized scream was ripped from my throat, brutal and unstoppable. My knees gave out as the force of the pain made bright lights pop behind my eyes. I sagged against the man, and I hated the sound of my wracking sobs.

"I'm coming back for you, Rosie. I promise." Greg's voice wavered with his own tears.

"No," I managed to gasp out. "Don't come ba -"

Pain exploded across my cheek again, cutting off my words. I could have sworn I felt my brain rattle against my skull, and my abused face throbbed. My captor released me, and I hit the ground hard, unable to catch myself. Through my watering eyes, I saw Jorje slip the camera phone into Greg's pocket before he pulled a black cloth sack over his head. "So you can't lead the FBI back here," he growled.

The horrible, bleak reality of my situation came crashing down on me: Clayton had no idea where I was, and Greg wasn't going to get a chance to figure it out. No one was coming to save me. No matter how desperately they might want to. My life and Greg's hung in the balance. And I was going to have to endure far worse abuse before it was all over. I prayed Clayton wouldn't give in to their demands. After these men were finished with me, I was as good as dead anyway. I knew I wouldn't be able to come back from that.

Jorje gripped Greg's upper arm and dragged him away. Blindly, my brother tripped up the stairs as he was led up out of what I could now tell was a basement. The concrete block walls were thick. No one would be able to hear me scream for help.

Once my brother was out of my sight, the man's attention turned back on me. The twisted lust in his eyes made me cringe, but I couldn't so much as scoot away from him with my hands bound as they were. I hated the terrified whimper that escaped me as he roughly turned me onto my back. He crouched beside me and lowered his face to mine, his fingers gripping my jaw hard. I hissed in pain as they dug into my rapidly-bruising flesh. But the horror of that was nothing compared to the disgust that tore through me when his hot, wet tongue licked its way up my cheek.

"It's just you and me now, *chica*," he said softly. "And Jorje. And we have you for as long as it takes for your Clayton to give us what we want." His grin was twisted, rictus. "I hope he takes a while."

Tears leaked from the corners of my eyes to stream down my temples, mingling with the sheen of terror-induced sweat that had broken out on my body.

The door at the top of the stairs banged open. "What the fuck are you doing, Ramirez?" An accented, angry voice demanded as the unfamiliar man descended the stairs.

My molester – Ramirez – jerked away from me to face the intruder. "Get out of here, Santiago, this is *Furiosos* territory," he snarled. "Go back to your *Muertos*. This is none of your fucking business."

Santiago's eyes narrowed and he folded his arms across his chest, his stance hard. "It is our business if you're going to fuck the rest of us over. We might be allies, but if you bring the fury of the FBI down on us, we will gut every one of you. I know you found a narc and are trying to manipulate the FBI into turning over the rest of them."

"How do you know that?" Ramirez asked suspiciously.

"We might be allies, but that doesn't mean we're not watching you, *muchacho.*" He imbued the word with as much venom as he could, clearly communicating the tenuousness of their alliance. I prayed they would tear each other apart before Ramirez could hurt me any more.

"What does she have to do with it?" Santiago jerked his chin in my direction.

Ramirez scowled, clearly pissed at his interference, but he decided to talk. "She's fucking one of the FBI agents. We sent him a little message with her brother, and he's going to give us the names of the snitches." He leered at me. "I'm just having a little fun before I have to give her back to him. That'll teach them not to fuck with the Latin Kings."

"*Maldito idiota,*" Santiago cursed. "If you damage her any more than you already have, it will only teach them that they have to eradicate us. We're gaining ground and getting rich. They don't have the resources to stop us. But if you mutilate this girl, this city is going to be crawling with so many FBI agents that we won't be able to hide."

Ramirez frowned, mulling over this information.

Please, I prayed, a spark of hope daring to flicker to life in my chest. *Please, listen to him.*

"What the fuck is this *Muerto* doing here?" Jorje demanded as he returned.

"Interfering," Ramirez snapped. My heart dropped as I watched his expression turn stony. Now that his friend had rejoined him, he wasn't going to be seen backing down. He spat on the floor. "Just because you can't get your dick hard enough to fuck a woman doesn't mean you can tell us not to," he flung the insult at Santiago.

The man's fists clenched angrily. "What the fuck is that supposed to mean, Ramirez?" He demanded.

My tormentor smiled at him cruelly. "It means you can't even fuck your own wife. Everyone knows she whores around to find some satisfaction."

His face contorted with rage, Santiago launched himself at Ramirez, shoving him back against the wall hard enough that I heard his head crack at the impact. "That's a lie," he hissed, his expression murderous.

Ramirez just laughed. "I saw her when I went to drag my Ana Lucia home from a club. She was rubbing up against every man in there like a bitch in heat. She wants what your limp dick can't give her."

Santiago snarled and wrapped his hands around Ramirez's throat. But Jorje was there in an instant, pressing the tip of his switchblade against Santiago's kidney. "You should leave now, *mi amigo*. Or you won't be leaving at all."

Santiago's expression was still livid, all of his muscles tense with the effort of reining in his violent urges, but he backed off, releasing Ramirez. He turned and headed for the stairs. The only man who might have protected me was going to leave me here.

"You should think about what I said," he called back over his shoulder. "Hurting her won't do any of us any favors. And if the FBI comes down on us, the alliance between *Los Furiosos* and *Los Muertos* is over. I'll be sure to personally be the one who rips your hearts out."

With that threat hanging in the air, he disappeared. The shattering of my heart at his absence was all the more painful for the hope I had allowed myself to indulge in.

Ramirez was looking down at me again, but his expression was pensive this time. "You know," he finally said to his friend, "I hate that *hijo de puta,* but he has a point. Maybe we should at least give them an hour to send Baker back to us. If they stall longer than that, we can send Vaughn another little movie."

I held my breath as I waited for Jorje's answer. *Please please please...*

After a long moment, he nodded his agreement. All of the air left my lungs in a rush as I heaved a sigh of relief. I still had no idea how I was going to get out of this, but at least I had some time to formulate a plan now.

Ramirez clapped his friend on the shoulder. "Let's grab a beer," he said as he turned from me. I almost wept with joy as they walked away from me and slammed the door behind them at the top of the stairs. I heard the lock click back, but I refused to allow myself to be disheartened at the sound. Without their terrifying presence, it would be easier to think.

Unfortunately, my mind turned in circles as I realized again just how hopeless my situation was. I couldn't dare to hope that anyone could find me. How could they possibly? Clayton had been sitting in the coffee shop when they had taken me; there was no way he would have been able to get to a vehicle in time to follow them. And Greg obviously hadn't been allowed to see where we had been taken. He wouldn't be able to find his way back to this hellhole. I started to cry again. It was going to be either Greg or me who died today. And I hoped it would be me. I wouldn't be able to live with the weight of my guilt if he traded his life for mine. Even though Clayton shared almost everything with me, I didn't have any information on the FBI's informants. I didn't possess any bargaining chips to talk my way out of this.

A horrible thought struck me. I shied away from it at first, unable to contemplate it. But the longer I lay there, my muscles growing stiff from lack of movement, the more the idea insistently pressed at my conscious mind. I did have something they wanted: my body.

They could take me unwillingly at any time if they chose to, and there would be nothing I could do to stop them. But if I offered myself to them, if I could please them enough, maybe they would let Greg go. Maybe they would decide to keep me, and that would buy Clayton some time to find me.

I had been with lots of strange men before. This would be no different. If I accepted them, it might not hurt as badly. If it was consensual, it might not destroy my soul.

By the time I heard them coming back for me, I had made my decision. This was my only hope. That thought made me want to laugh hollowly. What kind of hope was this?

But this way, I could survive it. I *would* survive it. And I would get Greg out alive as well.

I swallowed hard as they approached me, bracing myself. There was a third man with them this time. No, not a man. More of a boy. He was probably close to Greg's age. The hard, cruel lines of that young face made my heart twist.

"Your hour's up," Ramirez informed me coldly. "Vaughn obviously needs some more motivation."

I could see that the boy had a camera phone, and I knew both Ramirez and Jorje planned to take me, to torment Clayton with the images of them raping me.

Rape. I shuddered at the word. I couldn't let that happen.

As Ramirez crouched beside me, I saw the light of the camera turn on. They were ready to put on a cruel, brutal show.

"Wait," I gasped, my voice high and thin. I took a deep breath, trying to calm myself so I could speak rationally. "I want to offer you a deal," I said quickly.

Ramirez's eyes narrowed. "Do you know something? If you've been holding back on us, your brother will suffer before he dies."

"No!" I said quickly. "But I can give you something else. If you'll take the information from Greg and then let him go, I'll stay with you willingly. I'll…" I almost choked on the words. "I'll give myself to you."

Ramirez was still frowning, but there was an intrigued spark in his eyes. "And why would I agree to that when I could fuck you at any time without your consent?"

"Because Santiago was right. If you piss off the FBI by not holding up your end of the deal, they will destroy you. But if you show my brother mercy, you won't have to trade me for him. You... You can keep me."

He cocked his head at me. "And what's to stop me from doing that anyway if I decide I like your cunt?"

"Because I would fight you the whole time. If you agree to let Greg walk away unharmed, I'll make you feel good."

He grinned, and his fist tangled in my hair. He pulled me up sharply, and I cried out as some of the platinum strands parted company with my scalp. "I think we'll need a demonstration before we can agree to that," he said menacingly.

Fear spiked through me when he pulled out a knife, but he reached behind me and cut the cable tie that secured my wrists together. I hissed in pain as the plastic was pulled out of my torn skin.

"I want to see what you have to offer. Strip."

My hands were shaking madly, but I forced myself to comply, tearing at my clothes in order to get it over with as quickly as possible.

"No," Ramirez barked out. "Slow. Sexy. Make me believe you want our cocks."

I took a deep breath and closed my eyes, trying to mentally take myself out of the room and immerse myself in a memory in order to get through this. My first thought was of Clayton, of the hungry look in his eyes when he stared at my naked body.

But that thought almost made me break down. I was betraying him by offering myself to these men. And if they decided to send him the recording of my shameful behavior...

No. I couldn't think about that now, or I would collapse to the floor and my anguish would claim me.

Instead, I drew on my years of experience of flirting, of luring men in like the Siren that Penny had named me to be. But I longed to be a lioness in that moment. Still, I was able to fall back into my practiced movements, swaying my hips as I slowly peeled off my clothes.

My skin was freezing, and it wasn't from the cool air that hit my exposed body. I cried out in shock and my eyes flew open as Jorje's hands closed around my arms. The cable tie that he used to secure me this time was tightened even more cruelly than the first.

"What are you doing?" I asked, hating the way my voice quavered.

Ramirez pointed at the red lines on his cheek. "I'm not stupid. Your claws are staying sheathed."

Jorje's hands wrapped around my front, and I shuddered as he gripped my breasts. "Her tits are small, but they feel nice," he remarked, as though he was appraising cattle for purchase.

I agreed to this. This is consensual, this is consensual, I told myself over and over again. But if that was true, then why did I feel so dirty?

I had a moment to register Ramirez's merciless expression before he brutally drove two fingers inside of me. I screamed at the violation and the pain. My sex was bone dry and tight from my lack of arousal.

But it wasn't enough for Ramirez. "You really are a slut, aren't you?" He asked. "I hope your ass is tighter than your cunt."

Slut.

A defeated sob was torn from me as I realized I wasn't at all in control here. They were going to hurt me. But I had to pull it together, I had to try. Greg's life depended on me getting through this.

Chapter 18

Ramirez pulled his fingers out of me, but I didn't have a moment to experience any relief. Jorje's hands were on my shoulders, shoving me down so that I fell hard on my knees. He grabbed a fistful of hair at the nape of my neck and pulled my head back sharply.

"I want to see how good she sucks cock," he said to his friend. My stomach churned as Ramirez unzipped his pants and pulled his erection free.

Absorb the pain, I ordered myself desperately. *Embrace it. You can get through this. Clayton showed you how.*

But my joy from the pain he had given me had come from my ecstatic, willing submission to him.

You are willing. You are. You agreed to this.

Ramirez gripped my jaw, his fingers pressing against it viciously so that my mouth was forced open.

"Impress me," he growled.

I tried to brace myself, but my mind rebelled. This was so profoundly wrong. I had told myself I was doing this for my own survival, but I knew I wouldn't make it through this. Even if my body lived on, my soul would be destroyed so thoroughly that even Clayton wouldn't be able to piece it back together.

Ramirez's attention was jerked from me as the sound of shouting and heavy footsteps thundered above us.

"ROSE! Rose, where are you?!" Clayton bellowed.

I wanted to cry out his name, but Ramirez's grip on my jaw prevented me from forming a coherent word. Instead, I screamed as loudly as I could, the shrill, harsh sound echoing around the confined space.

My heart leapt as Clayton appeared at the top of the stairs, his face contorted with the unbridled ferocity of his fury. His enraged roar and two gunshots rent the air. I heard my captors' high, agonized screams, and something warm and wet splattered across my cheek.

Out of the corner of my eye, I saw Jorje and Ramirez crumple to the floor, writhing in agony. But all I could focus on was Clayton. He looked so angry. My betrayal burned through me, searing my flesh from the inside out. Clayton could see it now. And he would never be able to un-see it.

Slut.

"What the fuck did you do?!" Sharon asked, sounding alarmed. "They were unarmed!"

"They had knives, Silverman," Smith said coolly, his tone daring her say otherwise.

"Right," she nodded grimly in agreement.

Clayton was advancing on me, his expression thunderous. I fell back on my bound hands as I tried to scramble away from him, cringing. Oh, god, he had seen me allow those other men to touch me. I knew when he struck me this time, it wouldn't be meant for my benefit.

The furious light left his eyes instantly, replaced by concern and fear. "It's just me, Rose," he said soothingly as he bent to gather me up in his arms. "Don't be afraid." His voice sounded pained.

I began to cry as the taint on my skin touched him. "I'm so sorry," I sobbed. "I'm sorry I'm sorry I'm sorry..."

Clayton clutched me to him tighter. "It's okay, Rose," he reassured me, sounding alarmed. "You have nothing to apologize for."

That wasn't true. He just didn't realize it yet. My throat closed as my panic rose up in me, blocking my windpipe. I gasped, but I couldn't draw any air into my lungs.

"Breathe, Rose," Clayton commanded, shaking me slightly. "Breathe."

But I couldn't obey his order. He wasn't my Master anymore. He would reject me now that he could see my true nature.

"Get a medic down here now!" I heard Smith bark out. But I couldn't see him. I couldn't see anything. Darkness was rolling over me as my head spun. I threw myself into it, desperate to escape Clayton's piercing blue eyes.

▪▪▪

I became aware of an insistent throbbing in my head, but it was more annoying than it was painful. Something was dulling my senses, making my limbs feel heavy and my mind fuzzy. But the throbbing was rousing me from sleep. I tried to ignore it. I couldn't recall why, but I didn't want to wake up, didn't want to face reality.

"Rose?" His voice was low and ragged. "Rose, are you awake?"

No. Oh, no.

My worst fears were confirmed when I opened my eyes to find Clayton sitting beside the unfamiliar bed I was lying on. The memories of his anger, of my unspeakable betrayal, came rushing back, shoving ruthlessly through the fog in my brain to race across my mind with sharp, horrifying clarity. He had come here to torment me, to tell me that I disgusted him and he didn't love me anymore. I cringed away from him.

"Rose." Pain laced his tone as he said my name, and he reached for my hand. I jerked it back, a thin whine like the sound of a pained animal escaping me.

Something akin to anguish flared in his eyes, and he withdrew his hand reluctantly. "It's me, Rose," he said gently, but there was an underlying strain in his voice. "It's Clayton. I'm not going to hurt you. You're safe now. They're not going to touch you ever again." A shadow of his earlier fury flickered across his face, and I couldn't help shuddering.

He reined it in with a visible effort, taking a deep breath and forcing his taut muscles to relax. But even when his expression softened, my pain at his presence was undiminished. I wanted desperately to get away from him, but my heavy limbs wouldn't allow me to get two steps before he stopped me.

"Please," I begged in a strangled whisper. "Please don't hurt me. I'm sorry. I'm so sorry."

His expression turned stony, and he grabbed my hands in his, his fingers curling around mine tightly so I couldn't escape him. "Don't pull away from me, Rose. You're going to listen to me. And you're going to understand." His voice had that cool, assured quality to it that commanded my attention. His eyes burned down into mine with fervent sincerity. "I'm not going to hurt you. I will never hurt you. You have nothing to be sorry for. You've done nothing wrong. Those men touched you without your permission, and you're not responsible for that."

"But I am!" I wailed, unable to bear his firm reassurance. He was mistaken. He didn't understand. "I gave them my permission. I asked them for it because I'm… I'm a filthy slut."

I waited for his mouth to twist downward in disgust, but instead his expression was drawn and angry. "What have I told you about calling yourself that?" He demanded severely. "You are *not* a slut, Rose. And I will tan your hide so that you can't sit for a week if I ever hear you say it again."

"You don't understand," I protested. Knowing that I was about to destroy his fierce faith in me made my heart shatter. But I couldn't let him stay with me after what I had done to him. He deserved better than me. "I gave myself to them willingly. I wanted to please them."

Clayton's brows drew together, but the repulsed expression that I was expecting still hadn't registered. "Explain," he demanded.

"I… They were going to kill Greg. I couldn't let them do that. I thought if I could make them happy, they would let him go and they would keep me alive. I thought I was buying time, that they wouldn't hurt me as badly if I consented. I was wrong about that," I ended in a broken whisper as I recalled how Ramirez had brutally shoved his fingers into me.

Clayton's grip on my hands tightened, and he let out a low growl. "If I didn't love you so goddamn much, *I* would have killed your brother by now for what he's done to you. As it is, I have to remind myself of it with every passing second to stop myself from going to his hospital room and beating the shit out of him."

He loves me? He was too good. I really didn't deserve him.

"How?" I asked, my voice barely audible. "How can you possibly say you love me after what I've done?"

"I will always love you, Rose," he promised fiercely. "Nothing you could ever say or do will change that. And something that is done to you by someone else sure as hell won't change it." Electric blue sparks crackled and popped in his gorgeous eyes as he stared down at me with a furious intensity, impressing his will upon me with the full power of his dominant aura. "You are going to listen to what I'm saying, Rose. I love you more deeply than I have ever loved anything or anyone else. And you are going to accept that. You're going to believe it. I'm not giving you the option to do otherwise. Do you understand?"

"Yes, Master," I whispered, automatically submitting to his control.

"Tell me you love me," he ordered. "And mean every word of it."

"I love you, Master," I said, my voice ringing clear and true for the first time since I had awoken. "I love you, Clayton."

He lowered his face to mine, pausing when our lips were no more than a hair's breadth apart. His hot breath fanned across my skin as he spoke in a deep, approving rumble. "That's a good girl," he praised before he brought his mouth down on mine. The kiss was tender and soft. I knew Clayton was being careful with me because I was hurt, but I craved more of him. My fingers curled around his shoulders as I pulled him down into me.

But he had always been far stronger than I was, and I was unable to prevent him from pulling away from me slightly.

"No, Rose," he said softly. "You're hurt."

"I know," I said. "I need a painkiller." I reached for him, but he evaded me. He tried to look stern, but I could see a hint of regret in his eyes.

He gestured to the IV drip that was stuck into my arm. "You already have plenty of painkillers. But I can get you more if you want them."

He reached for the nurse's call button, but I grabbed his wrist to stop him. "No!" I cried, suddenly panicky. I didn't want to leave him again. Not when I had just gotten him back. "I don't want to sleep. I want to stay with you."

There was a soft knock on the open door, and I looked up to find Smith standing at the threshold to my room. He was holding a bouquet of roses and smiling at me softly. "Mind if I join you?" He asked.

Smith. At the sight of him, I suddenly recalled his presence in the basement, the screams of my tormentors as they writhed on the floor. I couldn't suppress a shiver at the memory, and Clayton stroked his thumb over the back of my hand to soothe me.

Smith looked uncertain at my reaction, but I didn't want him to leave. "Don't go," I said, my tone a touch pleading.

His gentle smile returned as he entered and settled himself down in a chair on the other side of my bed. "I'm not going anywhere unless you ask me to," he assured me.

"Thanks," I said softly, enveloped by a warm, safe feeling as the two powerful Doms watched over me. I knew nothing bad could happen to me so long as they were by my sides.

But now that I had overcome the hurdle of thinking that Clayton hated me, questions began to buzz through my fuzzy mind. "How did you find me?" I asked. I had thought locating me would be impossible.

Clayton looked slightly reticent, but Smith answered me smoothly. "Mr. Stickler here is hesitant to break the rules," he jerked his head in Clayton's direction. "But everyone's used to me not giving a shit about the rules, so I'll probably be able to get away with telling you this." He fixed me with a serious look. "But it is classified, Rose, and if it leaves this room an agent's life will be at stake. You can never talk about this to anyone."

I nodded my understanding. "I won't. I promise."

"Santiago – the man who tried to stop those motherfuckers from hurting you – is one of ours. He's been in deep cover with *Los Muertos* for over a year now. He risked his life by going into unstable *Furiosos* territory in order to locate you. As soon as he was able to get word to us about where you were being held, we came for you." His expression was slightly pained. "I'm just sorry we didn't get there sooner."

I dropped my eyes. "You got there in time," I said quietly. "I... They didn't..." I trailed off, unable to force out a description of the terrible things those men had wanted to do to me.

Smith's jaw tightened. "I know they didn't," he said angrily. "But it still wasn't soon enough. I saw the recording."

My stomach clenched painfully, and I shot a terrified look at Clayton. Oh, god. Had he seen...?

"I didn't watch it, Rose," he reassured me. He glanced over at his friend. "Smith wouldn't let me."

"Believe me," Smith said, "I'm going to have more than enough nightmares for the both of us after seeing that." His hands were clenched into fists, but his eyes were haunted.

"What did you do to them?" I asked quietly. "I heard gunshots and screaming."

"I didn't do enough," Smith said roughly. "Clayton was more vicious than I was for once. I shattered the leg of the guy who was holding you, but Clayton shot the other one's dick off.

Neither of them bled out, but I'm pretty sure Ramirez's time served will be short and incredibly painful." His mouth was twisted in grim satisfaction, and he was looking at Clayton with respect.

I nodded sharply. "That's good to hear." And I meant it. I wasn't a violent person, but that demon of a man deserved everything he had coming to him.

But the sharp movement sent pain spiking through my skull, and I cried out as I clutched my pounding head.

Something warm and wonderful oozed into my veins, and I dropped my hands from my face in puzzlement. I saw that Smith was holding down the button that dispensed my pain medication.

"Hey!" I protested. "You can't do that!" But my words were slurred as my tongue suddenly felt thick and unwieldy in my mouth.

Smith just shrugged, not looking apologetic in the slightest. "I just did," he informed me coolly.

My body became wonderfully light, and the bed fell away from beneath me, leaving me floating on warm, fluffy clouds. My vision began to waver at the edges, and Clayton's face blurred. I panicked. I didn't want to lose sight of him. I didn't want to be alone.

I tried to reach for him, but my hand barely twitched. A low, frustrated sound fought its way up my throat.

He was by my side in an instant, his face hovering just over mine. "It's okay, Rose," he reassured me. "You can sleep. I'm not going anywhere. I love you so much."

I love you too.

The world was a blur of shifting colors, but the multifaceted shades of his cerulean eyes were sharp and clear. I surrendered to the drugs as I allowed myself to fall into their blue depths, where no pain could ever possibly exist.

Epilogue

Clayton

One Month Later

Claudia was undeniably beautiful in her floor-length, form-fitting white gown, her beatific expression as she stared up into Sean's eyes only making her all the more breathtaking. I was standing at the altar, listening to the sweet, sincere vows she made to Sean and those he made to her in return. They were looking at one another as though no one else existed in the world as they pledged themselves to each other forever.

But I only noticed this with part of my mind, because I was staring at Rose with the same fervent light where she sat with the congregation. Trapped in the intensity of my gaze, I saw her blush slightly. Her eyes were shining as she was caught up in the palpable joy that filled the small chapel. She was the most heartbreakingly exquisite thing I had ever seen.

The service ended, and Rose cheered and whistled alongside everyone else as Claudia and Sean ran through the rose petals their guests tossed at them. Sean's grin was wide and almost boyish as he was completely possessed by the perfection of his happiness. And Claudia's answering grin was just as silly.

Only a few weeks ago, the sight of their happiness would have stirred up jealousy that I would have had to ruthlessly tamp down. But now that I had Rose in my life, I could fully appreciate the insurmountable depth of their feelings for one another. Because I felt exactly the same way about her. She had blown into my life like the force of nature she was, turning my world and all

of my preconceived notions about myself upside down. Before I
had known her, I had lived every day with the weight of what had
happened to Jen, struggling down my path to redemption that I
knew would never have an end. I had allowed myself to become
consumed by the need to make up for what I had done to her, and I
had allowed my life to stall out because of it.

But Rose hadn't given up on me, and even when she was
deeply hurt by the thought that I saw Jen every time I looked at
her, she had forced me to see that I wasn't responsible. I hadn't
even been aware of what a heavy burden I had been carrying all
those years until the weight of it was lifted from me. Rose's
refusal to allow me to continue blaming myself had freed me to be
the person I was supposed to be, to live the life I had been meant to
live.

And now I fully intended to live it with her.

An hour later, the sultry sound of Etta James singing "At
Last" surged around us as we danced, Rose's body pressed so
tightly against mine that it was almost obscene. But I didn't care.
Hell, I wanted people to see. She was mine and no one else's.
Unless I decided to share her.

Her delicious, sweet scent surrounded me. She always
smelled positively edible. It took all of my willpower to stop
myself from wrapping her hair around my fist and holding her
where I wanted her so I could plunder her mouth in an effort to
consume her. But now wasn't the time for that. This was Sean
and Claudia's night. I could devour Rose after the reception was
over.

In moments like this, I was struck by the incredible changes
that Rose had wrought within me. No. That wasn't right. She
hadn't changed me. She had shown me an integral, essential part
of me that I had never allowed myself to recognize, just as I had
done for her. If someone had told me two months ago that I would
own a beautiful submissive and be frequenting BDSM clubs, I
would have politely told them they were batshit insane. But now

nothing felt more natural or perfect than controlling Rose's body, than earning her sweet submission. I was overawed every time she willingly placed herself at my mercy, trusting me completely. The feeling was both heady and deeply passionate on a level that transcended physical pleasure. Although the physical pleasure itself was pretty fucking phenomenal.

The song ended, but I didn't let Rose go.

"Hey, Clayton. Do you think you could stop dry-humping Rose for long enough for me to get a chance to talk to her?"

I laughed and pulled away from Rose, but I kept my arm firmly around her waist where she stood at my side. "Okay," I told Claudia. "But you're only getting away with that because you're the bride."

She grinned at me. "Yes, I am. And as the bride, I demand to be allowed to talk to your girlfriend, if you can manage to let her go for more than thirty seconds." She turned her smile on Rose. "I'm pretty pissed at him for not bringing you to Indianola sooner. I hear all of these great things over the phone, but then he keeps turning me down every time I invite the two of you to come over for the weekend."

"Really?" Rose asked, shooting me a disapproving look. "I had no idea. It must have slipped Clayton's mind to ask whether or not I wanted to come."

"It didn't slip my mind," I shrugged. "I just thought you would want to stay focused on Greg and on your first semester at school."

I did my best to hide my disgust at the mention of Greg. He had gotten through rehab, and once he was clean he had been able to testify against *Los Furiosos.* The fact that he had helped us to eradicate one of the tribes of the Latin Kings did little to dilute my distaste for him. But despite what he had put her through, Rose still loved him fiercely, so I would put up with him for her sake. That didn't mean I had to like him, though.

"Rose is on a full scholarship at the Fashion Institute of Technology," I told Claudia proudly, deciding to focus on the positive.

Claudia rolled her eyes at me. "Yes, I know. You've told me that a time or twenty." But her exasperation melted when she turned her smile on Rose. "Congratulations! That is seriously awesome. Do you think I would be able to see any of your designs? Do you have a website or something?"

"You're looking at one right now," I told her. Even though Rose had said she was trying to wear something understated so that she wouldn't compete with Claudia, she still looked stunning in her indigo silk cocktail dress. The color highlighted the dark blue rings that surrounded her irises, making her remarkable ice green eyes pop.

"Wow!" Claudia said, sounding truly impressed. "You made this? I am *so* raiding your closet the next time Sean and I are in New York."

Rose smiled at her, blushing slightly at the praise. She still wasn't used to people being impressed with her designs. "No closet raiding will be necessary," she assured Claudia. "I'll make something for you."

"Really?" Claudia's eyes widened slightly. "That would be amazing. You really don't have to do that. I know how busy you are."

"I'm happy to do it," Rose assured her.

"You've been gone a long time, beautiful. I was worried you might have run off." Sean's arm snaked around Claudia's waist as he pulled her tightly up against him.

"Did you hear that?" She asked him. "America's Next Top Designer is going to make something just for me." She arched up onto her tiptoes and planted a swift kiss on his cheek. "And running would be futile. You would catch me in a heartbeat."

Sean wrapped his other arm around her back and pulled her up into his chest. His eyes narrowed dangerously, but there was a small smile playing around his lips. "I dare you to try, little one."

When Claudia answered, her voice was slightly breathless. "Oh, I wouldn't dare. Besides, we still have all of season three of *Game of Thrones* on our TiVo. I'm definitely not leaving until I've finished watching it."

Sean gave a low growl at her flippant words, and his hand closed around the nape of her neck as he crushed his lips to hers in a fierce, possessive kiss.

Rose tugged at my hand. "Ah, I think we should give the happy couple some space," she whispered. I allowed her to lead me through the crowd, following her out of the tent and into the cool night air. The reception was being held in a park just outside Indianola, and the lack of city lights allowed the stars to be visible overhead. Rose sat down on the edge of a picnic table, looking up at them and smiling.

"I really would like to come here again sometime," she said. "I love living in New York, but it would be nice to get away from the city from time to time. You feel so isolated out here. It's really quiet and peaceful."

The smile I turned on her was predatory as her words brought to mind a decidedly wicked scenario. I gripped her chin between my thumb and forefinger, holding her so she was forced to look into my eyes. Her breath quickened instantly at my touch.

"Yes," I agreed softly. "It is rather isolated out here. I think I'm beginning to share your appreciation for the great outdoors." I placed my hand on her shoulder, pushing her firmly down until her back was against the damp wood of the picnic table, her legs still dangling over the edge. I lowered my lips to her ear, loving the way she trembled beneath me as her desire began to claim her. "This would be one of those times when you'll call me 'Master' outside of the bedroom," I informed her in a low voice.

"Yes, Master," she moaned softly beneath me, arching her back so that her breasts were pressing up against my chest.

Just those two simple words were enough to make me rock hard for her. My hands were on her thighs, skimming along them as I slowly pushed her dress up to her waist. When I dipped my fingers between her legs, I was pleased to find that she was already soaking wet for me.

God, she was hotter than any fantasy I could have ever dreamed up even on my kinkiest day.

I pulled away from her, making her wait as I slowly freed myself from my slacks and put on a condom. I had to stifle a groan at the sight of her licking her lips as she watched me hungrily.

"Tell your Master what you want him to do to your body," I ordered roughly, my iron control slipping at the sight of her laid out before me, her pale skin and platinum hair practically glowing in the starlight.

Her head dropped back and she closed her eyes as she moaned at my crude words. "I want you to bend me over this table and fuck me hard from behind. I want you to use my body for your own pleasure. Please, Master…" She ground her hips up against nothing, her body instinctively seeking some way to release the need I awoke within her.

My need was just as strong, and I wasn't going to wait any longer.

I gripped her by the waist and roughly turned her onto her front. My fingers tangled in her long, silken hair, and I pulled back sharply. The way her back arched pushed her ass up to me like an offering. Keeping my hold on her hair, I wrapped my other arm around her waist, jerking her body back into me so that she was impaled on my cock.

Her strangled cry tore through the trees around us, filling the peaceful silence with the sound of her raw lust. I took her harshly, demanding she give me her pleasure with every punishing thrust. She ceded it eagerly, and I could feel her inner walls begin to flutter around me as she neared her orgasm.

I tugged on her hair, reminding her of my complete control of her body. "Not yet," I ground out. "Wait for me."

I loved the sound of her desperate whine. It let me know how badly she wanted me and how determined she was to obey me. It was her submission that pushed me over the edge.

"Come with me, Rose!" I ordered harshly as my own pleasure took me.

She followed me immediately, her orgasm all the more powerful for me making her wait. The way her core gripped my cock heightened the intensity of my release, and I threw my head back and bellowed as I reached my completion.

I waited until her final little ecstatic shudders subsided before withdrawing from her and settling down beside her on the table. I gathered her body up in my arms and draped her across me, idly stroking my hand up and down her back. We stayed there for long minutes, basking in the joy of holding one another.

There was something I had been wanting to ask her, and I decided this was the right moment. I reached into my pocket and pulled out a small, velvet-covered box. Rose's eyes widened when she saw it, and I thought I saw a hint of fear flash in their depths. I offered it to her, but she just stared at it, shaking her head slightly.

"Clayton, I…"

"Open it," I ordered.

She took the box with shaking fingers, swallowing hard as she flipped back the lid. When she saw what was inside, her brows drew together in confusion.

"I know you practically already live at my apartment, Rose," I said, "but I thought it was time we made it official. Will you move in with me?"

She brushed her fingertips over the key and then giggled. "Oh, thank god," she said, her relief evident in her tone. "I thought you were going to ask me to marry you."

I gave her my most dramatic affronted look. "I'm insulted you would think me incapable of coming up with a better proposal than that. I didn't even get down on one knee." Then a hint of true discomfort slipped into my expression. I frowned slightly as I reached out to cup her delicate face in my hand. "But I have to say I'm a little hurt to see you so relieved. Is the thought of marrying me really all that terrible?"

She pressed her palm against the back of my hand, holding it there so that she could lean her cheek into my touch. "Of course not," she said softly. "I want to spend the rest of my life with you. But I've only just started school, and I want to be successful in my own right before we get married."

I smiled at her, reassured. "I guess I'll have to re-schedule that proposal I had planned for next weekend then," I teased.

She laughed. "I'd mark your calendar for about two years from now."

"It's a date," I agreed firmly. I wasn't joking in the slightest. I gestured to the little box she was still holding. "That key won't burn you, you know. I promise it's safe to take it."

Grinning, she snapped the box closed and pushed it back into my pocket. "I didn't design this dress with any hidey-holes for storing away personal items," she told me flippantly.

"You should think about that next time," I said in mock-seriousness.

"But that key is mine," she declared fervently. "You're just holding onto it for me right now."

"I don't mind that one bit," I said, lust beginning to color my tone. "If I'm holding onto it, then you can't leave my side."

Her pupils dilated, and her voice turned low and breathy. "That sounds good to me. Screw the dress-pocket idea. I'll take any excuse I can get to keep you with me."

"A wedding ring would really tie me to you, you know. I wouldn't be able to escape you then." I gave her a wolfish smile, letting her know that *she* was the one who had no hope of escaping *me*.

"Two years," she reiterated, but her husky tone didn't hold the resolve it had before.

I lowered my face to hers so our lips were almost touching. Her warm breath played across my skin in little short, shallow gasps. "I have no problem waiting," I told her. "You've already given yourself to me. I own you, little sub, and that is one bond I am never releasing you from."

Her fingers curled into my shoulders as she held me tightly to her. "I wouldn't let you, Master," she declared softly.

I pressed my lips to hers, licking and nipping at them until she opened for me, a physical demonstration of her promise of everlasting submission. And the harsh, possessive thrusts of my tongue as I claimed her mouth communicated my own devotion to her.

Rose Baker was mine, and I was never going to let her go.

The End

Want more of the *Impossible* series? Check out *Knight* (An *Impossible* Novel)

Abducted. Drugged. Broken. I became a plaything, a possession. If I did ever have a name, I don't remember it now. Slaves don't have names.

My new Master stole me away from the man who tormented me. He saved me and took me for himself. I've found my salvation in his obsession, my freedom in his captivity.

Will his brand of rescue leave me more broken than ever?

Excerpt

I used to think pain wasn't real. At least, not in the sense of being a tangible thing. It was just the result of my primal brain's in-built response to inform me that damage was being inflicted on my body. If I trusted the person who was giving me pain, then I knew he wasn't going to damage me. If I understood my pain, it stopped being something to fear and became something... interesting. I could master the hurt and ride the high of the adrenaline that flooded my system. I could enter subspace, that gloriously blank place where nothing existed but the sweet endorphins released by the pain that I embraced.

But then He came along and turned that all on its head. He enjoyed administering pain to torture, not to pleasure. And I couldn't trust Him not to inflict damage. He claimed He didn't like it when I forced Him to damage me; He didn't want to mar his property. But that didn't mean He wasn't willing to do so in order to get what He wanted.

I had tried to fight the pain for so long, to hold on to my conviction that it wasn't real. It couldn't hurt me if I didn't let it. But He gave me so much that it overwhelmed me, claiming all of my senses until my whole world was agony. I was perpetually trapped in some twisted, inverted form of subspace where nothing existed but the pain, but it gave me no pleasure.

My only reprieve was the sweet reward that came with the merciful sting of a needle. If I was good, if I obeyed and screamed prettily enough, then He would give me my reward. I lived for it; that was the only time I *was* alive.

But I had become so dependent on it that now the denial of my reward was just as terrible as the agony He gave me. It had been so long since I had gotten my last fix.

Tonight, Master was testing me. He wanted to see just how obedient I was. He wanted the satisfaction of seeing just how thoroughly He had broken me.

I was broken. And I didn't even care. All I cared about was my reward. Right now, my need for it was so acute that my insides were twisting and my skin was on fire. I was desperate to give Him whatever He wanted so I could get my fix. If He hadn't ordered me to stand in the corner quietly and wait for Him to return, then I would have been curled up on the floor sobbing.

But I wasn't ensconced in the stark loneliness of the pitch black dungeon that had become my home, and I didn't have the luxury of going to pieces. His order for my silence denied me even the right to voice my agony. He had brought me out in public for the first time, and I recognized the place where He had brought me as a BDSM club. He would be able to torment me here in front of dozens of strangers, and no one would stop Him.

The thought of shouting out a safe word or screaming for help didn't even cross my mind. All I could think about was when He would come back and doing my best to please Him so that He would grant me my reprieve. He had been gone for so long, and I was starting to panic.

And now a strange man was talking to me, threatening to hurt me if I didn't tell him my name. But I didn't have a name. If I did ever have a name, I didn't remember it now. I was a slave, and slaves don't have names.

***Knight* is now available!**

Also by Julia Sykes

The Original *Impossible* Trilogy
Monster
Traitor
Avenger
Impossible: The Original Trilogy
Angel (A Companion Book to *Monster*)

The *Impossible* Novels
Savior (Impossible #1)
Knight (Impossible #2)
Rogue (Impossible #3) (Coming Soon!)

Dark Grove Plantation (The Complete Collection)

Made in the USA
Lexington, KY
22 July 2014